PENGUIN BOOKS

POE'S CAT

Brenda Walker is the author of two previous novels, the award-winning *Crush* and *One More River*. Her short stories have been widely anthologised and her novels have been translated into Italian.

POE'S CAT

BRENDA WALKER

PENGUIN BOOKS

PENGUIN BOOKS

Published by the Penguin Group
Penguin Books Ltd, 27 Wrights Lane, London w8 5tz, England
Penguin Putnam Inc., 375 Hudson Street, New York, New York 10014, USA
Penguin Books Australia Ltd, Ringwood, Victoria, Australia
Penguin Books Canada Ltd, 10 Alcorn Avenue, Toronto, Ontario, Canada m4v 3b2
Penguin Books (N.Z.) Ltd, Private Bag 102902, NSMC, Auckland, New Zealand

Penguin Books Ltd, Registered Offices: Harmondsworth, Middlesex, England

First published by Penguin Books Australia 1999
Published in Penguin Books 2000

1 3 5 7 9 10 8 6 4 2

Copyright © Brenda Walker, 1999
All rights reserved.

Designed by Anitra Blackford, Penguin Design Studio
Text illustration by Craig McGill
Printed and bound by Australian Print Group, Maryborough, Victoria

ACKNOWLEDGEMENTS

I would like to thank The Eleanor Dark Foundation for a Varuna Writers' Fellowship during which I began to write *Poe's Cat*; the Literature Board of The Australia Council for a Literature Board Grant in order to work on the book, and the University of Western Australia and the Institute for Research into Women and Gender at Stanford University for a Stanford Women's Fellowship which enabled me to do much of the research for the book.

Many people have provided insights into and comments on this work and in particular I would like to thank Shirley Walker, Peter Bishop, Tim Curnow, David Brooks, Nicholas Birns, Carmel Bird, Sari Hosie, Delia Falconer, Ava Caridad, Tim Coyle, Malcolm Mummery, Deb Westbury, Beth Yahp, Elizabeth Webby, Wendy Waring, Lisa Jenkins, Wolfgang Spinnler, John L'Heureux and David Halliburton.

'Poe's Cat', including 'The Story of Rowena' and 'The Salzburg Lovers' was originally published in *Southerly* and 'The Stonemason and the Sea' was originally published in *Salt*. I would like to thank the editors of these magazines for their interest in the book.

I would like to thank my publisher Clare Forster, editor Lisa Mills, Anitra Blackford, Dearne Sliskovic and Allison Scheffer at Penguin Books, for their warmth and precision.

I would like to thank my son Tom and Jill Ray, who each offered so much to my household at the time this book was written.

Our English friend described the poet as giving to his birds and flowers a delighted attention that seemed quite inconsistent with the gloomy and grotesque character of his writings. A favourite cat, too, enjoyed his friendly patronage, and often when he was engaged in composition it seated itself on his shoulder, purring as if in complacent approval of the work proceeding under its supervision.

Mrs Whitman, quoted in *Edgar Allan Poe*,
John Henry Ingram, New York, 1965

I

THE WINTER HOUSE

F inn's mother and my father were talking and talking behind the closed door of the study.

Finn is my first cousin. We're next to one another in all the family photographs, our heads tilting towards whoever is standing on either side of us so you hardly notice that we're touching, from our shoulders to our wrists.

The study had been built by the man who was my grand-father, as well as Finn's. He had built it well away from the main house, so he could write his parliamentary speeches there undisturbed. The study was like a small house, with window boxes and geraniums. There were clay dragons on the roof. Finn and I got a clear view of the roof from a back bedroom window on the first floor of the house. You could look straight down into the study. Finn and I were like a secret press gallery.

When he finally died, our grandfather was put in a coffin covered with an Australian flag. I could see that underneath all that cloth it was big, roomy enough for him to turn in his grave.

As a child I listened at the study door while he went over his delivery, his old crackling voice going up and down. By then even his own side had stopped listening. He set up a table at the markets and put a globe on it, a sepia globe with strips of paper splitting at the lines of longitude. People stopped for a spin, and wherever their finger landed he gave them a speech on trade policy. The Orkneys. Venezuela. Right in the middle of an argument about embargoes he tipped over and died.

The cousin who took a strong torch and a claw hammer to the cemetery at night didn't get much of a look at our dead grandfather. He climbed down into the vault but before he could get to work, one of the derelicts who slept in the warm grass piled against the headstones nearby decided to piss through the iron grille at the top of the vault and the cousin came home splashed and stinking.

My father took over the house and organised the caretaker, the repairs, the wood and ice deliveries and each family's share of holiday time.

The study was quiet for years. You could see the fireplace and bookshelves through the windows. Finn's family always came at the same time as we did. Then one year my father and Finn's mother started to go out to the study and talk. They made a joke of it. They called it their summer house. There were no lights in the windows, on dusk.

'While they're talking, they're safe,' said Finn.

We could hear the voices from the kitchen garden where

I was lying, hidden between the furrows, like some long blurry stripe in one of the paintings people often did, in summer, in the northern garden. The earth for the gardens was brought in drays from a silty river plain a long time ago. It was black and if a hoe sliced through it, the surface shone like thin glass. You could see shadows in the surface. It smelled good. It smelled as good as the inside of the machine which rolled our grandfather's cigarettes. Finn was sitting at the peak of a furrow between two staked vines. Every so often he leaned forward and ran a forefinger down each side of my sweaty collarbone. We practised a lot of things on each other, so we would know what to do when we grew up and met the people we wanted to do them with.

Finn got up to go inside. I didn't say anything. I rolled over to watch him at the kitchen window.

Firstly he slipped his forefinger inside his mouth. Then he drank a glass of water. Then he poured himself a glass of wine.

My mother was calling and calling, 'Thea! Thea!' She wanted to call my father, but she couldn't bring herself to say his name.

My father is a surgeon. He could pull your liver out from under your ribs as if it were a stiff drawer.

One night he showed his postcard collection around the table. We'd eaten. It was late, and hot, and the food had been left uncovered for too long to save. I could see my mother watching it.

My father collected postcards from the early twentieth century. He could have opened one of the cupboards upstairs and found bundles of them in old rubber bands. The Pyramids. Thickset bare-breasted girls with an urn held at the waist or balanced on a shoulder. Any number of cathedrals. My father's postcards were unusual. He collected pictures of death.

He had the odd ordinary person with the lank hair of recent illness spread over an embroidered pillow. If the picture was taken from the foot of the bed you could see plugs in the nostrils. Babies had a hard settled look, not like the live babies in the family, cousins or the babies of cousins, who relaxed into your shoulder like some heavy liquid. He had real postcards of executions from all over the world. If he set himself up behind a globe in the market, like my grandfather, and showed a postcard for every country where a finger pointed, he would have given people something to think about. He had gangsters with chests laid open under gunfire. He had the hanged. Women too huge to be carried through their doorways were photographed before being dragged onto a hammock and winched out over the street to an undertaker's van. Their flesh was dappled with black spots. My mother always waved her hand over the picture of the face with the insects. She couldn't help it. She'd seen them all and she'd been doing it for years. Earthquakes, mud slides, firing squads; there was a mania for pictures taken afterwards. A nurse was about to be shot as a spy, and when one of the men in the firing squad refused to take aim at her he was shot as well. There was a postcard of both of them.

It was Finn's mother's favourite card.

Finn thought that while his mother and my father were talking in the summer house everything was safe. When Finn and I practised our kissing it was soft and cushiony, we almost had to stop and smile. We didn't break free to talk.

The talking between our parents wasn't safe.

They were planning to leave us all, or rather, they were planning for us to leave.

Finn's father was brave, he was written up in all the war histories, but he couldn't bear to lose his wife. He had to be cared for by a special nurse.

My mother went back to the country where she always got a good price at the cattle auctions because everyone in the district knew that she was alone. She wasn't completely alone. She had me, and her sister lived nearby. She had my grandmother, too.

Somewhere in the old albums and scrapbooks you can find the pages where my grandparents are together, or where she is performing some duty on her own. There she is in a fair copy of a Worth dress, at twilight, in the grounds of Government House. She is walking along a row of Girl Guides. She is sharing a recipe with a miner's wife. Turn the page and she's completely gone. A photo of my grandfather will be cropped to the elbow, and a mark which looks like a ribbon in the crook of his arm will indicate that a woman's hand is resting there, and you know it isn't my grandmother's hand because the press have sliced the rest of this woman away.

My mother loved her mother-in-law. They lived close to one another. The rest of the family kept their distance. Finn didn't know our grandmother.

She wasn't pleasant or beautiful. Our grandfather sent her maintenance cheques, but they didn't amount to much. She was doing her best to die, but in fact she lasted years and years, until long after I had grown up.

My mother could eventually say my father's name, in between picking up the telephone and passing the old black receiver across to me. My old dolls were kept in a basket near the telephone. While my father talked to me my mother picked out each doll and plaited her hair very tight.

We didn't ever go back to my grandfather's house in the mountains, and the years passed. When I came across scraps of blue wool in the back of a drawer in my mother's house I had to think for a while before I realised that I'd saved them for my grandfather's bowerbird. I could hardly remember the bower under the rhododendrons in the northern garden.

Finn turned into a journalist. He had a column about Australian history which was syndicated across the country. It even turned up in our local newspaper. I saw his photograph and remembered the feel of his shaggy hair. Nobody could get a comb through it except me. I sat him on a kitchen chair with a towel over his shoulders and I dribbled the best olive oil through his hair until there were green drops on the towel, then I worked from the tips to the scalp with a comb. It was full but sleek, even after he washed it. His mother was very pleased.

After I left school, the stock and station agent gave me a job. I saved for a few years and then I went backpacking in America. The parliamentary grandfather was excited about America, he thought our west would follow theirs, and he loved to talk about the gold in California from behind his table at the markets. At a youth hostel in Boston I met a scientist who was working on blood clots and I stayed on for a while. When I came back I wrote a small book.

Finn and I passed for writers, in the family.

His mother thought that we should see each other.

He sent a postcard with a picture of a child crouched down in a vegetable garden. On the back was an invitation to meet him for lunch.

I didn't reply.

I was walking past the old black telephone when it started to ring. My mother had a new calf in an eiderdown in front of the slow combustion stove. The cow had died of snakebite and she'd had to use her bloat knife to cut the little one free. I was shaking up warm formula in a baby bottle and I picked up the phone with my free hand.

I didn't know his voice. Then I did.

He said he'd meet me at the railway station. I thought about the station where we dragged our luggage free and porters wheeled it to the cars which would drive us up to our grandfather's house in the mountains. The station smelled like coal smoke from the last century. There was a mortuary platform with a line out to some great necropolis. My father always pointed it out. It looked like the set of a wartime film.

I said, 'Everything will drop to black and white. Everything will go grainy.'

Finn said, 'I know. I've seen it. I was in tears every time I saw it. I was in tears.'

We both started to laugh.

The milk for the new calf was dripping from the upside-down bottle onto the floor.

He was thinner than I expected. He patted my shoulder. We sat down on the plastic crescent-shaped seats in front of the clocks and the old platform timetables which riffled through the names of stations like hard leaves turning over in the wind. Springwood. Blackheath.

I put my ankle on my knee and it got uncomfortable so I switched to the other ankle. Finn put his arm over the back of the seat behind me. He brought a big umbrella, in case it rained. I looked down at his beautifully polished shoes and remembered that his father was in the military. Pigeons landed at our feet, pacing, thickening their feathers at the throat.

'You can come to the staff club at the newspaper and eat something light or we can go to a restaurant for the afternoon.'

'You choose,' I said. 'You're the one with all the appetite.'

He let this pass. He asked if I ever thought about the summer house. I said that I thought of the whole place as the winter house. He told me I was right. He went there often, to write his column or to work on a book he was putting together. In winter he camped in front of the fireplace downstairs. He said that it was very cold.

Long after the calf was grown and sent to the saleyards, long after I forgot about Finn's harbourside lunch, I came to the winter house to distract myself. To escape.

My father asked if I'd like to go up there for a break. I was outside a church in my formal clothes. My parents were pretending that they'd never met. The black hat which felt so snugly comforting when I put it on in a shop that morning was tight, headachy.

My father explained that I wouldn't be alone, Finn would be there.

I was feeling alone. We were at the church because we were going to bury my grandmother.

Her death was expected, from the time before I was born. I said so to my mother. She said that all death is sudden, even when you've been waiting for a long, long time. The coffin had silver animals, foxes, on the handles. I was one of the six who carried her. She was small, so it must have been the wood and the silver handles which made her so very heavy. I had to swing my free arm a little outwards, to balance. When she was finally settled I looked down, thinking about how deep she was. The woman next to me was a friend of my mother's. Her hand had covered mine when we both automatically slid our palms flat under the box to lift our end, to keep it level so the whole thing wouldn't tip as we all carried it down the steps at the front of the church. She looked down into the hole with me.

'Sure is deep,' she said.

I could still feel the cool wood and her hand sliding over mine. The teethmarks of the machine which dug the grave were still there in the clay walls.

Afterwards I walked by myself for a while, over pits for stillborn babies and over the poor who were buried, at the end of the nineteenth century, in kerosine-tin coffins. There were the usual angels and glass domes protecting bleached plastic flowers. I could see why mourners bought them. I could see why children shattered them with stones.

My father had reminded me about the winter house. 'It's just above the cliffs,' he said. He talked awkwardly, like a tour guide, like someone introducing a place that the other person has never visited. 'There are plenty of walks. You can go for walks along the paths between the cliff face and the sky.' He was worried that I'd fall. I said that I'd be fine.

The drive still climbs through a rhododendron thicket. The son of the bowerbird must have a place in there, lit up with stolen blue clothes pegs. There are low fast-moving clouds, snow clouds, above.

I'm carrying my suitcase and the drive is much longer than I remember.

I let myself into the house. The hall, yes, and then the dining room.

The wooden draining board in the kitchen looks swollen and miserable. The sink has cracked three ways. When I turn on a tap to fill the kettle I can hear water pouring down into the wall behind. The pantry door is painted a dirty pale blue. Tiles lift; paint curls away from the walls. The pantry is stacked up with croquet hoops, old Hansards, wire birdcages, cardboard boxes and Fowlers Vacola bottles full of brown liquid and peeled white shapes. Eggs. Onions. The clamps over the lids are spotted with rust. A rum bottle with the lid unscrewed is thick with dead cockroaches. I don't know what the boxes hold. Envelopes of baby teeth. Letters from a boy sent off to school, who failed Latin and missed his rabbit.

There is a gardenia in a blue vase on the windowsill.

The fireplace is broad and deep. A shed out in the garden is filled with dried split timber. The door must have been left open in autumn because the wood is packed with leaves which are still, after months in dry darkness, the deepest red. The leaves burn first. They explode in quick white flame. I'm thinking of the ordinary words for fire; yes, it's crackling, it's licking at the wood, the upper unburned ridge of wood. Licking. *The fire tongues my dry life away.* I read it in one of the books which are stacked in piles in front of the bookshelves. The fire. My life. Sparks chip at the wire screen. Finn has propped it up to protect the rug with the spider design that someone dragged back from Afghanistan.

He's got an old anatomy book open in front of the fire.

'Did you know that there's a map of the nerves in the brain?' he asks.

I tell him I'm almost sure that the brain can't feel anything.

'No no,' he says.

I'm not with him. He's talking about a pattern of tissue and cells on the surface of the brain, a pattern which traces the whole body.

'A map of the nerves. The lips and hands are huge. And listen, it changes. If you cut off your arm, that arm is wiped right off the map.'

He starts to read aloud. Apparently the map on the brain isn't visible, like the pattern made by drystone walls when you look down from the second-storey windows, or the widow's walk on the roof of the house. I'm disappointed. I say that I would have liked a plan. A picture. Something completely clear.

'Wouldn't we all,' says Finn.

His hair is still shaggy, but it's completely, amazingly white. He's asked me to cut it in the kitchen with a towel around his shoulders and old newspapers under his chair. It's annoying him. He wants it clipped back to the skin. I imagine him with his head bent and his lap full of white. For the first time I'll see the exact shape of his head.

There are pictures of split heads in the anatomy book.

I can read the upside-down heading on the page in front of him. Even upside-down, it sounds more complicated than Finn is saying. But if he's right, I'm glad that this true map of the self and its state of pleasure or injury, its secret numbnesses, is hidden in darkness, under strong bone.

Finn has stopped turning the pages. He's lying face down, his head turned to one side, his cheek resting on the back of his hand.

It's my turn to move aside the screen and lift on more wood. I do it, wait, and the leaves burn in a quick white rush, lighting up the room. It looks like a library after a cataloguer's argument. The walls are lined with bookshelves and pile after pile of our grandfather's books are stacked on the floor. There are theatre programs and museum catalogues.

A cover shines briefly in the light cast by the burning leaves. I go over to pick it up. There are six pictures on the cover. A raven in profile. A red-eyed ape showing pointed predator's teeth. A church spire with a swirl of dark birds. An unconscious girl in a sprawl of yellow hair. A robust upright mummy, tightly wrapped, not at all like the photographs of mummies in the *Catalogue Général des Antiquités Egyptiennes du Musée du Caire* of 1912 – also in these piles of books – where the bodies seem so helpless and even the feet are dislocated, trapped in resin and webbing. The central image is a worried-looking man. A full moon shines through black branches behind him. He's completely alone.

The name of the book is *The Extraordinary Mr Poe*.

It's easy enough, since I'm already wedged against the shelves, to look up Poe in an old *Dictionary of Literary Biography*.

Edgar Allan Poe was born in 1809 in Boston, and died of drink or exhaustion or, according to some authorities, of rabies caused by a cat bite, in Baltimore, in 1849.

Poe's mother, an English actress, died in a rooming house in Richmond, Virginia, when Poe was three. Poe was the second of three children. His father had disappeared. He was brought up as the foster-child of wealthy southerners and cast off when he reached adulthood. He joined his father's family, who lived in great poverty, and married his thirteen-year-old cousin Virginia.

Poe wrote and worked on literary journals for a living, but he was often in want and usually in dispute with other editors and writers. When Virginia Poe was nineteen she had a lung haemorrhage and from then until her death at twenty-five she was extremely frail. Poe wrote that he could endure her death, but not the uncertainty of her illness, where he was constantly subject to false hope.

He endured for two years after her death, writing, lecturing and courting a number of women in the hope of making a stable home for himself and his mother-in-law, who was also his aunt.

Debussy was obsessed by him.

I know this because my mother played Debussy on her small upright piano at night, when she was bored with the radio. She played Schumann, as well, and other music which I've forgotten. Sometimes she told me about composers' lives. I remember Schumann, because he ruined his own hands.

The fire chips and chips at the screen. Finn is asleep, white-haired as a child and breathing in a slow deep rhythm. His arm is getting hot. He moves it, without waking up. On the map of the nerves, where the body billows or shrivels into nothingness, the shape of his warm arm must be suddenly large.

Finn's father was in British Intelligence. He was there when Rudolf Hess flew into Scotland to try to end the war. He stood by as Hess was questioned and finally shut away. You could say there was little enthusiasm for this in Intelligence. You could say more. They liked Hess, and Spandau Prison or in fact any kind of confinement, any place where you can have an effect only on yourself, was a nightmare for people like Finn's father.

When I was small I slept in this house with all the preparations for Christmas outside my door and wisteria under my window. My grandfather made me a nest of pillows: one above, one on each side. I've set myself up in the corner room over-looking the wisteria courtyard where I slept as a child. The clay dragons on the roof of the summer house are in view.

I'm trying for the feeling of Christmas and the scent of wisteria, but the season is all wrong. Now I can hardly sleep. I postpone the time when I go to bed.

I remember how on my first night here I woke up in sickening fear.

There were footsteps in the corridor of the long gallery at the top of the stairs. An arm lay coldly across my eyes.

I realised in a matter of seconds that the footsteps were Finn's. He always had trouble getting to sleep. The arm is no mystery, either. It prickled, warmed. I'd slept awkwardly and lost the circulation. If I'd got up and pulled on my jeans and sweater Finn would probably have made us both a cup of tea.

I'm gripping Finn's shoulder, shaking him, whispering. If he stays here all night the fire will burn out and he'll wake up icy, aching, in the early hours. He opens his eyes. I see, suddenly, that he doesn't recognise me. He has no idea where he is. Then he returns, relaxes, smiles.

He waits while I gather some books to read in bed and we part at the top of the stairs.

I've picked up the Poe section. As well as *The Extraordinary Mr Poe* I have three biographies and a collection of letters. There's even a *Children's Poe*. The books are still in the bedclothes when I wake, towards dawn.

I wake in the utter dark.

Surely this is my own arm, numb, across my eyes.

Surely.

Finn and I are out tramping on the cliff paths in a stiff wind. He writes in the morning, then he comes out for a walk. I've started to do the same, or rather, I've been leafing through books in the morning, waiting for him to knock on my door.

He can't see me. I'm behind him. I'm opening my mouth to the wind as children do, feeling that cool dryness in my mouth. My coat flaps open and my sweater flattens against my chest. My eyes are weeping at the outer corners. The path is so uneven that I have to watch each step. I'm missing the views: the blue air, a visible blue; the treetops so far below that they look like the small soft tops of blue–green clouds.

There's a secret pleasure in watching every step. I'm looking down at my hiking boots which are thick and supple with strong brass catches up each ankle, for the laces.

I wear a kind of uniform: jeans and solid boots. I wear a red sweater for a few days and when I get tired of it I switch to an identical one in green. Finn is dressed in much the same way, except his sweater is grey. My legs, when I look down, could be the legs of any tall thin man.

I'm wearing my grandmother's ring. In a way I don't like it. It slips and scrapes the inside of my little finger. It isn't even the ring she was married with. Most of the diamonds fell out and were lost. I'm wearing the final two, clotted in reworked platinum, a metal which always looks to me like the grey and black pattern on the back of a housefly. I'm wearing this ring, then, not for decoration, but because there are times when I'm absorbed in some task and I catch sight of it, from the corner of my eye, and briefly my hand looks just like hers.

Finn knows the way down clay paths over ferns and duckboards. The waterfalls shine like ribbon on brown stone. They're not thundering and vaporous, like some slipped ocean at the end of the world, like Niagara, which was my last waterfall. I held onto a railing, but I wasn't afraid.

'Ah, the mountain forests,' said Finn next to me. 'The mountain forests are funereal, secret, stern.'

'These forests?' The trees look soft and faintly blue. The sky is a nursery blue.

'A hundred years ago they saw things differently. Someone said the feeling in the bush came straight out of Poe. Lonely. Sinister. It helps if you're on horseback, late at night.'

We stop at the kiosk beside the highway for good coffee and chocolate on our way home.

I'm still thirsty. Cupboard doors are closed on shelf after shelf of glasses. Someone has begun to use them to organise and store small domestic things: rubber bands, pencils. Finn held up a glass of carpet tacks. In one quick unexpected action he mimed tossing them to the back of his throat. He could have been sixteen again.

There's an old black beret hanging next to a fireplace in one of the rooms off the dining room. It's a proper Basque beret from northern Spain: thick wool bound in leather. Our grand-father wore it at the markets. I'm cold, but I haven't put it on. I'm not in favour, I say to Finn, of historical re-enactments. With our history, it's just as well.

When I was small our grandmother lived in a building that is now a museum, with each room set up to imitate the way it could have looked in the past. The past is all polished mahogany and blue and white china with lightly crackled glaze.

I remember her sitting in an old brown armchair with a lit cigarette. Her mouth moved slightly, compulsively. It was the side effect of some drug. I often escaped from her armchair and her cigarette into the long grass and roses outside. There was a statue of a woman in the garden. A curve of sculpted drapery fell from her shoulder. I could scramble up and fit myself into this curve, which felt like a wide supportive arm. When it got too hard I went back inside. My grandmother had three rooms and each room had a door which was nailed shut, because someone else rented the room on the other side. I put my eye to the crack between the door and the architrave and imagined slipping through.

After she got too old to live alone she went to a nursing home where she had a small morgue as a smoking room. She sat in a plastic chair between a drawn curtain and a door. Around her neck was a chain and a copper merit badge in the shape of a shield, which her sister was given in 1915. Her sister died in 1919, in the flu epidemic. It was my grandmother's turn to look after a sick aunt, she refused, her sister went in her place, caught the infection and died. Smoking was only allowed in this small room. There was a plain bench for a corpse, usually empty, on the other side of the curtain.

She was just a frail jumble of limbs when she died.

When I dream about her she's solid as her armchair.

I think that the saddest photographs I've ever seen are the pictures of unwrapped mummies in my grandfather's catalogue. We used to leaf through it when we were children. We'd never seen such nakedness. The bodies have elongated and tightened on themselves. Some have a thin straight penis between their legs, some have long knobbled hands.

Someone from Cairo University unbandaged the bodies and wrote a description of each one.

He sifted through the linen and sawdust which is packed inside an ancient Egyptian corpse. He identified beads, teeth, wire and small wax gods. He admits that the fist-sized lump he found in one chest cavity is a mystery to him. It may be a precious stone, a carnelian, or a dried heart, pushed sideways when the body was cleared.

Sometimes a kind of tact stopped him. In a small tight parcel of bandages he could feel the skull of a child, just the skull, above a bunch of material which might be reeds. Another small parcel had the curved shape of a baby resting against a breast. They were wrapped for death as tightly as a living baby is swaddled. He didn't unroll these bandages.

Twice a coffin bearing the name of a famous king was found to hold the body of a woman. He noticed that the skin split under pressure from the material which was put in the mouth to make the cheeks look round and lifelike. Earlier writers thought that this split and lifting skin was a mask overlaying the real face. He corrects them. But he's the first to admit that he can't always tell the difference between a heart, after death, and a piece of stone.

We're out walking, Finn and I, on another afternoon.

We come to a valley which is like a scoop in the face of the cliff. Pale trees have grown to a great height, out of the valley's shadow. One has fallen over the path. Finn climbs over it and stops to rest on a flat rock on the other side. I sit with him. He passes me biscuits wrapped in greaseproof paper.

We sit for a little while in silence, then he tells me something about the famous General whose biography he is writing. He speaks about the General quickly, between mouthfuls of biscuit, as if he's a secret lover. He's irritated but he can't shut up.

I've been reading all the books on Poe, deliberately digging them out of the furthermost piles, disturbing the library. His stories are so dark and crisp. He flicks about like a gymnast and he makes a clean finish, every time. You could break your back just trying for that quick flick into stillness, at the end.

Finn stops complaining about the General. He surprises me. 'What are you writing about? You've been doing a lot of sighing, down in your room.'

I surprise myself. I hadn't been writing anything. Just copying a few lines into an old notebook. *The life still there, upon her hair — the death upon her eyes.* That kind of thing. Suddenly I say, 'I want to write another book. About Poe. I want to put the love back into Poe.'

'There's plenty of love in "Annabel Lee". It's the love poem of the century. His century. It's practically comatose with love.'

'Exactly. I mean alive love. Not just adoration.'

'Big job,' says Finn.

'There's a story I can't stop thinking about. A Poe story. Well, there's more than one. But the one that's on my mind is about a man who marries twice. Both wives die and when the second one dies part of her shroud or whatever falls away and he sees the hair of his first wife, underneath.'

'Gruesome,' he says. 'Imagine making up something like that.' He starts to roll a cigarette. He does it as neatly as a machine.

The facts are worse. When Poe's own wife died, the place where she was buried was due to be demolished and a man called Gill, who was writing a book about Poe, picked out her bones and put them in a box and forgot about them. When he remembered he showed them around. He said they were the bones of Annabel Lee.

The rim of paper at the edge of Finn's cigarette flares up for half a second and settles down.

Before I came up here I stayed in the city at the foot of the mountains. I had a few people I wanted to see. One was a woman friend, an actor. We met in a café near her theatre and she told me about shooting a love scene. The man lay between her legs with the lights and cameras behind him. Both were naked, but his body covered her up. I asked about the contact with the man. She laughed. He wrapped himself in an elastic bandage and held the end between his teeth, so it couldn't come adrift as he moved. They never really touched. When I see this film I'll see rapture in her face, although I know that at the time she was looking up at a bandage and a set of teeth. She says the camera angle is everything, in a vision of love.

Poe loved his cat and his cousin Virginia. He married her. He was Eddie. She was Sissy to him. Cousins. No ordinary romance.

There's just one picture of her, done straight after her death. Her eyes are half open. Her head tips loosely to one side. It looks less strange and uncomfortable if you imagine a pillow instead of the dark cross-hatching in the portrait.

In one of the books I've piled up next to my bed a man wrote that *one can never visualise Virginia as a woman. She remains a pale shadow, an Annabel Lee to be mourned as a spirit rather than as a once living human animal, and when she is spoken of it is usually as though she were a child.*

I copied it into my notebook. I've got it with me in my backpack.

I can't let this man have the last word on Virginia.

I can't lift the top of her skull and copy the map of her particular nerves.

I can't pull on the black beret of re-enactment, or a tight mourning hat. A bare-headed imagining is the best that I can do, a kind of dream of her.

My dead grandmother's head rested on thin cushioned wood, then on the flat of my hand, supported by another woman's hand, when we came carefully down the steps of the church, lifting her head so she wouldn't tip, imagining her comfort, when she was beyond all feeling of her own.

My old room is comfortable and warm. On the windowsill, at eye level, I've got a bunch of narcissuses in a glass from the big cupboard downstairs. They're more brilliant, more strong-smelling than wisteria. The man I met in Boston brought me a good deal of narcissuses, a bunch a day, throughout the late winter and into the spring. When I focus on the flowers I remember his face. What I remember most clearly is a line which was starting to form by the corner of his mouth. I wonder if it's a crease these days. The window here overlooks immense black ragged pines.

Under the narcissuses I've put a clay Buddha dipped in gold paint which a Chinese student gave me in Boston after I took him to a gallery. I know that the Buddha is clay inside the gold, because once I dropped it and it broke neatly in two. One of the halves formed the exact shape of the palm of whoever worked the clay and pressed that half into a mould. The palm-print was so perfect that I left the halves unglued for a while. Then I closed the Buddha on the secret Chinese palm.

The wind pours through the pines, the gutters of the summer house are thick with orange pine needles, the window rocks in its frame.

I close my notebook and begin to write, on the back of a sheet of my grandfather's old letterhead. I write a page and salvage one clean sentence and copy it onto a fresh page. The side of my hand slides over the impression of the emu and the kangaroo. When I finish in the early hours I have something called 'Poe's Cat'.

POE'S CAT

A MAN LIES AWAKE with a forgotten box of bones under his bed. He moves pillows, lights a lamp, takes a book and stares at the words. A window near his bed sways backwards and forwards in its casement with a squeak, a thud and a squeak. The fire is low, a single flame flares up in the dark. He turns down the lamp and pushes and shivers his way into sleep.

The bones under the bed are long and hard with slightly porous ends. They're wrapped in dark hair which is dull now, dull with dead sweat and traces of old soap. The teeth are dry but glossy and are all still in place. Scattered through bones, teeth, hair and the white linen threads of the burial dress are polished hairs from the coat of a well-groomed winter cat.

The cat sees all of this in a trance. It is so cold the cat and the woman, Virginia, are both dazed with the cold; it has found its way into the hollows inside their faces where it seems to swell. Their eyes are wet with cold.

The house in Amity Street and other places and events beyond this room, even beyond its own experience, appear. The cat sees into the future.

A man it doesn't recognise reaches into the collapsed wood of a coffin for the woman's bones. The graveyard is to be cleared and he has a new small box for her. The cat sees inside. There are no boundaries, no sealed places in its imaginings. It sees the woman catching cherries, stitching the red seams of the last dress which she wore visiting.

Their ears hurt. It is so very cold, too cold for the woman to talk or for the cat to listen. Speechless, bedridden, Virginia turns up the collar of the greatcoat which has been put around her and slips her small hands under the cat.

Muddy stands at the door in her neat cap and collar. The cap isn't tied. Wide bands of starched linen which would make an uncomfortable bow under her chin sit loosely above her black dress. Her face is encased in white cloth like the veil of a nun. She has lived a frugal, disciplined life, but it's all been self-discipline, not submission. Her face is square, thin-lipped, pouchy at the jawline. She could head the kind of Order which harries legalistic bishops, and she is often called a saint, but a life of spiritual or any other kind of obedience doesn't seem right for her. Besides, she's not a nun, she's a mother. Virginia's mother. She is important. Without her there would never have been a marriage, strong shoes, a roof, fire and food. Not that fire and food are plentiful at the moment. This is a plain country cottage, all sweet grass and honeysuckle in the summer, now deeply cold, and shoes, fire and food are hard for Muddy to find. Her luck is running low. It will rise, just a little, in the next few weeks before Virginia dies.

Muddy has brought a visitor to Virginia. Visitors come from New York, out to the country cottage at Fordham which is supposed to have such fine reviving air. Mary Gove Nichols is welcomed in, commenting on the cold. She looks at the straw bed where Virginia rests, the military coat that is the only warm covering. She has a friend, Marie Louise. Louise sits with the dying and the mad, offers diagnoses, reaches for whatever is most needed at every bedside: a facecloth, the first line of a poem. She's exactly the person this household needs. Right now, looking at Virginia, Mary is dismayed. The scene is so entirely comfortless. Then she notices. She says, 'The wonderful cat is trying to keep Virginia warm.' She's weeping as she speaks. Muddy rubs Virginia's feet, which have flung aside the prickling coat.

Suddenly, thanks to the visitor, a feather bed and eider-downs arrive. Louise comes over the hard earth to Virginia's bedside. She brings her medical intelligence, her painting materials and her quick pen. Muddy has something to cook and the stove is hot. The cat sits by it, looking across for passing feet and up at the underside of all the furniture, the rough unfinished places where insects wait without concealment.

When it's warm enough it goes back and settles next to Virginia.

When Louise comes the cat insists on her attention. She writes about it later: *The cat always left her cushion to rub my hands and I had always to speak to the cat before it would retire to its place of rest again.* She's troubled by the knowingness of the cat, forgetting the magic cats of fairytales and how they protect their owners. Louise looks into the cat's eyes, which are open wide with unnatural alertness, not panic, wide as an owl's eyes, and green. *She seemed possessed and I was nervous and almost afraid of her, this wonderful cat.*

Through the dark afternoons at Virginia's bedside, when the only movement is the white mist which her own breath forms repeatedly, and the slide of her brush as it makes a thin wash over paper, Louise suspects the cat of secret knowledge: the ability to speak, the knowledge of all human things and more, of things beyond our understanding, such as death.

Poor Eddie. He stands at the door; he's pigeon-chested and his arms are thin. These are the last weeks of his family life. For so long he has gauged the extremes of night-time sweats and daytime coughing. There can be no hope, just slight relief on occasional days. It's been an unusual marriage. A cluster, perhaps, rather than a marriage. When Eddie has taken too much alcohol or opium, Muddy scolds him and pulls off his boots. Virginia, on the other hand, is his pupil and his child. Muddy is not expected to be entertaining and Virginia is not expected to organise a house. It's an unusual marriage. At best playful, instructive, full of laughter and dearness. These aren't the best of times. 'My wife,' he says, 'my mother.' Muddy is not his mother, nor, these days, is Virginia much of a wife.

Virginia's hands move through fur. 'Actors,' she says, imitating the tone of his voice. 'The true son of actors.'

At least when the cat plays with sewing thread or the shadow of an insect on the wall it knows when to stop. When the game is over it moves to a high spot and cleans itself. Virginia strokes the red blotches of the coat, then the white, then the black. A tortoiseshell cat can only be female. It shows the world exactly what it is. Virginia touches the fur in patches, the red for blood, the white for the mother and then the black. She quickly smooths them together under her hands.

The man who scoops Virginia's bones into his box in the cat's cold trance has never met her. Perhaps he thinks she was scholarly and thin with a sweet voice. He's never felt her warm impatience in his body, as the cat has. He's confusing her with Eddie's stories. He shows people her bones, when he remembers them, under the name of one of Eddie's imaginary women: Annabel Lee. He wants to write about Eddie's life.

Eddie's mother was an actress. Eddie once told Louise that his mother was born at sea. Perhaps she was born in a bed in a room somewhere in London, and Eddie was making up a story to impress Louise.

His father was a lawyer who wanted to act, and did appear onstage. A lawyer must have conviction in the character he represents, and a fine carrying voice. David Poe, judging by reviews, needed to work on both.

Their first son, William Henry, was sent to his father's relatives.

Eddie was the second. He stayed with his mother, sleeping

in the space she made for him between her thin arm and her breast, watching the stage from the side as the houselights flared and simple hessian sets became weighty and majestic. Her voice and her limbs seemed to float. The lamps made her light and strong. He watched from the end of one cheap lodging-house bed after another as his mother's substantial whalebone stays pulled her stomach flat and gave her an unnatural waist. It was her last pregnancy. Already she was glittering and feverish. His father was gone, dead or just gone, by the time Eddie's mother died.

Her baby girl and her little son were with her when she was finally carried to her grave. They were separated and dispersed, with her few belongings and her cherished, secret letters. What was in these letters? Nobody knows exactly, although plenty of people would like to know, given the disappearance of Eddie's father and the harsh rumours about the parentage of the baby girl. They are a cherished set of letters, cherished, then finally burned.

Eddie was scooped up by a merchant's wife, dressed in floppy velvet and trained to recite. When he grew up he dressed in a military greatcoat and trained to drill.

The wife of the merchant died. Eddie didn't understand simple human hatred; how it is often said to be part of love, but entering it, tunnelling, will not bring you through to love. Time and again he stepped into the hatred of his foster-father and tried to dig through to something else. After many scenes, feints, denunciations and reunions, the merchant angrily, decisively abandoned him.

Where was he to go? He was twenty-six; his life insisted,

repeatedly, that he should be orphaned and alone. He was to sleep in solitary rooms, his greatcoat over some bed, stiff with the shape of his own emptiness. He wrote the merchant letters. Sometimes he was sent a little money.

He went back to his father's family, to Muddy, who was his widowed aunt. He had stayed with her once before. His older brother Henry was already part of her household. His decrepit grandmother watched them all from her nest of knitted rugs: Muddy and her children, Henry and Virginia; the new arrival, Eddie, and his brother Henry, who told stories about his time at sea and coughed with the consumption. The other Henry worked and drank. Their grandmother died before Eddie married his cousin Virginia, adding eight years to her age for the benefit of the deputy clerk who provided the certificate. Muddy endorsed Virginia's false age. There might have been an earlier, private wedding. A woman guest commented on the *very youthful appearance* of the bride. It was not the same woman who earlier spoke of Virginia's *abandon* in the company of her cousin, now her husband.

That is the first part of Eddie's story.

The man with the box of bones thinks Eddie was a genius.

The cat has heard Eddie's tales, read aloud.

The cat has heard Virginia tell stories, too. When she was a young girl Muddy sat her down by the stove or butter churn and made her talk about what Eddie did: the letters he wrote to an older girl, which Virginia delivered, and the puffy lock of hair she carried back; what he read in the lamplight when the others were asleep. Muddy was interested in everything. Virginia remembers the fire and the slapping churn.

Virginia told her mother all about the wooing of the girl with puffy hair but she gave nothing else away, beyond the titles of the books whose pages she and Eddie turned together, at night.

All these stories, with their events and particulars, and each one carries only a small part of the truth.

The cat in its trance half-dreams about all of this, as the cold swells within. Eddie is at least correct in his story about a man given to opium trances who desecrates his cousin's grave. He writes about a trance as a dangerously truthful state, a state in which a man who thinks about teeth might tear them from a dying jaw and gather them, without remembering he has done so, in a box.

There are proper coverings, now, but Virginia's breathing is much worse and sometimes she shivers. Eddie stops writing, briefly, and half-hears the sound of her breath. She's too sick to paste lengths of paper together for him to copy out his work. Virginia hears the scratch of his pen; when he pauses he hears her rasping breath. Her hands are slow in the cat's fur. Ordinary things alarm her: a pile of candles or the quality soap and strips of cloth which Muddy has put aside on a shelf for some unspecified purpose.

She's frightened after Louise goes, and she turns to the wall and makes a hollow for the cat under the eiderdown. When all she can see is the white wall her breathing softens and she whispers so quietly that her voice does not carry, even to the other side of the bed. The bed is warmed by the cat and Virginia's hands, or her poor breath or the breast feathers of some bird in the eiderdown.

She whispers about all kinds of things. She talks about her father, who is never mentioned in their household. His beard was full and very soft. She remembers him swinging her about in his arms. She has dreamed of flying ever since. When she flies in her dreams she sometimes smells his coffee and cotton shirts and something else, between aniseed and bitter chocolate, that might be his tobacco.

He died, as Muddy says, without making provision for her. 'Except,' Virginia whispers to her cat, 'for this secret gift of dreams.'

Someone is sending her unsigned letters. She reads them in the chair she asks to be carried to on brighter days.

These letters are about Eddie. Whoever writes them detests him. Muddy explains that one of the women who writes to Eddie has been offended by him: she is trying now to wound him through his wife. Plenty of women write to Eddie since he became famous. He encourages correspondence. When some of the women find out what is in another's letters there are all kinds of difficulties. Virginia has an unsigned letter in her lap. She looks at the open hatred in the words, thinking that the letters are the end of an original correspondence which she will never read, although once it lay to hand, on his desk or somewhere else in the house. She can only imagine the fervour of these vanished, loving letters. She infers it, through the existing hate.

Everything which is written, she tells her cat, makes you wonder why it was written, and leaves you imagining what might have been written instead.

She asks to be carried to bed. Eddie lifts her and the skirt of her donated nightdress bunches uncomfortably behind her knees.

The cat watches her slight movements, listens to her sounds. She sleeps, forgetting everything except the smell of cotton and coffee as she dreams, floating away from open masculine arms.

Later, the cat can hear a voice telling a story and it listens, in the hollow of the eiderdown, sighing briefly if Virginia's body moves.

Finn and I are at the kitchen window where he stood with the light behind him, licking my sweat from his finger, so long ago. We're both looking out into the kitchen garden. Something shaped like a squirrel is moving out of a cavity in the drystone wall that separates the rows of tomatoes and beans from the trunks of the elms which shadow the northern garden. It's as big as a squirrel. It glides to a trunk and freezes, then when it feels safe it scrambles up the bark. I can see the creamy belly, the long rubbery tail. It's a healthy rat.

'An outdoor rat,' I say to Finn. 'Feeding on the compost.'

'So long as it stays outdoors.'

There are no fences, and terriers come bustling through the garden occasionally, but I haven't seen a cat.

'You'd think a cat would come.'

'Grandfather shot a few after he lost a bowerbird.'

I think of the old man and his speeches, his easy policies, getting simpler and simpler the further away he got from any chance at power. Bad luck for the cats.

'I'm writing about a cat.'

I've put Finn in the wing chair, myself on the edge of the unmade bed.

I start to read the story of Poe's cat in the crooning voice of someone in our family who carried her child around like a teddy bear. I can only just remember her. Her husband died when she was well into her pregnancy. She spoke to her baby in a sing-song voice until my father snapped at her.

Finn is looking at me without blinking. 'Cut it out,' he says.

'Okay. Fine. I'm sorry,' I say.

I start again. I get to the end and Finn's eyes are closed. He sighs.

'A touch morbid,' he says.

'Not me,' I say brightly. 'I'm not morbid. It's all here in Poe.' I push at the pile of books with my foot.

'Yes, but you don't have to make a meal of it.'

I'm furious. He can see that I'm furious.

'Look. I know you're not trying to fall in line with Poe. I know you're not digging a hole in the ground and falling in. But he wrote miserable stuff. I read some poems at school. Miserable. Listen. This is what our housemaster said. Listen. I'll try to remember. Here goes. "The world has had enough of bards who wish that they were dead. 'Tis time the people passed a law to knock 'em on the head."'

'I'm not interested in the stuff your housemaster made up.'

Finn is pleased. 'He didn't make it up. It's Henry Lawson. There's plenty more, if I can remember it.'

'Please try,' I say as spitefully as a fourteen year old.

'"They say that life's an awful thing, and full of care and gloom,/They talk of peace and restfulness connected with the tomb."'

'Well, it was pretty awful. Life in the nineteenth century. Unless you had money.'

'"Some are made of common mud, and some are made of grit;/Some try to help the world along, while others fret and fume/And wish that they were slumbering in the silence of the tomb."'

When we were little our grandfather gave us threepence for recitations. He'd shout, '"The Sick Stockrider"!' and we'd leap to our feet and start. I want to throw a coin at Finn.

'Have a heart. His mother died. His wife died. She was so young, and he knew she was going to die. And she was his cousin, too.'

'That makes it worse?'

He's blurry, through my unexpected tears. 'It makes it so much worse.'

'Why?'

I'm looking for a way to tell him about how it was, for me, when we were practising by the summer house, or in each other's rooms, in this room. Finn and Thea. Cousins. The favourites of the grandfather.

We didn't stop at the collarbones. We had no words for this, no *making love*. We slid over and through one another. There was no break between us. All surge and no retraction. I never felt him shrink and slip clear of me. I couldn't speak. There was no need. We were like a socket and bone in the one limb.

It was my idea to say that we were only practising so we would know what to do when we grew up. It was fun, then it was more than fun. I couldn't speak. I was gasping; I've never taken in more air in my life and still I couldn't breathe.

'It was so close. You and me. I couldn't be bothered to breathe, when I was fucking you.'

He looks shocked. I can tell he was hoping I wouldn't bring this up. 'If you couldn't breathe when we were lovers, yes, *lovers*, how come you got asthma when we stopped?'

It's true. We had a discussion, Finn and I. We were as grave, as self-important as wartime parliamentarians. We decided not to do it any more. His mother and my father made it all seem so wrong and sad.

We decided not to do it and I got asthma straight away. It was years before my chest stopped closing up.

I don't want to be reminded of all this. I climb down from the old high bed and stamp out of my own room. It feels good, but it doesn't feel as good as winning an argument.

Later on I come back in with two mugs of tea and an explanation. 'I don't want to write about Poe. I want to write about Virginia.' Another breathless girl.

'Fine. Let me in on it. If you let me in on it I'll tell you if you're slipping into a crypt.'

There's a room directly under my own that looks straight out into the wisteria courtyard. The woman who helped in the kitchen slept there. It still looks like the room of someone who didn't sit down with the family. There's a small armchair draped in too many knitted rugs. She stitched her squares up and added another layer of rug to the chair and sat straight down and started in on the next one. The first few must be matted together like felt. The bed looks as if no one has ever slept in it with a man, or even with a bent knee jutting out over the mattress edge.

I'm down here because I remember this woman turning up at my bedside in a storm which had brought down all the power lines. My grandfather sent her to check on me. She was carrying a candle in a chipped enamel holder and she left it at my bedside so I wouldn't be afraid. The flame was out of sight. It seemed that the walls themselves had begun to softly glow.

I've found it. A box of six candles and matches. The holder. She left behind a hairnet too, dusty brown and so fine I thought it was old hair pulled from a brush, until I held it open in my fingers. It had little glittery chips of glass, blue and rose and clear glass, fastened throughout the net. She would have sat in that chair, knitting, glittering. I can't remember her name.

I'm up in my own room in a pool of candlelight. I want to write another Poe story for Finn. So he'll understand why the idea of Virginia follows me about the corridors and will not be blown aside by the wind on the cliff paths. I feel like I'm in high school. 'Ligeia' appears, under the address of our grandfather's electoral office.

LIGEIA

A MAN IS TELLING a story about a series of terrible events which befell him a long time ago. He was once married to Ligeia, a tall, thin, scholarly woman, dark and very beautiful. He was so engrossed in her beauty and erudition that he now remembers nothing else about her, no details of her family or even her father's name; nothing except her body and her ideas. They lived in an ancient town somewhere on the Rhine. He doesn't say where.

When I read this back to myself I think about another kind of romance where the family needs no introduction. Cousins. I try to remember loving Finn. The blurriness of love where there is nothing fresh or new: no meeting each other's parents for the first time, no discoveries of tastes or separate memories. Nothing but bodies and ideas.

His wife's health begins to decline. As she dies she clings to her husband's hand, speaking with frightening forcefulness of her great love for him, and insisting that death is only a failure of the will to live.

The man leaves the German town and buys a ruined abbey in a bleak part of England. He restores it and decorates it with great extravagance and passes the time smoking opium.

He marries a fair Englishwoman.

The new wife does have a lineage. She is Lady Rowena Trevanion, of Tramaine.

He treats her cruelly. He roams about the countryside calling his first wife's name. His temper is atrocious. Rowena hides from him. Then she becomes mysteriously ill. She is thin and terrified. She sees and hears things which are not there. Once, after a good deal of opium, he hears odd noises in the room, and sees drops of strange liquid materialise in the air and fall into the cup from which Rowena drinks.

Rowena dies.

He sits up with the corpse. He isn't in mourning for Rowena, he is still longing for his first wife. With all possible intensity he imagines her alive. The body seems to revive, then slip back into death. He thinks passionately about Ligeia. The dead woman's pulse starts, then stops. He imagines Ligeia and hears a slight cry.

Towards morning the woman stands up in her grave-clothes and pulls the bindings from her face. Her hair is plentiful, and black. His longings are requited. It is Ligeia.

The Story of Rowena

Once upon a time, Virginia says, there was a small monastery in a remote part of England. It didn't have a vineyard or a bakery or books bound in thick caramel-coloured skin. The walls were built by the monks themselves from local stone. These particular monks had taken vows of silence, so they worked carefully from copied drawings and made signs to one another with their fingers. They developed strong and supple hands. When the walls and the tower were finished, a vine with glossy leaves was planted against the walls and soon the simple building had a covering which moved in the wind and offered birds a place to nest.

The abbot's great ambition was to have a sheet of glass set in the window of the turret. He asked the local people to help and although it was not a wealthy region, the gold for the window was finally gathered and taken to Venice by one of the brothers, where this great expanse of glass could be poured.

Years passed and the silent monks went about their devotions, but the abbot was increasingly angry and distracted because his glass didn't arrive. Finally he set out on foot with the senior monks to see what had become of the gold and the window.

For the first few months of the abbot's absence the bare feet of the monks followed their usual disciplined paths. Yet as time passed and the abbot failed to return breaches occurred, so slight as to seem a consequence of forgetfulness. Eyes were raised from the stone paths to the sky, which wasn't always dark and overcast. New harmonies grew in the choir. The language of hands was used for jokes and conversations as well as for instructions. One after another, their garments of mortification were left unworn and they slept in shy nakedness under woollen cloth which the abbot had laid aside for his own vestments. Pines sighed beyond the stone, owls cried out and deer skittered fearfully from some enemy in the grounds. It was good to be inside.

More months passed and the monks stopped watering down their wine. They began to visit the sick and poor whom they had simply prayed for in the past. They repaired stone walls and thatching for the villagers and, since the local people couldn't understand their language of signs, they learned, again, to speak. One by one the monks left the monastery to join the women of the town, who welcomed them, delighted with their patient supple hands. Tonsures grew out and beards grew in. New fathers soothed their babies with liturgical chants.

The last monk to leave was the nephew of the abbot. As he was dragging the great iron-studded gates closed a cart appeared, pushed by the brother who had been sent to Venice years before. They unwrapped the glass together in the tower. It was disappointingly grey but they fixed it in place as the abbot would have wished, before making their way together down the winding stairs to the gates and the village beyond.

Long after the children of the monks and their children were grown, when the monastery buildings were just a scatter of stone and a tower, a man in deep mourning came to the village.

Children were playing around the great oak cask in the village square where women poured the urine of their households, which was used to clean hearths and clothing.

Rowena was the child of the poorest widow in the village. She stood by the cask with her mother's iron dipper and he nodded to her, through the startling fumes of ammonia.

At a meeting of the local guilds he announced his plan to restore the deserted monastery. Someone found the original plans with their ancestor's notes on the edge of the parchment. There was a story, in another family, about the unusual carving of the ruined ceiling in the turret. Tools were unearthed and the local people set to work, hammering and winching stones into place.

The stranger was black and birdlike, watching everything with quick shifts of attention and a slightly tilted head.

When he went to the city work slowed and Rowena joined the other children who carried baskets of fruit and bread to their fathers, then rolled in the high grass under silver birches until the pollen made them sneeze.

The stranger returned with the means of decorating his new home. He showed the children plain blue paper for the walls of his library and marbled paper for a lesser room. He had a piece of tapestry in black and gold with a peculiar design of limbs and faces, which they could only see in part. When the others left he showed Rowena the entire pattern; she saw strange connections between the bodies. She kept forgetting to ask her mother what it meant.

The people of the village talked continually about his treasure, but she never freed him, in her mind, from the smell of piss, and she thought the spouting men in his tapestry were simply passing water, inexplicably, in a black design on cloth of gold.

At last the draperies were hung, the abbot's old glass was polished, candles were wedged into their sconces and the local people were invited to the building to enjoy the sight of the restoration. Rowena thought the rooms were as strange as the props and costumes of the travelling players who set up in the village square each year. She and her playmates hid and sprang out at one another. The monastery was full of children laughing, crouching behind the ottomans or the marble bath.

In the turret she found matching cupboards, painted to look like granite, but made of a light wood. She stepped inside one and half pulled it shut, then she realised that the paint was so recent it was blackening her hand and she found somewhere else to hide. The stranger had a special word for the cupboard, it was a sarcophagus, supposed to have been carried all the way from Egypt.

The stranger's wealth was said to have been bequeathed to him by his wife, a German princess who died of a goitre. Village women hoped at least to see a portrait in court dress and they weren't disappointed. The stranger had painted the picture himself. The German's pink breasts and her collarbones were shaded with grey. She had bulbous eyes and her hair was completely black.

The stranger suggested to Rowena's mother that he teach Rowena another language, perhaps German. At first she refused. She dreamed that Rowena walked through the stones of a black wall and she could not follow, although she beat on it with the palms of her hands. The guilds didn't like to see Rowena's mother offending their patron and they threatened her with eviction if she didn't comply. She thought of the homeless and their hollow-eyed children sleeping under shelters of rough logs in the forest.

Rowena had no aptitude for languages. The only word she remembered was *Mutti*: mother. Her hands were dirty from making mud men with the other children on the riverbank. He told her the story of the young huntsman who is tempted into casting infallible bullets, with the help of a ritual involving the skull of a woman who has died in childbirth, a dagger and crucible. One of the bullets almost takes the life of his bride. Rowena nodded and sweated. He liked her best when he'd taken his dose of opium and he sat her on his desk with her back to him and undid her plait, combing out her pale hair with his fingers and twitching it, one way and then another, to catch the light. She was supposed to keep quite still. Finally Rowena was allowed to leave and she ran so fast down the road to the village that she tripped and grazed her knees.

Later, when she walked into the chapel where the monks had once prayed in temporary obedience, her wedding gown snagged with every step on the brown scabs across her knees.

Virginia stops whispering and her hands are still. The cat and the woman can hear the wind in the bare lilac and the cherry tree outside. Eddie's chair scrapes back in the next room and his new boots creak across the boards. He'll go for a walk to deliver a poem or a letter and he'll forget them, lose his coat in a tavern, court a woman or, without a pistol to his name, become involved in a duel. Muddy will have to calm him and wipe him down, when he turns up.

Virginia's breath comes deeply, evenly; the cat feels the warmth of her suddenly healthy breath in its fur. Muddy has put some scented winter flower on the table next to Virginia's bed. It's perhaps not quite as pleasant for the cat as the honey smell of blood which often comes from Virginia's mouth.

She wakes naturally and her eyes open. She yawns. Where was I? she says. She talks about the composer, Weber, and how she has heard slaves singing his 'Bridesmaid's Song'. She knows some of the details of his life. He loved cherries, she says, and his hands were odd because the thumbs came halfway down the fingers and the fourth finger was at least as strong as all the others.

Rowena's mother told her what she might expect of her marriage and this explained the figures on the tapestry. But when Rowena put her arms around her new husband he felt as empty as a cylinder of paper, as dry as a scroll. She didn't press too hard. Each day she knelt on the window seat, curved her hands around her eyes and pressed her face to the grey glass. She ran along the colonnades with a hoop and at night he put her to bed with a glass of milk. He tucked her tightly into the sheets and, in his only attempt at play, drew a single corner over her face. She decided it was a foreign custom and slept soundly in the bed between the two black cupboards. Every day she sat up on her husband's desk and he twitched her hair, or tugged it without exactly hurting her. The pressure on her scalp was almost pleasurable. She remembered that when she was small and comfortless she didn't suck her thumb, she twirled the end of her plait around and pulled it, over and over again.

One night her husband swept his candle over her as she lay asleep. The light glinted on the carpet by the bed, which was woven with the same design as the tapestries. He noticed a strange irregularity in the pattern. Bending closer, he saw that the silk was splotched with blood.

Virginia stops telling the story. 'I keep thinking about Weber's hands,' she says. 'He had a big reach and a strong fourth finger himself, so his music is difficult for a person with normal hands to play. He didn't recognise other people's weaknesses. As for the marksman and his infallible bullets,' she says, 'he was so caught up in his own weakness that he didn't notice that it could all end in the death of his wife.'

After her first bleed Rowena began to have peculiar dreams. There was no moon and the turret room was completely dark. She thought she woke to something warm and soft, very close to her face. She sat up quickly and freed her arms from the sheet. She seemed to be alone. When she relaxed and closed her eyes the sensation of warmth returned. She dreamed of kisses: dry splashes of kisses on her shoulders and her face. Fingertips moved her hair aside and touched her mouth and ears. She took a strange finger into her mouth and held it between her teeth. It was cool on her tongue.

Her husband decided that Rowena's portrait should be painted. She waited on the window seat while his brushes swept across the canvas. It took a long time. She finished each day rubbing her arms and stamping her feet to bring back the circulation. Food was forgotten, in his creative intensity. She was often hungry and she lived for the moment when she could sink into sleep. The picture was kept covered because she wasn't to see it until it was complete. She wished her husband would interest himself in music or translation, as in the past. Months wore on while the canvas was scraped in places and re-worked.

She woke in the night and examined her dreams, as a monk might have examined his conscience.

She dreamed of bundled letters and fine scented soap. In her dream her mother was beside her, saying to whoever was listening, 'I lie with her until she goes to sleep.' If the moonlight was bright enough when she woke she could see the pines at the edge of the monastery grounds. Some were dying, their trunks bare except for the jagged stumps of branches. Healthy trees had a huge disordered reach and clumps of shadowy needles, like the fur of a cat, but dark, dark green. They gave the wind a soothing voice.

She closed her eyes and waited, listening to the wind until it stopped sounding like the wind and became a rushing sound, the sound of light breath blown on her face and over her ear. She was being kissed; it was soft and cushiony and her mouth opened on a vast dark warmth. She had the impression of the interior of the mouth as a place of warm expansion, not an opening of jaws. Then the mouths separated and she felt, on her face, sensations of warmth so light they might have been produced by her own happy skin.

All day she sat for her portrait, cherishing the prickle of a small abrasion on her favourite breast.

'Cherries,' says Virginia. 'What I'd give for a lapful of cherries.' She moves the eiderdown around the cat. 'No use to you. You want the real thing, don't you? Blood for you, cherries for me, please.'

In the autumn she was sitting under the cherry tree in a white dress, catching the fruit as Eddie threw it down into her hands. He was no climber, he leaned against the trunk, not high off the ground. They were both laughing for a change. Then a cough interrupted her laugh and her dress was suddenly splashed with brilliant red.

'Back to Rowena and her little chafed breast,' says Virginia.

Rowena sat obediently watching the back of the canvas. Her husband scraped at the paint so fiercely that she saw the impression of the knife in the weave. At his feet lay curls of greasy paint, exactly the pale colour of her hair. She could move a little, when his attention was held by the canvas. She examined the tapestries. The pattern seemed dull and obvious, after her dreams. As time wore on she noticed that her husband rarely looked up to check his image against his subject. He spent hours with his face close to the canvas. She discovered that she was able to slip down from the window seat and walk in the colonnades, or out under the pine trees, without him missing her. He worked steadily, then slept on an ottoman directly beside his work. She found him asleep in this position after one of her walks, and, curiosity overcoming her obedience, she stood in front of her portrait. She recognised the features from a looking-glass. Yes, it was her. But it was not her alert daily face: her eyes were closed, her head tipped to one side: the angle gave her chin an abnormal fullness and looped above her ear was the glossiest black hair.

There was a peculiar stillness about the face on the canvas.

Rowena once heard a story about a man so obsessed with a portrait of his new wife that he failed to notice her illness. The completion of the painting coincided with her death.

The grey glass pane rippled in places. It had been poured imperfectly. It gave her an idea.

Standing on a high fine chair, she reached for every candle

in every sconce throughout the turret and the lower rooms. She melted them in an iron dish over the great fire in the kitchens. When the wax was liquid she poured it onto the flagstones, where it cooled into a malleable sheet. She carried it up the turret stairs to where her husband lay sleeping and spread it over him, taking care to make a hole so he could breathe. As he lay under the heavy warmth of the wax he felt, as if in a dream, small hands smoothing his limbs and sealing the wax around his head and chest. Rowena looked down at the drift of grey bubbles in the wax blanket. It was kinder than tying his hands and feet, she thought. As the wax hardened he tried to smile in his sleep and she realised that he was enjoying the complete and cooling embrace she had provided for him.

She took up his palette and brushes and set to work on the canvas. Low on each closed eye she painted a lid and lashes, so her portrait stopped showing the face of a dead woman and became, instead, the face of a woman half awake, in a relaxed and languorous trance.

When she finished she gathered the white nightgowns and dresses of her marriage and carefully tied them into a bundle. As she walked down the road to the village with the bundle on her back it occurred to her that she and her mother could join the travelling players. The clothing would make fine costumes for both of them. She could play Juliet in white batiste, in some easily dismantled tomb.

'There you are,' says Virginia, 'a story, a romance, in fact, all finished.' She's bright-eyed, very warm. The cat stretches and rolls. 'No loose ends?' she asks.

It would be good to move to the stove, but Virginia holds her cat.

'Just the one, perhaps. The letters in Rowena's dream. Listen.'

The Salzburg Lovers

Once there was a pair of musicians who first met in Salzburg. Although they lived far, far apart and spoke different languages a friendship developed between them and they corresponded for many years.

Both travelled a great deal with their work and from time to time one would stand on a quay between the stone and the harbour of a great city and consider that the other was due to embark or to depart from that place soon, but not soon enough for a meeting to take place.

At first their letters were full of professional discoveries. Then one was briefly displaced from his position at the same time as the other fell in love with a cruel first violin. Each remembered with relief the touch of the other through formal cloth as they had embraced on their last meeting, now so very long ago. In time they developed a habit of including occasional dreams in their letters, as well as words of consolation, quotations, opinions and descriptions of events. Over the years the dreams revealed many coincidences and anticipations. Each discovered a great deal about himself, as well as the other, through the correspondence of these dreams.

One set of dreams recurred, but was never committed to

paper by either man. Each knew, but kept secret, the manner of the other's death.

I'm sitting on the floor by the candle and Finn is in the wing chair.

I read the last word, *death*, and turn the page so the crest and the old electoral address are all that I can see.

Finn is looking straight ahead. From here I can see the underside of his top lip. He has his mother's mouth. Soft and full.

'Would it change anything, if you knew?'

'Our grandmother thought she knew when she was going to die.'

'She got hope and facts mixed up.'

I am thinking that before I die I'd like to run the edge of my hand lightly over the dip that Finn's spine makes down the length of his back.

I nearly forgot. 'The writing?'

He smiles and I can almost see inside his mouth.

II

A Woman Had First to Die

Today I opened the ladder room because I wanted to climb up through the roof and look down on the northern garden.

Nobody ever wanted to sleep in the ladder room except the big cousins with the ouija board. They had a friend whose motorbike slid over on a wet curve. A truck was coming the other way. They wanted this friend to tell them what was going to be in their next exam. I think the dead boy did his best, spelling things out slowly, like a person with a terrible disability.

'Remember the ouija board?' I say to Finn, at the top of the stairs.

He walks slowly towards me, like any one of the fathers in the family. The same stare, the same slow tread.

'Thea, you are not, absolutely not, to use the ouija board to call up Poe.'

He's gone before I realise what he's talking about.

The ladder room made a good darkroom, and for a while there was a lot of splashing about with chemicals behind the door, until someone's mother walked in and saw pictures of a great-uncle's extender in full use. The extender came in a cardboard box. It was a glass tube, narrow at one end, with a hose and a pump-bulb at the other. The narrow end fitted over an adolescent penis, and the results, in terms of size, were brief but spectacular. The adolescent penises were pretty spectacular to begin with. The extender was now bundled up with all the developing equipment.

The ladder room is one of the internal rooms, flanked by the gallery on one side and the long study on the other. Three rooms open into the long study. Nobody ever studied there. The windows are huge and the light is too strong. Books and prints are best left downstairs.

I can see why Finn set himself up in the rooms at the end of the first floor. He has a bedroom where I was taken, when I was small, by someone much older, and shown the shadow of a man on the rug. Lamps were moved over the shadow to convince me that it wasn't a trick of the light. I should have squatted down and patted it with the palm of my hand. It was just a patch of dampness from a fallen vase. At the time it looked like drained body-fluids, and it didn't smell good either. If you don't imagine a corpse on the floor the room is very pretty. It has a high bed which must be climbed up into, like an old car without the doors, and a sunroom to one side, with windows opening on to birds and lichen. Finn has set up a desk out there. He seems to write from a platform in the winter sky.

I like to sit quietly in the darkness of the ladder room. Until today I've never climbed the ladder. Nobody has, for years and years. The ladder is bolted flat to the wall. I can only manage toeholds on the rungs. At the top there's a framed wooden square with an iron handle. I force it aside and keep climbing. I'm crouching in a big shallow roofspace. To one side and ahead of me I can see another ladder. It must end in a door or a trap-door, yes, it does. My mother used to come out on this narrow balcony calling, 'Thea! Thea!', trying to spot my father on his way to the summer house. I could hear her as far away as the fern paths that lead to the cliffs.

The northern garden is a sea of copper leaves. Each leaf is a stiff hand-sized scoop, like a wave. They've fallen in thick drifts. I know they're copper-coloured because they show orange, or gold, against the reddish black of the iron boats which have appeared in the garden. These boats are too beautiful to be the cast-offs of someone's welding class. My father must have bought them in a gallery in the city. Without the boats for contrast the leaves would look much more red and ordinary. There are benches, too, in this sea of leaves. They've been painted, or their paint has weathered, to a light bluish green, the colour of copper salts or corrosion.

The boats move about each day. Someone knocked on the door and introduced himself as a photographer who is working in the garden and I think he drags the boats into different positions, using them as props. Sometimes a sail is missing, or it reappears.

I wake and listen to the garden, in the night. A man walks in sandshoes, up and down the gravel under my window. I listen to the squeak, squeak, squeak. It's a frog. A nightbird whistles, closer and closer. It's a man whistling up a dog. I think of the dog trotting and pausing and trotting further on, down the stone steps under the rhododendrons. The man claps softly and whistles. There are no fences. He passes through the grounds and goes away. I'm listening for the drag and scrape of the boats in the darkness. It doesn't come.

The boat I like best is empty except for an iron basket filled with big white stones. It has a curved iron sail. This boat keeps appearing in the northern garden. It's the kind of boat you might find a baby in.

I'm climbing the second ladder. When I break through to the widow's walk on the roof of the house I half-expect to see the daughter of a pharoah far below, very cross and cold in her thin pleated linen, tapping her fingers on her upper arms and frowning down at the baby Moses in the belly of this boat.

Perhaps a baby is the very thing she needs. Or perhaps what she needs is an empty boat with a swivelling sail.

My mother always says that a woman must have three things of her very own. She started to make lists like this after my father left her. Three things, she says, like a good godmother at the foot of a cradle, or like the queen in the fairytale who pricks her finger as she sits at a window in the wintertime, stitching clothing for her unborn child. Blood falls on the snowy windowsill and the queen wishes for a daughter as white as snow, as red as blood and as dark as the window frame.

My mother wouldn't wish beauty on a baby girl. She says what a woman needs in life is her own money, her own car and a gun.

I've never seen her with a gun. Somehow it isn't a handgun I imagine for her. Her wrists are too small. Besides, a handgun for most of us is just a shape on a television screen and she doesn't watch much television. She's a country woman; a woman feeding the wood she has just chopped into the firebox of a slow-combustion stove while cats crouch and stretch in the narrow space between the stove and the side of the chimney. When I think of her with a gun I think of a light rifle with a stock as warmly polished as a cathedral pew; a stock with a brief and painless recoil. Or a shotgun which can be broken up like a metal puzzle and scattered in pieces throughout the innocent cupboards of the house.

I have one of the things she would wish for me. For the moment, I have a little money of my own. I don't have a car, but I can walk to the cliff paths or to the cafés and the supermarket. I catch the train down to the city. In the morning I sit with old women holding baskets on their knees and at night boys run the length of the train or light matches and hold the flame against one another's jeans. I'm not frightened, in the train at night. If the boys stumble against my seat they're quick to apologise. I've never held a gun. A calm silence is the best defence.

When I was little my mother and I spent each Sunday after-noon with my grandmother, the one who just died. Long after her Government House frocks were too grubby and torn for the dress-up box under the stairs, long after the broken pieces of her Minton dinner service were piled into a pothole in the driveway along with the top of a finely smashed marble wash-stand, she survived in her brown armchair with her pack of cigarettes. My father sent her a gold lighter once. She wasn't impressed by the brand name. She had forgotten what Cartier meant. My father didn't visit her.

We drove away from the wooden farmhouse on the river-bank along roads that were twin ruts, with a crown of grass in the centre which brushed the underside of the car.

Her three rooms were in a house in town. On the wall outside her rooms, above each window, there was a semicircle of stone. On either side of the windowsills stone was carved to look like a burst of flame. Inside, my grandmother sat in her armchair, moving only to light a cigarette or pass a letter to my mother. Once she unbuttoned her dress and put her hand across a white and oddly young breast to show my mother something: a rash, or a bruise where she had bumped against a doorway. Otherwise she was still and often silent.

In one story of Sleeping Beauty the princess is pricked with a spindle and falls asleep, but she isn't woken with a kiss. She's raped. Still fast asleep, she gives birth to a boy and a girl. The girl sucks her mother's finger and a splinter comes out. The spell is broken. In this story only a daughter has the power to heal a mother. Perhaps this was the problem. My mother was only a daughter-in-law.

My mother has walked down hospital corridors past a woman lying on a trolley with her throat cut, through bath-rooms where the basins were streaked with human waste, past the slow unravelling of a wicker chair by another woman who is hoping to hang herself with the twine. Once my mother stood at a bus stop outside a big hospital and an old lover who knew the place came by. She told him which ward she was going to. He said, 'You can't go in there,' but she did. She found my grandmother and carried her away, and nothing changed. We used to sit in silence until the hours pass and sometimes my mother knitted and sometimes my grandmother drank from a glass, because the drug which keeps her calm and still also dried her mouth.

When I wasn't playing in the garden, or watching in the stables for what I thought were very large mice, I learned to enjoy settling into a calm silence, almost a trance, within myself.

I've pushed the last obstacle aside. I'm on a ledge behind a railing on the roof of the house, looking down on the sea of copper leaves. There is no boat of motherhood far below, no shivering Egyptian girl. There's no boat to sail away in. The sea is empty, except for the benches in their pale corrosive green.

'What was your mother like, Finn?' I know her as a woman carrying a tartan rug across a lawn; as a voice in tune with my father's, in the twilight; as a name which made my mother sick, really sick, to hear. There's more to her than all of this. After she began to love my father she must have worried about him in the same way that my mother did. He was a surgeon. He liked to show off his stainless steel tables with their convenient drains. He liked to show off his electric saw. She must have worried that a cloud of tuberculosis, or something even more deadly and invisible, would drift up from some opened breastbone. She must have grieved over Finn, who stayed with his own father.

We're on the floor in front of the fire again. It's early in the evening and we're sitting cross-legged on the spider rug with our plates in our laps. We could eat formally, sitting up at the polished table in the dining room. We could eat from a painted table which is fixed to the kitchen floor. I like it, though, between the sofa and the fire.

The food is good. Finn can cook. He doesn't keep his supplies in the old pantry. Tonight he's baked rich meat with an undertone of citrus and red wine. All the flavours have merged into each other. Before I came here food seemed to separate into grease and salt, or sugar, in my mouth. I lived on boiled eggs and sharp Greek yoghurt. I ate apples and rye bread. Yet here I am, spooning out more and more for both of us until there are just puddles of sauce left in the dishes.

Finn is lying along the sofa behind me in the darkness.

It's his father he wants to talk about. My uncle. His father was in North Africa in the war. The nights were bitter. The days were burning hot. Water was in short supply, men wiped the worst of the dirt off their uniforms with petrol. Troops dug holes for themselves in the sand at night, or crept under the flaps of ammunition tents and woke up sick from the cordite fumes. When he was approached by British Intelligence he didn't hesitate. He was sent to Scotland to interrogate German fliers.

'His German must have been good.'

'No,' says Finn. 'His Latin was very good.'

The interrogation was more like a conversation, both sides

listening, less for hard information than for shifts in tone and attitude, signals of allegiances. I remember that after the war he was sent to China, then South America, which was where Finn, who was six, met him for the very first time.

I remind him about his mother. His mother, he says, was not really with his father, even when they lived under the same roof. This explains a lot. His parents seldom lived together. They wrote, over long distances. Finn was the only son and his mother's favourite. But something odd happened after the big break-up, when he was left to look after his father. 'She expected me to be in charge,' he says. I can tell it's not the time to turn around, to catch his eye. 'Then,' he says, 'she began to hate me.'

No wonder so many stories are about the adventures of someone who travels alone.

The next morning I'm down in the kitchen, cutting sandwiches for a train journey. I'm going down to the city to see my father. Sometimes it just has to be done.

When I was little my mother and I shared a bunk in a wood-panelled country train with clip-up silver washbasins and a chained bottle of dirty water which shifted, in a silver holder, all through the night. I know, because I watched it. I sat up between the rocking wall of our compartment and the wall of my mother's back. I've never ridden in another train like that, although I've always hoped for one.

The train to the city has rows of orange acrylic seats. It's the kind of thing I want to know about Poe's life. I want to know about the ship which took him to England when he was a child.

I want to know about lanterns and the china on the captain's table. I want to know how he travelled between Richmond and Baltimore, where he first met Virginia. I want the colour of cushions, if there were cushions, and the painted wood. I want the sway of a tilting ship or a train.

I read over my Poe notes, but they don't help. I try to read the *Children's Poe*. Howard R. Howard wrote it, he says in the preface, to *render Poe more friendly to the childish mind*. He brought it out in 1911. I'm up to 'The Oblong Box', where everyone is saved from a shipwreck, including a man who wanted to drown with the remains of his dead wife. In Howard's version the wife isn't very dead, in fact she comes to, in a lifeboat. It's a lot less nasty than the original. Poe's man goes down with the corpse and the ship. When I was a child I wouldn't have found Howard's story friendly, I would have found it dull.

This must be the same station. My mother must have lifted me down to this very platform and whoever was minding me must have led me away. I see myself, walking away in patent shoes and a light woollen coat with a brown velvet collar, sewn by my mother. She had things to do in the city. She was still married to my father then, but there were plenty of things he wouldn't do. My grandmother was in hospital again, a different hospital with something special to offer. It sounded like something any unhappy person would want. Deep-sleep therapy.

My father lives above the harbour, on a steep bank a few metres from the waterline. He's done his best with dinner. Fish and salad. Finn's mother has disappeared for the night. They do this at my own mother's insistence. Finn's mother and I are not to meet, or at least, we're not to meet with smiles and glasses of wine while cooking smells waft from the kitchen. My father doesn't pretend to be living alone, but he doesn't mention her.

Wash from passing ferries hisses just outside the windows. As the night wears on the voices on deck rise in excitement or argument or, once, in song. I listen for a splash but nobody seems to go overboard, as I would expect in the kind of novel where a dripping intruder appears at the door.

On the train as I was reading the notes I've made from the books on Poe, I couldn't get past a particular sentence. *In order that Poe might become the kind of artist he was, a woman had first to die.* It's stark. I have to remind myself that this is a death, not a murder.

'How are you getting on up there?' It's the first time he's asked after me. He's filled the evening with talk about the headlines. Morgue workers have been filmed stealing from the bodies that the police bring in. It isn't only watches and rings and money. Shoes are pulled from the feet of the drowned and dried out by the staffroom radiator. Belts are unbuckled and whipped free of their loops. I thought the papers had printed the whole story; I couldn't see how this story could be any bigger than it is, but my father had some extra information that he thought I ought to hear.

'I'm in my old room. You're right about walking beside the cliffs. It's wonderful. Finn and I go out every day.' He's nodding and looking at his whisky, which is running low. 'And I've started on a new book.'

'Oh yes,' he says. I sent him a copy of my first book. I don't think he read it. He sent me chocolates. I don't think Finn's mother read the book either. My mother says all she reads is the labels in dress shops, and even then she doesn't read the price.

'I've started a new book about Edgar Allan Poe. You know. Horror. Mystery.'

'Poe? Can't say I've ever heard of him.'

'He's never read Poe.'

Finn is making us both a cup of tea. I'm sliding around him, barefoot on the kitchen linoleum. 'Watch out,' he says when I get too close to the boiling water slopping over the lip of the jug.

'Think what he's missing. "The lips became doubly shrivelled and pinched up in the ghastly expression of death; a repulsive clamminess and coldness overspread rapidly the surface of the body; and all the usual rigorous stiffness immediately supervened." Like it? It's from "Ligeia". He could practically take notes.' Finn knows that I can trash my father but he mustn't join in.

'Send him some Poe then,' he says carefully.

'He doesn't read. He doesn't want to listen to me talk about my book.' I'm trying not to make it come out like a whine.

'Just as well I'm here,' he says.

I'm standing a little way back from him. There's a metre or so between us and I'm thinking, suddenly, about the things we use to fill that space. Tea. Talk. The loose pages of my book. It's like a ceremony; an arrangement of words and objects that will keep us just far enough apart for me to breathe. He smiles at me. These things all sit between us so that we can have enough space to love and breathe.

I'm back at my writing table, listening to the wind. The windows rattle. I think of all the ropes and lead counterweights which are hidden in the sides of the casements. Finn jammed pieces of cardboard into the frames for me, to keep the windows still. Now they are quiet, except in the most abrupt gusts of wind. I think of the lead swaying slightly in its dark enclosure, registering the quick force of the wind.

I'm trying to write about some of the places where Poe and Virginia lived. Place quickly shifts to personality. I'm writing about Muddy, as if she were a structure that could be unbolted and moved from place to place, and in a way she was. She was a shelter. Her back held off the winter wind.

Muddy made a home for her children, their cousins and their grandmother in Baltimore. When the family had dwindled to three starving cold adults at Fordham, where Virginia died, Muddy pulled turnips from neighbouring fields and scraped them and cooked them up. She had a begging basket which she carried with her when she went visiting and she wrote letters to friends and acquaintances which were not plaintive. They were letters of demand. She was tough. Yet perhaps there was a price to pay. Perhaps her own son paid a high price for his mother's choices and ambitions. Perhaps Poe paid a price, as well. Louise wrote that Muddy *was like a cat, often, treacherous and cruel.* She says this comes from having had absolute power over other people, in the past. *She had a hard side to her nature like many*

Southern persons, who are, or have been brought up with slaves as
servants and associates in childhood.

In the train on the way up the mountain I watched a young
mother and her children. The baby was asleep on her lap. She
smiled slightly, turning to the window. As we passed through a
cutting the black wall behind the glass showed me her reflection. Her eyes were closed. It was the most private of smiles,
the adult equivalent of the baby's relaxed trusting happiness:
arms wide, mouth open. An older child slept against them both.

I can remember the fact of sitting on my mother's knee, but
not the actual sensation. I do remember our kitchen chairs.
They were blue-grey, picked out in some brighter colour. I
remember her brushing down the old farmhouse chairs and
stirring the paint. The hopeful smell of fresh paint comes to me.

The baby woke, arched and began to cry. It didn't stop.
Other passengers looked away. The older child was roused, told
to reach into a bag, to do this, to do that, no, the other way, the
other way. A bottle was assembled, the baby was suddenly quiet
and everyone in the carriage could forget that there is such a
thing as loud, pure anxiety. The smiles, the rapture could begin
again. But not for the older disturbed child, who sat frowning
and unthanked.

I'm in the dark. I've gathered all the books on Poe around me,
and they contradict themselves. I'm picking my way through

contradictions. Poe called Louise 'Marie Louise', or just Louise. Muddy called her Loui. I've had to choose a name for her, and I've chosen to call her Louise. I've written confidently about Poe's mother's death. One book I've been reading has his brother Henry present in the room, another has him away with Poe's relatives. In some, he lives with Muddy and her children, in others he isn't mentioned. He's like a shadow of Poe, a shadow that only shows up in a certain light. I can't be sure about anything. I could walk through the Fordham house where Virginia died and lay my hands on the walls, I could close my eyes and read the walls with my fingertips and I'd still be none the wiser. All I have are my own imaginings.

I sit quietly with my books and manuscript, imagining the shifting pressures of the Baltimore house where Poe first met his cousin Virginia and the Fordham house where she died; trying to imagine the invisible forces of anger and assent.

In a house as crowded as the one in Baltimore people lay claim to small territories: a chair; the brief attention of whoever else is in the room. I think of Muddy's son Henry, whom nobody knows much about, except that he worked in a brick-yard or a stonemason's yard. After Poe's death Muddy was *every hour more <u>desolate</u>*. She was desolate for twenty years. She lost her children, as she puts it: her Eddie and Virginia. No mention is made of Eddie's brother Henry, or her own son.

I try to imagine these lost boys and the Baltimore house.

I'm not the only person who has tried to imagine what it might have been like to live in Muddy's house. Mostly it's all cosy, a picture of cheerful, scrupulously managed poverty. Grandma Poe is paralysed, and Henry Poe is dying, yet the point, after all, is not death and paralysis, but the onward move-ment of Poe's pen.

I wonder how it might have really felt to live in a house like that.

I am imagining a sound so pervasive that it is as present in the rooms as the air. The sound is barely heard, except perhaps in the dreams of the people who live there. It's a constant unan-swered cry of pure anxiety. I make a heading. 'Amity Street'.

AMITY STREET, BALTIMORE

COUSIN HENRY'S SPITTLE LANDS on the side of the copper cooking pot, spreads to a quick web and turns black.

Brother Henry sits on his stool under the arc of spit, immovable, as still as the red coals under the pot; stone dust on the back of his hands. He doesn't turn to his cousin. His hands rest on his knees. He waits in silence. Eventually boards creak in the attic above his head; the other must be gone. He is alone, a stonecutter with a man's muscular arms and the round boneless face of a child.

All day a great shock travels, again and again, from stone to iron to Brother Henry's arms as he pounds the massive chisel and the stone splits along its hidden fault. At night the shock is still felt, the blows repeat themselves in his body like a heart-beat, like something essential to his life. Free of the weight of the iron chisel, his body heats and seems to spread; soon this sensation will grow as he sips from a small bottle of almost raw spirit he carries next to his chest. The last thing he wants, at the end of the day, is Cousin Henry chattering about his poetry, or his time as a sailor, meaning deckhand, or lawyer, meaning copy clerk. Brother Henry turns his back, hence the angry spit.

The stonemason has a sudden vision of ships locked into a frozen river, ice and metal under pressure, as solid as stone. As he watches, the ships thaw, they melt; wood, metal and the odd perfect circle of glass dissolve and trickle into blackness, as the ice with its hull-shaped holes remains firm. He reaches for the bottle of spirit, eyes on the black smudge on the glowing copper, the smudge like a spread city, a net, a web of compli-cated taste. Here and there within the web, scattered now and burst, lie the bacilli of tuberculosis.

This is how Muddy finds him when she comes to lift her pot from the fire and dip the soup out into bowls which little Virginia, just seven years old, has placed in a row on the table. She calls him the cigar store Indian. Her only son, her firstborn, unwilling to so much as turn to her or meet her eye. He looks like a wooden Indian, with this exception: the master carver usually did the head with skill and character, leaving assistants to put together a rough blocky body. Brother Henry's body seems to have been carved with great attention. It is his face which is unformed, like the knife-work of an amateur.

He won't come to the table. He won't sit in a row with Cousin Henry and Eddie, opposite Muddy. He tells himself he's a free man, not a man in a chained line of three at the slave market, Muddy holding her great purse. She has already chosen. Not Cousin Henry, chattering and spitting blood. Not her great son with his father's disturbing frame. It's Eddie she wants; she will choose the man to be her son and she has chosen.

At night Virginia, lying between a wall and the wall of her sleeping mother's back, hears a snuffling sound. She thinks of small anxious creatures, moving quickly, then hesitating, in the cavities of the house. She often dreams that when she puts her eye to a single crack it will widen, the space inside will open to accept her and she will find herself in another, safer place with the crack closed tight behind her. She listens for the sounds of this safe place. She hears rustling, snuffling, then it comes to her: she is listening to her brother the stonemason, in tears.

In the attic Cousin Henry's breath scrapes and scrapes. His breath is as difficult as chiselling the surface of stone.

Once Cousin Henry saw a burial at sea. The corpse of the ship's barber was sewn into canvas with a ball of shot at the feet. It was laid on a plank. At a signal the plank was raised to shoulder height and the grey figure slid into the sea. It was pulled smoothly, like a ribbon, down. He's salvaged this memory. It's far more important than his memories of the great cities of Paris and St Petersburg. He knows, at some deep level, that death can be as smooth, as easy as a ribbon drawn through water.

Eddie is awake at his table with his pen in his hand, writing a letter to a girl, wondering how to deliver it.

He thinks he'll use Virginia.

One other person lies awake in the house, barely a person, now, but still watchful, aware. Her spine curls, her feet have dropped. Plates of skin lift from her scalp. Her chin and throat are wet again. She's everybody's grandmother: Henry and Virginia; their cousins Henry and Eddie.

There is grey dust and death in the house. Virginia leans too hard on Eddie's knee. The grandmother thinks that the house needs something to move from person to person, something to make that grey boy smile and calm the other, dying boy. Something to touch them all. A big wise cat.

I put my pen down. The window chatters and falls silent in its hollow frame. Lead counterweights move a little in the darkness. 'Tell me about your mother, Finn,' I remember having said. His last words on the subject were: *Then she began to hate me.*

FORDHAM

LOUISE CLIPPED PAPER TO her easel and set down her jar. The cat shook itself as drops flew from the brush to the plank floor. Louise was painting the cherry tree, to please Virginia. She was taking as her model an old watercolour of Boston harbour which Eddie's mother left to him. Muddy had no use for it. She called it Louise's antique and lost it, or gave it away, in later years. Eddie's mother had written a message to him, on the back. *Love the place of your birth.* She could have meant

Boston, thought Louise. Or perhaps she was writing about herself: remember the body of your mother, which gave you birth.

Virginia propped the opalescent painting of the harbour on the windowsill below the cherry tree. Louise was not confident. That shine was light on water, she and Virginia knew it was water and would have known, even if the painter had been unskilled, because of the sailing ships. Could she paint the cherry tree in liquid, opalescent light?

The mesmerists, as Virginia reminded her, would say that the tree was already swimming in an invisible fluid, which flows through and around us all.

Louise wondered aloud why the mesmerist had to be so very close to his subject to adjust this flow of internal fluid, so close, she has heard, that a woman's legs may be gripped between his knees.

Virginia smiled but she wasn't listening. She was thinking about Eddie's absorption in his work. Often when he wrote he couldn't hear or even recognise her. It must be like standing in a heavy shower with the sound of the rain blotting out all voices except your own, internal voice; the rain veiling in grey the features of every other person.

The tree was bare and strong. Branches ended in webs of dead twigs, which were to cause difficulties for Louise, disrupting her bright wash. The tree had oblique holds in the air, as if it sought spaces for itself, in some solidity.

As Louise painted, she talked. She had never been to medical school, but she was skilled in doctoring. She was present at many births, easing infants from their mother's wet rippling grip. Virginia was interested in all the details of birth.

Once Louise saw a movement in the purple mess at the bottom of a chamberpot. She lifted a fist-sized head and a smaller body out, put her own mouth to the tiny stretching hole of a baby's mouth and breathed. The baby lived. The mother didn't thank her, nor did the registrar at the foundling hospital, though Louise doesn't mention this to Virginia.

She doesn't talk, either, about the glassy-eyed bundle in wet expensive cloth on the icy parquetry of a grand hallway. The cook called her in, hoping for a miracle. Madame had dismissed the servants for the night, opened the fanlight and made a cold parcel of her latest child.

Mothers die, too. Louise has watched them buckle in hot pain, white-faced, teeth clacking together, not a genteel chattering but a great uncontrollable clatter. Then the mother is gone, leaving a fat-eyed sleeping baby under some rug she has stitched or knitted so hopefully, months or weeks before.

Louise would like to tell Virginia that we are not, even as infants, or before our births, swimming in some kind, connecting fluid. She has delivered, along with a healthy child, the skin of an incomplete twin, flattened and absorbed by its partner.

Muddy stood at Louise's elbow, offering tea and advice on the colour or angle of a cherry tree bough. She seemed suspicious of the conversation, concerned, perhaps, that Louise was offering her daughter information more proper to mature women in commonplace marriages. Louise's brushes clinked in the jar, coloured water splashed a little on the floor.

The cherry tree is stubby under Louise's brush. She finds a

stroke which works, repeats it and it stales. Muddy is behind her, insisting that she move her brush this way or that, softly rebuking. It is as annoying as someone humming the melody of a difficult piece of sight-reading. Muddy gives up, finally, and finds something else to do. As soon as she has gone Virginia begins to speak. Lately she has been telling story after story, to fill in the time. Louise, listening to her story about the stone-mason and the sea, half forgets what she is doing with the cherry tree. She plays with it, shaking unseasonal red over the paper, trailing drips.

Louise is a gifted painter and she sees the work of other artists, even famous foreign artists, in households and various galleries. She will never see the picture which proves her point about separation, which shows that even, or especially, in kinship there can be a terrible threat. In one of Gustav Dore's famous engravings of Eddie's poem 'The Raven', a skeleton with enlarged leg bones floats above a sea at night. A child with its head in its hands is also floating or bumping against the bony chest, almost received into the pelvic cavity: mothered by death, above the dark water.

In an hour dinner will be ready, and after dinner Finn will settle in the wing chair and I will settle on the edge of the bed and he will listen while I read. He closes his eyes when I read to him. I flick quick looks at him, over the page. He looks as if he's asleep, but he snaps to attention if he thinks that he can't quite follow me. I take up Poe's story of 'The Oblong Box' and try to make it clear, for Finn.

THE OBLONG BOX

A MAN SETS OUT on an ocean voyage for reasons which are never quite explained. One of his fellow passengers is a painter whom he knew when they were students at the same university. He is deeply curious about this man. He is as curious as if he were in love. No detail of the painter's travel arrangements escapes him.

The painter boards the ship just before she sails. His new wife and his two sisters are with him. He also has an unusual piece of luggage: a long narrow box which his old friend assumes contains valuable canvases.

The painter is not friendly. He is grim and remote. His sisters are not forthcoming, either. The painter's wife is not the kind of woman he would be expected to marry. She is plain but extremely lively and flirtatious. The other passengers think she is ridiculous. The man assumes that his friend is already regretting the marriage.

At night the painter can be heard tapping open the lid of his strange box.

The ship runs into bad weather. Sails, then masts are lost and the hull begins to fill. The pumps don't work. The passengers must abandon the wreck.

At first the painter sits quietly in the heavily laden lifeboat. Then he begs the captain to return for his oblong box. He is on his feet. The lifeboat is in jeopardy. When the captain refuses to go back he dives overboard and swims to the wreck. He can be seen on deck, tying himself to the box, before leaping, with the box, into the sea.

He disappears.

Much later, on dry land, the captain tells the painter's friend that the woman who passed herself off as the painter's wife was hired for the role. The painter's wife died just before the ship sailed. He wished to take her body home to her mother. He and the captain knew the passengers would not knowingly travel with a corpse, so they smuggled the body on board and paid the dead woman's maid to impersonate her. At the end, the painter left this world of substitutions, for his wife.

The Stonemason and the Sea

'Once there was a rich man, a stonemason by trade.'

Virginia stops speaking. Her chest suddenly feels hard, inside. She is thinking of her brother, who worked in a mason's yard and came home to sit in his stone dust and stare into the fire, until the day when he didn't come home at all. *Gone to dwell with the angels,* Muddy says; she will say it of Virginia, soon.

Once there was a stonemason, said Virginia. He had three wives and many children. The first wife was plain and wealthy. She caught the typhoid from an open drain. The second wife ran away with a sailor and was washed ashore, quite dead, after his ship left the harbour. The third honoured her marriage vows as best she could.

The third wife carried just one child herself. In her pregnancy her husband's children caught whooping cough and the house was filled with cries, like the cries of great seabirds in lonely distress. The third wife had been friendly with the second. Indeed, they had been sitting in a park by the harbour, tracing patterns in the dust at their feet with green willow twigs when the sailor appeared with a bunch of violets for whoever would take them from his hands. It would have been improper for the third wife, who was then an unmarried woman, to accept, and in any case, she always thought that violets had a secret bloody smell. The sailor told them stories about ghost ships and whirlpools. They met him more than once. He told them how albatross were hung alive on hooks at the stern of the ship so their feathers could be stripped without damage and sold, in port, for decoration. The women were ashamed of the plumage on their hats.

The third wife thought of the albatross as she stood in a cold hallway trying to decide which of her friend's children to go to first. The eldest child of the typhoid wife lit candles and the heel of the third wife's own unborn child moved over some gaspingly painful internal place which would, in time, open to allow it birth.

During the time of the whooping cough the third wife

learned that every act of giving involved an unbearable with-drawal. Each minute she spent rubbing something aromatic into a small chest or back meant that another child with her dead friend's eyes cried out like a seabird on a sharp hook, inhumanly.

The third wife became aware of the eldest child of the typhoid wife. She was almost grown, her adolescent limbs were too long for the clothes her father provided.

When this child was born her mother had saved the petals of a tulip and placed them between the pages of a book, to mark the occasion. The book drew off any dampness and by the time the child brought the tulip fragments to her new step-mother they were as translucent as the underwings of an insect. These wings were a secret, between the third wife and her stepdaughter.

As they were awake through the night, dividing the nursing between them, it made sense to share a bed. To her surprise, it came to the third wife in a dream that it was this grown child she loved best, not the children of her friend, whose husband she had married in order to care for, or even her own baby, now quiet, within her. She was unaware that in her sleep her step-daughter's hand had crept guilelessly across to the warm place between her breasts. It would be gone before she woke.

The rich man came looking for his wife in the dawn after the sick children had settled. He found the exhausted women asleep, face to face, the pregnancy between them. With thick blankets drawn over them, concealing their limbs, it was hard to see whose pregnancy this was, or rather, the rise of the unborn child was something that they shared.

He went to the kitchen and with his own hands he lit the

stove and carried a wooden bucket to the pump. He was awake and he was completely alone.

By day he travelled between the brickyards where he watched men tread his clay or burn his stacks of bricks; and the place where his stone was split and shaped. Men fell silent at his approach. He had once split stone, himself. It was something that could never be forgiven. An owner from the proper class was an owner. This man held certain deeds, and only by virtue of his first wife's money.

One day, after the defection and then death of his second wife, he noticed a covered shape behind rubble in one corner of the yard. He tried to ask about it, but he could not make himself heard over the sound of the hammers. Men closed their eyes against stone dust and the shock of the impact of their work. He could not make himself seen. In the end he was told it was a figurehead for a ship which had met with an accident in the harbour. A stowaway was discovered on board and ran the length of the deck before leaping to the back of the figurehead, which was rotten with sea worm and had collapsed into the water, far below. One of the stonemasons who had a reputation for carving had agreed to make a replacement, working in his own time by candlelight and using oak provided by the sailors. The figure, he was told, must be covered to protect it from the drying effects of the stone dust. He noticed chisels scattered about the corner of the yard. Then tools as fine as weapons appeared, with abrasives, for smoothing the wood. In time, there was a smell of paint. Suddenly the whole shape disappeared. Before it did, the youngest apprentice hid himself behind the rubble and lifted the hem of the cloth covering the figurehead. It was a woman with a tilted chin and eyes which would eventually fix on the stars. Her clothing was pressed back from her body as if she had been sculpted in a high wind. Her wrists crossed at her chest. Her face was carved and painted to resemble his employer's runaway wife.

At about this time the rich man began to worry. His third wife had quickly agreed to marry him. When she lay below him, or swayed above him, her breath fast, he thought he might be making her happy, although her eyes were always closed and at times she turned her face to avoid his mouth. If he separated the long strands of her hair and smoothed them behind her ears she shook her head, as if to free herself from his hands.

He looked at a picture, taken some days after the wedding. It was the children's idea to have a picture made and they managed to keep very still as the operator crouched, draped in black, behind his machine. They were excited about their new mother, who had often held them or read to them when she visited her friend. She was wearing a black velvet hat which he had given her, with an explosion of feathers at the side. On the day of the wedding they were not explosive. He remembered how lightly they drifted in air.

The stonemason's second wife was not, in fact, dead.

She hadn't drowned and been defaced by shrimp and other small creatures on the harbour floor. She stepped out of her clothes on the quay and swam through garbage and phosphorescence towards her lover's ship. A woman whose skirts had been torn on the previous night found the dress and shawl and slipped them on in place of her own. The second wife turned in the water and watched. She shouted, but the sound seemed to pool around her, unheard. For a moment she thought of striking out for the shore, covering herself with the rags of the thief and pursuing her through the streets, following a flicker of the silk which she and her daughters had stitched. It would be like rushing after her earlier, married, self. Shrimp tickled her skin. She turned slowly in the water, back to the anchored ships.

The shawl was quickly exchanged for a bottle of gin, which was swallowed as the thief leaned against a rotten balustrade. It had taken her weight without difficulty on other occasions. This was different. The railing gave way and she was tipped into the sea and drowned.

It was a cold tiring swim. The second wife was glad of the long discipline of childbirth; the knowledge that the body can safely move through unthinkable phases of exhaustion. At first the slip of the water was delicious. Then her arms began to ache; soon she was gasping and spitting. Her eyes were stinging. She made her way through beds of oily weed. The ships were just as small and bright as when she left the quay. She turned on her back and closed her eyes. Pebbles of tar, rope fibre, a clot of human waste and a single pearl-shell button caught in her hair. As she rested under the calm stars a current swept her into the middle of the harbour and when she looked about her she found she could not distinguish between the ships. A carved eagle stared down from a sternboard. Someone poured galley slops from a deck. Shadows of masts slid over her as she was carried towards the open sea. She turned again and swam with strong even strokes to a rope cast over the side of the final ship. It rode low in the water so the climb was not as difficult as it might have been. Just as she was about to reach the deck she heard two men speaking softly, above her. One said the same thing, again and again.

'My wife will sail with me. We cannot be parted. She will sail with me.'

Virginia turns to Louise. 'Can you imagine always being with the same person, in the same company, night and day, as if you were their infant, or as if they were yours?'

Louise wonders if the great relief she saw on Virginia's face when she first settled by the sick woman's bed was only caused by the things she brought: the eiderdown, the food and wine, the money for clothing and fuel. 'Nobody ever stays exactly the same,' says Louise, cautiously. She herself was first married to a doctor, then divorced. Her second marriage, to a minister of religion, did not last, although in its early days she was his *beloved wife,* his *Heart's ever, his all. God help my elastic soul,* she wrote, towards the end of her life. *It did not break or die, and I am thankful that I am emancipated from the love of this man, altho' he is the father of my children.* 'Everybody has to change. That's the hardest thing. To be resolute, in the face of change.'

'Exactly,' says Virginia. She has spoken as loudly as she is able. Muddy comes quickly, soothingly, calling her an angel. All she is wanting is a pair of wings. 'I'm no chicken,' says Virginia. 'I don't have the need for wings.' She takes up her story again, when she is alone with Louise.

The second wife pulled herself onto the deck. Her legs shook, but she scrambled to her feet. She had climbed aboard a trim well-fitted ship. Thick ropes as grey and silky as a grand-mother's plait were coiled around stumps of iron. Places where a hand might fall were plated with highly polished brass. Even the holes where bolts were sunk into the deck were fitted with wooden plugs. She crouched over an open hatch and looked down on a vat of rice and melting butter. She could have reached down and touched the head of the cook.

'Does she have to always be called the second wife?'

Virginia thinks for a minute. 'Let's call her Stella,' she says. Both women laugh. Stella is Eddie's most annoying acolyte, *fat*, says Louise, *and gaudily dressed*. She is generous when Eddie praises her writing sufficiently, but although he needs the money he avoids her when he can. Muddy sends Louise to fetch him when Stella Lewis visits. When she finds him he tells her he *would like to die, and get rid of literary bores.*

'Will we still like her, if she's a Stella?'

'She's our Stella now,' says Virginia.

The captain and his argumentative passenger caught sight of Stella.

She quickly introduced herself as a woman from the country who had lost her way and wandered in the narrow streets by the harbour until night fell. She lost her footing on the quay, slipped into deep water and was carried away in the current. She explained that she had struggled free of her heavy skirts and the bodice and sleeves which kept her chest tight and her arms moving in the smallest of circles.

As she spoke she picked at a knot in her hair. The strands

slid aside and a single white button popped free. She could not meet the eyes of these strange men. Beyond the first glances at her teeth and skin they were not, in fact, looking at her, or even listening to the substance of her tale. They were listening, purely, to the tone and accent of her voice.

The captain spoke first. His passenger found himself placed in a peculiar difficulty. His passenger had urgent need of a woman of exactly her height and colouring. Would she be happy to discuss this in a less exposed situation? The deck felt steady beneath her feet. Stella smelled warm butter and listened to someone singing as he scraped a pan. She followed them to a cabin below.

The passenger passed her a greatcoat. She wrapped herself up and perched on a bunk, resting her feet on a high wooden box which took up most of the space on the floor. The men remained standing, as if they should hold themselves formally until a particular woman gave them permission to sit.

'My passenger had a great fondness for his wife,' the captain began.

'Has,' corrected the passenger. 'She is still my wife.'

'Unfortunately the lady is gone from us, unexpectedly. She is dead.' Stella tucked her feet under her, on the bunk. 'She is dead, and he will not be parted with her remains. He wishes her to be carried with him and put ashore at her birthplace, where she may lie in her family vault. Now as you may know, there is a particular prejudice against sailing with the dead. It is not a prejudice I share. Yet no other soul will put to sea with us if the contents of this box become well known.'

'Conceal it in the hold,' said Stella.

'Our difficulty is not in the concealment or display of the body,' said the captain. 'The couple were already settled for the voyage. Until today the lady was about on the deck and apparently fit. Her disappearance will be a point for discussion. What we need,' and here he slid the top of the box aside, so Stella could peer in, 'is a substitute. It happens that you look like the woman who died.' Stella saw the corpse. It had hair as lank and dark as her own and two rows of dry, strong teeth. She leaned back as far as she could in the bunk. 'We sail on the next tide,' he said.

Her instinct was to scramble down and away. But where could she scramble to, naked, exhausted, and so far from shore?

Stella suddenly realised that what she had left so far behind when the night began had been waiting at the end of her adventure. Her sailor was lost to her. She was to be confined, again, as a wife. The men watched her sadly from the far side of the box. Stella smiled. The passenger lifted the top of the box entirely clear and began to work his wife's rings free of her hands. They made a little cold chiming sound as he dropped them into Stella's outstretched palm.

The boat ducked and stretched upward in the open sea. Stella thought of the thin bobbing neck of a climbing horse. She couldn't see a great deal. She was veiled, for the time being, in case those who had seen the dead woman made comparisons, although the general resemblence was surprisingly strong. She was promised that in a matter of days she could remove the veil.

At night she slept, or crouched awake on the bunk. Her new husband did not sleep. He lit a slow burning lantern and opened the box.

He was a painter with a reputation as a portraitist. The dead woman had been one of his subjects: his best commission, he explained to Stella, although the picture itself was never satisfactory. He wanted to make one last attempt. Stella watched him outline the shape of a woman's face on the inside of the lid. She had never realised that a portrait begins with blocks of shadow, competing with one another for the greatest depth. The high structures of the face push forward from the deepest areas of shadow, before the features are distinctly brushed in. The planes of the dead woman's face were easy enough to replicate. Her eyes and mouth, which had suffered most change in the course of her death, were another matter. He unpacked the earlier, unsuccessful portrait and propped it against a trunk. He looked from Stella to the corpse to the picture on the trunk. Each woman was substantially, maddeningly wrong.

In time Stella stopped looking like the woman in the box. The surface of the dead eyes dimpled and turned grey. The face puffed up and the neck was suddenly thin. Whalebone stays creaked softly against the straining waist and chest and one night the mouth opened on a froth of old blood and the woman seemed to moan. Stella knew it was just gas, working its way up through the closed throat. The painter mixed more colour and continued with his work. His palette had to change, night after night.

Stella began to vomit from the stern of the ship, and had to brush aside the advice of older women with their remedies for seasickness or kind words about pregnancy. Two of these women agreed to share a bunk so that Stella could have a cabin to herself. After they dragged the dead woman's clothing trunk into this empty cabin and arranged her brushes, mirror, jars of cream and bottles of scent in the small space which was available, Stella began to experience the pleasures of the ship.

Firstly there was the fresh spray and the motion of the deck itself as the boat lifted and skimmed, again and again, through the waves. Even in calm weather, in her cabin, she felt a pleasant tremor beneath her feet.

Then she made friends with the ship's cat, a white cat which had had its ears clipped back hard against its skull after they were damaged in some harbourside mauling. Its tail had been docked at birth. It looked like a creature from the far south: the cub of a white bear or a seal. This cat brought Stella parts of the rats which it killed in the hold. Often it settled on a wide brass railing on the deck and when she stroked it and spoke its name, it pushed its head politely up into her palm. It was the purest, uniform white. Its eyes were grey and green.

Once a sailor joined Stella and the cat. He was tall and tanned, with thick whiskers and a stumpy plait dipped in fresh tar. She expected him to tell her stories about ghost ships and whirlpools. Instead he brushed his fingertips down the length of the cat. He told her that once he had sailed to an eastern port where the people believed that the markings of a tabby cat were traces left by the fingertips of the Prophet Mahommed. The white cat stood and shook herself. The sailor's fingermarks were not so indelible.

The sailor said that he himself travelled with a large kind of monkey, an orang-utan, which loved to climb the rigging in a high wind. It had the run of the ship but it crept back to lie beneath his hammock at nightfall. It learned to tie the ribbon at the end of his plait in the particular way favoured among his countrymen and it was at its most busy and happy when he allowed it to sift repeatedly through his hair. He stopped tarring his pigtail to please this ape. Sometimes he thought he could still feel its strong narrow fingers as he drifted off to sleep. He took it to Paris, where it became confused and angry and finally escaped from his control.

Stella thought about her lost sailor. He passed through her dreams. The man on the other side of this white cat had his smell. That was all.

The shipboard husband joined Stella on the deck, although he was exhausted and the light hurt his eyes. His hand, stained with dark paint, was always at her elbow or flat on the small of her back, directing her from one side to another. The women who had moved aside to give her a free cabin smiled at this. The husband was afraid of a particular passenger; a man who claimed to have been his friend. This man often asked Stella about her husband's paintings, in particular, the paintings he was travelling with. The box on the cabin floor had been noticed. The man assumed that it contained valuable canvases and pestered Stella about them until she agreed.

One was a still life, she told him, of red pears. She had been thinking about pears, now that the novelty of buttered rice, biscuits, dried meat and the fish which the sailors caught had worn off. Pears, in her memory, seemed to be just the sweetest water held in a structure that did not resist the mouth, dissolving by themselves into liquid and light pulp. Then there was the skin of the pear: green and scattered with fine solid points of black, or glowing yellow, or red and marked with stripes like the strokes of a brush. Yes, pears, she said, in white cloth with blue shadows.

The man asked about the other work.

Spray touched her face. Her silk dress had begun to dull from the spray. The touch of water was enjoyable, but she wondered if she would ever again be completely dry. Mary and baby Jesus, she told him, on a donkey led by Joseph through the waterless deserts of Egypt. The remarkable thing about this picture was the rendition of warm sand, in pale gold.

The stranger wanted to know if there were seascapes or floating wrecks. She told him her husband's habits made it obvious that the ocean did not interest him.

Was there anything of herself in the box? Her husband's admiration, and his hope that her picture would be the best of his paintings, had been conveyed to the stranger in many letters, during the period of courtship. Stella said no, there was nothing of herself in the box.

At this point her husband appeared and touched her waist uncomfortably. The stranger asked after his most recent work. 'I am making studies for another portrait of my wife,' he said, 'before a high sea.'

That night a storm was threatening. The air chilled and the stars could not be seen. Nobody was strolling on the deck. Stella went to her husband's cabin and tried not to choke on the smell of the corpse when she opened the door. He, too, must have found the atmosphere more than he could bear, because he had fainted across the bunk. She secured his paints and his jar of turpentine and helped him to his feet.

Stella listened to rain sweep the deck, above. A sudden lurch of the ship thrust her husband from her grasp and caused the lid to clatter against the box. The face in the painting was now covered in a drift of black hair with one thumbnail-sized circle of white. Stella saw that it was a pearl-shell button.

She sat on her own bunk with her knees drawn up and he braced himself on the edge of the closed trunk. The floor tipped and tipped; the ship fought its way to the crest of a wave, then flicked back in the other direction as it fell towards the trough. He reached out and held her ankles. Then, slowly, he made his way to her. He leaned forward and kissed her eyelids. She slipped his limbs free of his clothes. So much tense fibre, she thought, between the toes and the crown. Calf muscles, thigh muscles, the flat slabs of the chest. She painted her own designs down the breastbone and around the nipples with small strokes of her tongue.

In whispers, in the warmth and lightness she has made between them, he tells her about his dreams. He dreams, again and again, of a hunt. The quarry is an antelope, tottering under the weight of her young. When she senses his presence she pauses and takes a step in his direction, then waits just long enough for him to aim and fire. Dogs rush foward, he follows; the meat he was sure of is always, mysteriously, gone.

She shushed him. The floor was falling beneath them. There was so much more work to be done.

Finally he slept in the wildly swaying lantern light. Her ears began to ache with cold. Once she watched as her stonemason husband demolished a brick kiln. Holes were knocked in the base and great chains were passed through the holes and pulled sideways to bring the structure down. The crash was the loudest thing she had ever heard. Now waves were crashing on the deck, each, it seemed, with the force of that demolition in the stonemason's yard. There was a greatcoat somewhere on the floor. She crept down on her hands and knees and discovered it. She waited for the morning, while water gradually made its way into the hold and up to the cabins, where it sloshed one way, then another, across the floor.

Long before morning came, the tanned sailor waded to the cabin door. They were to make their way up to the lifeboat. The pumps had failed; there was no time to be lost. Stella took the sailor's arm and forced her way beside him, into the flood. Her husband was to dress and follow. She climbed a ladder by touch. As she settled in the bow of the lifeboat someone handed her a hessian bag. In it, stiff and shivering, was the white ship's cat. Shadows appeared in the black spray and climbed aboard the boat. It was so dark and Stella was hemmed in so tightly that she could not see whether one of the shadows was her husband. Surely he was among the saved. The lifeboat was winched from the deck.

Afterwards she read in a newspaper that a salvage vessel had put out for the ship the day after it foundered, but had been unable to board because of the high seas. A man was standing on the deck with what looked like a tall awkward doll in his arms. It was too thin and tattered to be human, although it had a woman's dark plentiful hair. No rescue could be attempted.

'Well I guess he died happy,' Louise says to Virginia. 'He sure saw it through.'

'Yes,' she whispers, smiling, 'he saw it through.' She lifts her head slightly and Louise turns the pillow, then draws the comforter up to Virginia's chin. Virginia speaks once, very softly, before she turns and sleeps. 'What a fool,' she says.

They all want Eddie to live long and happily. Louise has given Muddy her recipe for strong yeast bread. She brings shell-fish for him to eat. He must have plenty of oysters and clams, she tells Muddy, because he needs phosphates; and plenty of boiled wheat. She tries to keep him calm, which is not easy, given the cheap alcohol, the wanderings. Late in their friend-ship, she takes him to church, where he sings in a sweet tenor voice, but the sermon is suddenly unbearable to him. The Lord, says the voice from the pulpit, watches over us in our difficul-ties, he is *a man of sorrows and acquainted with grief*. Eddie has to leave the church. Louise is worried, she's seen the results of his impulsiveness, but she decides to sit out the rest of the service. He comes back before the end and sings the final hymn, 'Jesus Saviour of My Soul'. He knows the words by heart. He's come back out of concern for her, not acceptance of the doctrine. Then again, he likes to sing, he does it well and he also likes to impress Louise. Louise is most impressed by the way that his symptoms line up with textbook cases of physical brain disor-ders. She thinks he has a lesion of the brain. If he will believe this, if the household will believe that he is sick, and not only temperamental, he will have the stable care she thinks he needs. At home she sits him well away from the fire and explains, again and again, the value of proper nourishment and of a predictable daily routine. She is young, and if she is severe she is also amusing. She has provided for the household. For the moment, she has authority.

Muddy bakes the bread, but she is not interested in much of what Louise has to say about Eddie's health. Louise says, privately, that *such women never respect the intellect or judgment of their own sex.*

Virginia has turned on her side and drawn her knees up to her chest. She's very still. Louise puts her fingertips to the side of the throat and counts the slow beats. The breath can sink, the breath can be barely there, what matters is the pulse. Louise reads her father's medical books, she writes long letters and keeps a journal and a memorandum book, but she is, as Eddie says, a country maiden. He means that she is uneducated. Virginia, at least, speaks French and could write a fine acrostic poem. Mary Gove, who brought Louise here when she saw how stricken Virginia was, has read much more, and much less practically. She knows about homeopathy and hypnotism. But when she sees starvation and consumption she calls for Louise. Mary has read Swedenborg. Once she told Louise that the spirit can only leave the body when the heart is completely still. Louise remembers that the spirit is supposed to be attached to the rhythms of the breath and heart. Swedenborg heard this from an angel, or more than one angel. He writes about the community of angels and how they organise themselves. The dead can do almost anything we can do; they talk with each other, they fall in love, they marry. They can even die again, in the sulphurous lake. The only thing they can't do is have children. Louise has attended at plenty of happy births. Most births are huge with happiness. The angels leave her cold.

She listens to the light rasp of a broom and the cries of the cat, excited by the smell of shellfish cooking on the stove. It is pushing its way between the broom and Muddy's ankles. Muddy is making soft angry noises at the cat.

Louise strokes Virginia's head. She can feel the unevenness of the bone, all the dips and roundnesses. What does it mean? A phrenologist would know. Mary Gove would know. All that Louise knows is that there is no other skull shaped exactly like Virginia's. Muddy has had two daughters and Virginia is named for the eldest, who died very young. In a way, she is a replacement, a substitute, or so it must have seemed at her birth and baptism, before the needs of the living child pushed aside the memory of the dead. Louise rubs backwards and forwards across the hollow at the back of the neck. There is a small lump like a button or a fine brooch above this hollow where the neck meets the base of the skull. Louise rests her palm lightly on Virginia's head. Nobody else is shaped like this. Her own hand could belong on no other wrist. Not the wrist of a sister or an angel.

Louise thinks miserably of the parts of Virginia which work so very well. The voice. The eyes which miss nothing. She sews seventeen, twenty stitches to the inch. The red dress which was the last thing she made is folded away now, but Louise has seen the fine seams and hem. Everything about Virginia is well and capable, except her breath. Louise feels pressure at her own throat and eyes. Wetness and pressure.

Muddy takes up the broom again. It slides and rests. The floor cannot need so much attention. Louise counts the strokes as she would count a pulse, as she would count stitches if she were a seamstress or a very young wife, marking the passing time, waiting for a husband to return in the night, or waiting for a note from a husband who has decided not to return that night. Muddy sweeps and sweeps.

Virginia must find her mother unbearable. She showed Louise a story which Eddie wrote about a passionate suicide pact. Louise can't believe in the doomed lovers, but an early detail of the story sticks in her mind. A child is drowning in a black canal. His mother is just above the surface, on the marble flagstones at the edge of the water, but she cannot swim. Louise remembers the child *deep beneath the murky water*, trying to call to the mother who cannot save him, whose love is made point-less by the fact that she cannot save him, so the drowning child, resentful and unheard, is *thinking in bitterness of heart upon her sweet caresses*.

Louise stands and stretches. She should make coffee for Muddy and herself.

Muddy wants to talk. Her great worry is that Virginia will have to be buried in a cotton dress. Louise remembers the canal scene, again. The mother in the story is not looking down into the water for the face of her child, she is gazing at a prison in the distance. Louise understands the need to look away. She discusses the burial dress. She says that she will provide one herself, in good linen. There is something else. All the whispering in the sick room. Can it be good for Virginia? Louise promises her that it makes no difference, either way.

'I've dreamed of Stella,' says Virginia, who is sipping from a bowl of clear soup. 'It can only be Stella, with all that black hair. She was sitting on a woolwork cushion on the floor of a small boat. Not a very seaworthy boat. More like a boat you'd sail to an island in a shallow lake. A holiday boat. She had something like a picnic basket at her feet. A basket, or a bowl with a handle. She stood up and I was worried that she might upset the boat. She picked up the basket and stepped over the side of the boat and into the sea.'

Louise thinks of a body floating, until the skirts soak through, then slipping down like a ribbon drawn through water.

'The waves were really drifts of leaves. The wind blew some aside and I could see moss and white quartz underneath.'

'Any footprints?' asks Louise.

The survivors of the shipwreck slept in a wooden community hall with a curtain strung across the centre for privacy. The ship had foundered near a town which had a group of charitable Episcopalians who stuffed sheets with clean straw for mattresses and set up a decent kitchen. The white cat settled at the head of Stella's mattress, or nosed through the curtain on its way down to hunt beneath the floor of the hall.

Personal effects were salvaged from the shoreline and returned to their owners and this is how the trunk which Stella had strapped shut on the night of the storm made its way back to her. She had never explored it fully, she had only lifted out a single dress and a bag of brushes and creams and handkerchiefs. Now it would need to be properly unpacked so that everything inside could be laid out to dry.

What had the dead woman packed for the long sea voyage back to her birthplace and her mother?

The Episcopalians had set up drying racks in front of an arched fireplace at one end of the hall. They gave the shipwrecked women basins of fresh rinsing water. Stella hung up a sodden, dark silk dress with rows of false buttons at the arms and chest. A ballgown was ruined because the colours of the wet embroidery had run into the white gauze. Stains had spread across lawn nightdresses, but these could be bleached out, in sunshine. Petticoats survived the immersion well. Each had a border with a simple picture worked and repeated in crochet. Stella's favourite one was in the shape of a cat.

Under all the clothes she came upon a wedding quilt, sewn with determined precision. Her favourite motif was a cherry wreath. The heart and linked wedding rings were in the centre, where they should have been, but the finest blocks, the blocks which would have strained the eyes and then the whole body until the middle finger stung with unnoticed needle pricks, showed wreaths of padded cherries. An Episcopalian woman brushed past Stella as she spread it out to dry. 'There's four years' work,' she said. Stella agreed. She could feel hard cotton seeds in the wadding as she lifted the quilt over a rack. The trunk was nearly empty. The bonnet in its octagonal box would have to be thrown away. Shoes were drying into twisted shapes before the fireplace. At the very bottom of the trunk, under a tin full of dense cake which smelled of alcohol and sea water Stella found a flat envelope, like a folder, of heavy paper. Inside were three or four letters which would need to dry before they could be read, and even then, the ink may have run irreparably.

In the evenings some of the southern women sang hymns and thanked the Lord for their deliverance. They swayed and clapped their hands as they sang. Stella remembered the row of small whispering children, her own and the children of the typhoid wife, who sat between her and her stonemason husband in church in the years before she met the sailor in the park. The children swung their feet and scuffed joylessly at the pew in front of them. She was forever settling a small knee with the pressure of her hand. Now Stella sang with dizzying loudness, her voice lost in the general song and the splash of rhythmic clapping hands. Then one of the southern women read from a family Bible. She read about the water of life in the new Jerusalem, the city for clean true worshippers. Stella imagined she was offered the water of the spring of life in the cupped hands of the Lord who promised to make all things new. She sang. There was no mention of the burning lake. It was as if there was no such thing as faithlessness.

That night she dreamed of her lost friend, the friend who had refused the sailor's violets. She dreamed that her friend was big with the stonemason's child. Each time her own waters had broken this friend had been at her side in a wide apron with her hair bound so tightly that there was no chance of a strand escaping and spreading an infection. Stella knew that the binding caused a headache. Her friend had warm basins and white cloths, folded and baked in the oven for cleanliness. She had a special knack of gently turning the head of the infant as it was pushed free.

Stella woke in the dark of the community hall among all of the saved and she prayed that the cat would return soon to comfort her.

The shipwreck made important news. Relatives scanned the survivor list and the accounts of the great storm sent shivers down the spines of city folk as they drank their morning coffee. Some made a difficult journey with spare horses and carried their loved ones away. There were weeping reunions on the steps of the hall and weeping farewells within. Everybody promised that they would write. Those bodies which had been washed up on the shoreline had been buried immediately and the mourners who slowly arrived knelt, one by one, on a hill overlooking the sea. A man planted a row of cypresses.

A reporter came all the way from the harbourside city where the voyage began. He interviewed a sailor and a child who had lost her favourite doll and he wanted to talk to Stella, but she would give no account of herself. She picked up one of the copies of his paper and took it back to the hall, where she curled up on a mattress and fell asleep reading notices of impending marriages. It must have been this which gave her such a shocking dream.

Her stonemason husband and her closest friend were standing at an altar rail with all the children dressed up behind them. Her friend wore a white veil.

There was a path over the smooth hill where browning cypress seedlings stood in the wind from the sea. Stella walked across this path and back until nothing about her abandoned husband caused her pain. She had thought of him, if at all, as in a state of noble constancy, surrounded by children, absorbed in his work and memories. She made herself imagine the tips of his fingers and the pretty ears of her friend. She thought of this friend with her children. Her friend's hands had accepted them into the world, gently turning each small face uppermost.

She walked and walked. In the end, if she could have flown to the side of the stonemason in a dream, she would have wished him well. She might even have said in the grand voice of a woman in a dream, *Thou art absolved, for reasons which shall be made known to thee in Heaven, of thy vows to me.*

While she was out walking a message was brought to her. It was from the mother of the woman whose husband would not part with her corpse. This mother was not to be put off, it was obvious from the handwriting, or rather the strong printing, and from the announcement itself. Despite the unpredictability of travel in this place and at this season the mother was convinced of the date and even the time of her arrival. Stella was told that she must be packed and waiting. The woman who carried the note to the hill expected Stella to be very pleased. It was not Stella's own mother, of course, it was the mother of the painter's wife. Stella wondered if the real daughter, who had probably never been permitted to sing loudly and sway and sleep on sweet straw, or even walk some distance alone, would have been dismayed as well.

Sadly, she laid the quilt and clothing in the trunk. She kept aside the cat petticoat and the dark dress. She snipped off all the false buttons on the wrists and chest. The captain and the painter had not agreed on a fee for her impersonation, so she must decide what she might be worth, herself. She chose a pair of glass earrings in the same green as her eyes. She fastened them with the help of the dead wife's mirror. Finally she read the letters in the heavy paper folder. They were letters from another woman and they were not the kind of letters which any mother ought to read. Stella tucked them into a pocket in the petticoat.

When the Episcopalians heard that she wished to ride out to meet her mother they found her a kind horse and, since nobody would take her oddly amputated cat, a wicker basket for it to travel in and a packet of fish for it to eat.

The horse's ears pointed sharply forward and its neck bobbed up and down like the prow of a ship as it climbed the hill on the road leading away from the town. Stella sang one of the southern women's songs and when she reached the top of the hill she stopped the horse, steadied the wicker basket, and gladly breathed the free air of Heaven.

This is where it should finish, thinks Louise. At this peak of possibility. Virginia's colour is high, soon there will be a risk, Louise knows, of exhaustion, or worse, depletion. A sinking, from which she will not be able to rise.

Louise finds she is not able to say, Stop there. Stop talking, now. Enough. She cannot snip this thread.

There is more story on the spool.

Stella came to a great sea port in the south, says Virginia, where tobacco was loaded onto boats which would sail to the far side of the world. Captains and merchants met over the wines they had withheld from their cargoes and as they drank they planned the fastest and most weighty of voyages. When these conspiracies ended and the bottles were finished, or almost finished, coins might be flicked in the direction of a pretty, solitary girl, which is how Stella found the price of a small bare room with a windowsill wide enough for the cat to perch on in comfort. The horse was sent back on a lead rein with a traveller who, in all honesty, may or may not have been going in the right direction.

The wine they were drinking was exactly eleven years old, as old as it could be, she was told, without risk of spoilage and the age it ought to be to bring the most pleasure to the palate. Stella could read the year on the label but the rest of the language was strange to her. It tasted of warm raisins. So did the mouth of the large Scottish merchant who kissed her, in daylight, in the street. Stella accepted him. The taste of raisins was still with her when she arranged to take the white room with a sash window opening onto a view of ships and water, and a high single bed. The whole world, it seemed, was simple, warm and laughable.

A merchant needs shirts with stitching as fine as the weight of the linen they were cut from, and a merchant needs a companion for conversation as he waits for his ships to return, or to watch with him for the first sight of a sail lifting above the edge of the world. A merchant needs to share the wine kept aside from his common cargo.

Anyone walking along Stella's street in the morning might have seen her sitting crossways in a wide chair with her feet tucked underneath her, holding her sewing and her face into the light. Over the years her face lost its pretty roundness and the white cat no longer stretched on the windowsill but some evenings the same voices could be heard: the voice of a man whose chair was set back within the room so he could not be seen by passers-by; the voice of the stitching woman, suggesting, calmly answering, making something for him out of everything she had noticed and gathered in her stillness and her voyaging.

'Why a merchant, in the end?' Louise asks.

'Because the stonemason was stuck fast in his life and the sailor had slipped away.'

'And the merchant?'

'He came and went, in leisurely hopefulness.' Virginia spits into a handkerchief. 'And it isn't the end.'

A beautiful young sailor with very white teeth and translucent winter skin passed under Stella's window, on his way to a meeting with a captain who he was hoping would add his name to a crew. The sailor was very sad. His old captain had decided to retire. His shipmates had gone in different directions and he missed them. He missed his ship. It was not only the familiarity of the vessel which he was sad to lose – the perfect sway of her in the heaviest seas, the convenience of her rigs and fittings – something else drew and attached him to this particular ship.

The young sailor was not on board on the legendary day when a stowaway who was disturbed in the hold ran from stern to prow and climbed out on the figurehead, which collapsed beneath the extra weight. He was on board, though, when the new figurehead was lifted into position and secured. She had been carved by a local stonemason, working in old oak. It was said that this stonemason held a grudge against his employer. He carved the figurehead to resemble the employer's wife, who had recently deserted him. The young sailor paid little attention to this story, but he was entranced by the figurehead herself. Her face was tipped up to him as he worked in the rigging. High among grey ropes and stars he would pause in his work to look down at the secret folds in her hair; invisible from the deck. He told himself that nobody had ever seen her quite like this. He made excuses to do the highest and most difficult work, out of turn, so that he could glimpse her face.

He had gone to sea when he was barely more than a child. He was afraid of storms, whirlpools, pirates, cannibals and desert islands. He hoped to be pitted against them all. He was afraid that he would make his final home in the belly of some fish. Indeed he did sail through ferocious storms and vast herds of whales, but that was the limit of his adventuring. He worked in the rigging, took his turn at the helm or at the handles of the pumps or at the oars, in port. It was a most orderly life. At night he dreamed of the figurehead. She did not unstiffen and climb across the deck to his arms. In his dreams she did exactly as she did when he was awake. Her face tipped down to the deep and up to him, where he stood among the stars.

The ship was lost in a harbour collision. A barge with a new and awkward crew stove in the starboard side and she sank immediately. When she was raised the figurehead was gone. He dived for her himself, but she was gone.

The young sailor walked under Stella's window, on his way to a meeting with a strange captain. Stella's voice meant nothing to him. He did not look up to see her living face in the light.

'At least you'll get to travel, for this book,' says Finn.

I know I should be travelling. There are museums, shrines. I read that Poe bought a stuffed raven from Dickens. It's supposed to be in a glass case in a library in Philadelphia. I suppose I should take a look at it. And the places where people in this story were buried or reburied. Pinned down, under final words. Then I think of the story of Poe's tomb-stone, which was propped up outside the monumental works after the inscription had been cut. Before it could be carried to the grave it was smashed to pieces by a derailed train.

Finn has been to the war cemeteries in France. He has walked through forests, through plantations, of crosses.

It's been so long since I travelled in America.

It was with the narcissus man, the one who brought me flowers from the country every morning, through late winter into spring. This was in Boston. I moved out of the youth hostel and went to live with him. I tried to make my mother's recipes in share kitchens. I remember aluminium saucepans; skimming stock in a corridor with the top of a broken washing-machine for a bench. The mattress was narrower than the base of the bed. He slept in his lab. He was working on platelets: things which clump together in the blood. He could keep them alive and do things to them in fresh umbilical cords. He observed them when veins were split in autopsies. He watched a lot of autopsies. He wasn't disturbed, just irritable. He was always coming back to our room complaining about some dead impacted bowel.

It finished at Niagara in winter. The hotels were cheap; almost empty. Everything was stiff with cold. I stood for long minutes with my gloved hands on a railing. Before me a whole lake fell down so far that if you fell with it you'd be lucky to survive.

III

Smiling and Bowing

at the Madman Poe

'Everyone said that she was raving mad.'

'They would have said the same thing about your father if he hadn't been a war hero. And rich.'

We're talking about our grandmother. Finn can't remember ever seeing her. I've just broken the rule about criticising each other's parents. Finn doesn't react. He sticks to the point: our grandmother.

'Everyone said she was mad and nobody could live with her.'

Her ring is scraping the inside of my finger. I twist it upright again. 'I don't think it was put to the test. He only tried to live with her for ten years. Then he farmed out the kids and got rid of her.' My father and Finn's were sent to boarding school. Finn's father was practically a baby. Four. A house-master's wife carried him about on her hip for a year. He had blisters on his wrist where he sucked himself at night. He called everybody Mummy: my grandfather, the housemaster's wife. My father told me about it. My father was six and disgusted.

'Ten years is long enough. He gave her everything she asked for. He built the house for her.'

'No.' This is news to me. But then, my mother and my grandmother weren't exactly reminiscing, in the cigarette smoke on Sunday afternoons.

'Look at the date on the house. 1922. She married him in London in 1920. They came out on a liner. She hated it, in the city. She couldn't get used to the heat. So he bought this block up in the mountains and built the house for her. He had her draw up a list of everything she missed and he worked his way through.' The garden must be all that's left of her list. The garden and the flowery curtains in the upstairs bedrooms. She had a chair covered in the same material. Lilac. Rhododendrons. I think of the bowerbird making his curved walls of pine needles and his dancefloor under the canopy of the garden my grandfather made, to draw his wife to him. 'It didn't work. What do you do? He wore himself out, trying to make it work.'

I don't know where he got all this from, and how I came to miss out. Family. I thought I knew everything he knew. That was the problem with us. We couldn't match stories of the past, lovers' stories. There was nothing to disclose. Or so I thought.

'How do you know?'

'I've got his old diaries.' I'm surprised. In fact I'm hot with envy and resentment. I imagine my grandfather, who told me I was his best, his favourite girl when he tucked pillows all around me in the dark, heading down the staircase afterwards to a manly glass of port with Finn. I imagine him placing his diaries in Finn's hands. 'When I say I've got them, I mean that I've read them. Anyone can. They're down in the pantry. They look like old Hansards.'

'And they give you the full picture? If they're anything like his trade policy they won't be models of clarity and even-handedness.'

'OK, he was stupid when he got old. But he wasn't always stupid. He did make a fair Foreign Minister, before he was past it.'

'So what's his side of the story? From where I sit, he got sick of her and he paid her off. She ended up on my mother's hands. It was my mother who organised a fresh toothbrush and took her washing home from hospital. My mother had to deal with the psychiatrists. One was wearing shoes that didn't match. Brown and black. When my mother pointed it out he said he had another pair the same, at home. My mother got her out of the deep-sleep therapy.'

'I didn't know,' says Finn.

'She'd tried to kill herself. She was on an iron bedstead. Naked. Comatose. Some of the others who were with her died. My mother got her out.' It was difficult. My mother was heavy and unfashionable in her bushwoman's clothes. But she dealt every day with angry cattle. She could sort out a psychiatrist.

'Why do you think your mother went to all that trouble?'

'I know everyone says it was more or less revenge. She was trying to show up the rest of the family. To get back at Dad. But that's just not her. She loved her mother-in-law. No obvious reason. Sometimes in a family you pick the person you'll stick with, and it isn't the obvious one. Look at Muddy and Poe. She had her own son and Virginia, she had Poe's brother and Poe. She stuck to Poe. It wasn't easy. He was trouble. But she wanted him. She looked after him. He was hers.'

'That's just the difficulty with our grandparents. Or so he says in his diaries. She married him and sailed off with him but she couldn't decide whether or not she really wanted him. Even when he was planting out the garden, in 1922, he thought she might be mad. He thought he might be mad, as well. He had crying jags. He didn't know what to do. He took his work seriously, and in the early days it was serious work. He couldn't get on with it. He wrote the diaries to convince himself that he was sane.'

'Therapy.'

'He didn't put it like that. He wouldn't use a word like that. He thought if he could string together an account of the situation he was basically fine.'

'It's a pretty standard diagnosis.'

'It's easy to blame him for what happened, and I'm not saying we shouldn't judge. We should. Being moral means making judgments and it isn't such a bad thing. But I've read the diaries and I don't think he's entirely to blame.'

There's a little silence. The wind starts up in the pines.

'Remember the story you read out last night? The Poe bit? About the box?'

'Of course.'

'Tell me about the man in the lifeboat again.'

'He goes mad. That's what the captain says. *Mr Wyatt, you are* mad. *I cannot listen to you.* Then the painter, Wyatt, goes over the side and swims back to the ship and his dead wife.'

'She's dead. She doesn't care if he's with her or not. It doesn't stop him destroying himself.'

'I know.'

'You say you watched our grandmother every Sunday afternoon, in her armchair with her cigarettes. I don't think it would have mattered if the armchair had been parked downstairs. She could have stayed in this house, and in her marriage, and still been miserable.'

'It would have been easier on my mother if she'd been parked downstairs.'

'You said yourself that your mother made her choice.'

The wind is still drifting in the pines. I don't want an argument.

'Thea?'

'Yes?'

'My father wasn't raving mad. He was betrayed. My mother betrayed him. It bent him out of shape for a little while.'

I'm ashamed of myself. The remedy is a walk on the cliffs, alone.

The steps down the cliff face are made of earth packed behind bolted slabs of wood, or steep, ladder-like prefabricated steel with treads angled for a very short stride. Earth and wood are strewn with leaves trodden into earlier leaves but the wind has blown the steel treads clean. The earth steps can look natural, as if shallow terraces had formed behind fallen saplings. In the places where young trees provide the protection of a railing all that can be seen, beyond the trees, are the forested valleys below.

The railings are so cold that at first touch they seem wet, and perhaps they're glossed with light vapour from a distant waterfall. Generations of ferns use their own dead stems for support on the rock face; if you look up there's a spume of grey. From above the fern is a single arch of green. Moss grows thick and high; then sends fine hairs even higher. The air is full of light mist and the sound of falling water. At certain times of the day every lookout, every tongue of rock is occupied by backpackers or families, grouped before a camera with their backs to the railing and the empty blue air, and beyond that, in the distance, rock and a long postcard view of a waterfall.

Children run down flight after flight of steps. Everyone stops to share chocolate or cellophane bags of nuts and dried fruit from the kiosk where the paths begin. Backpackers' straps creak and babies riding in slings look calmly over the valley, not knowing what it is to fall.

When people stop to rest or eat or to be photographed someone always says the same thing. This is after they've caught their breath and got to the end of the roll of film or the choco-late. I overhear them say *imagine*. Then there are two variations. *Imagine if* leads to a conversation about flying. From behind the railing it seems possible to soar out straight and level across the valley floor. The other thing people ask of one another is to *imagine when* this cliff and the whole forest below were unknown to Europeans. Imagine standing lean and naked under loose furs on the pathless cliffs, eating, if not exactly nuts and fruit in cellophane, some natural meal.

I can't do it. Not the flying, not the lean nakedness.

Finn's room is on the far side of the staircase which leads to a corridor, or gallery, where a big lithograph is hanging, along with some linocuts showing different views of the house. There is only one painting: a portrait, close to Finn's door. It is the portrait of a man in uniform, some relative that I don't know about. Finn would know what the decorations mean. It's a confident portrait, painted by someone who has done a good deal of official work. The soldier himself is pink, whiskery, responsible. The tones are warm. Red and khaki. Red: the colour of the poppies around the Acropolis where the young men who were the officers in France in 1914 wandered on their Grand Tour; the colour, too, of the Flanders poppies which finally covered their battlefields.

Next to the portrait of the soldier is a black and white photograph of a man climbing a rock chimney. It must be one of the postcard peaks. It isn't a view; for him, it's a place where he finds handholds and dangerous, irregular steps. He's climbing without safety gear and his body is capable and relaxed. The face, in silhouette, is the face in the painting of the soldier.

I'm staring at this when Finn opens his door.

'Ah,' he says, 'the warrior on the mountainside. No cable car for him. Listen.' He disappears and comes back with a book. '"He who climbs without knowing to where he climbs, will reach the highest peak."'

'Not necessarily,' I have to say.

Finn shows me the spine. He's quoting from a life of Rudolph Hess. Hess believed this stuff. Then he hanged himself. I wonder what he climbed onto, finally, to tie the electric flex around his neck, and then to tie it to the handle of the window which took his weight.

Finn looks shaggy, after the man in the portrait. I remember a promise I made one night in front of the fire.

'Isn't it time I cut your hair?'

It's harder than it looks. Finn's hair is thick and white like the hair of a stage professor. It slips away from the scissor blades. And the scissors have been in this kitchen too long, they've jointed chickens and taken off bacon rind. I grip tufts and the scissors chew away until there's a circle of white around us both and Finn can run his palms over the lumpy mess I've made of his hair. I don't offer to get a mirror. He glances at his reflection in the window above the sink.

'I saw clippers in the pantry.'

He's right, they're there, among rusting Farex tins in a shape I've never seen on supermarket shelves. They're still sharp. He tucks his chin down and I work away at the stiff handles of the clippers.

After I've finished he has a head of strokable prickling fur. We both stroke it. It's compulsive. The stubble springs up against the hand. He doesn't look too bad. Younger, and his eyes are huge.

'Well? Will they all think I'm a great-looking guy?'

'They?'

'Women.'

I'm women, suddenly. 'I don't know. How would I know? I finished with romance pages and pages ago. Remember? Stella ends up on her own. Except for a visitor.'

Finn laughs. 'Where do you go when you've finished with romance?'

What comes after romance? Cold, I could say. Safety railings at Niagara. I can't go into all of that. The opposite of love. 'What about war?' His territory.

He laughs. 'You think you can have war without romance?'

I imagine blackouts. The world reduced to touch. Welted uniform seams, under cold hands.

In daylight the strong aeroplanes of the first war, aeroplanes of wood and tight painted cloth, loop noisily above small groups of mechanics and young girls. There are curves of black smoke in the sky. Engines stall and cut in, seconds before the half-expected smash. It's a whole lot more exciting than watching a Zeppelin or the sea above a submarine. And some loose sweet mobility stays with the pilot, stepping down from a wing and walking to the girls as mechanics in overalls crouch with chocks behind the wheels. The girls pretend to be unimpressed. The pilot. The young girls. It's easy enough to imagine.

'You have to win every point,' I say, trying to make it sound like a fault. I leave him with the clippings and the broom.

There are still so many books on Poe that I've barely read. Our grandfather must have had a passion for him. Poe and Japanese fairytales and Australian poetry. You wonder how one head could hold it together.

The windows in my old room are set low in the wall, so when I sit cross-legged on the bed to read I can look down into the garden. I can watch for a bird and wait to hear it cry. Parrots come for the pine cones and the plums. They take the fruit before it has a chance to get properly ripe. They walk clumsily along the branches, using their beaks as an extra foot. A wing flicks out, for balance. I could watch until dusk.

I open my notebook and pick up my pen.

In 1915 a Lithuanian composer named Karnovitch was captured by Germans in Galacia. He was interned in a small town for three years with nothing to do but write. *Separated from the world, we had plenty of time to read, meditate and dream.* He put together a piece of music called 'Remembrances of the House of Usher'. I've never travelled in Bohemia, so I have no way of knowing what his small town looked like. In my imagination I give him a room with windows overlooking a tower and a bell-shaped dome. I give him a flock of geese in the streets below. I give him linen as white as the confident geese. I give him a table under the window and a soft pencil and plenty of paper. I give him the sounds of trains and running water. Nobody speaks Lithuanian in the town, but his Russian and German are good. At night, in candlelight, he rules up his pages and, forgetting where he is, whispers to himself in Lithuanian.

Perhaps he wrote his music behind rough planks in a barracks, in deadly cold. But I've given him a room and a beautiful dome in a spirit of sympathy, because in a fragment of a letter, which is all I have been able to discover of his, he speaks for both of us. He writes that, *The night is waning in reality and I am sitting at my table. Do forgive me this endless letter! You see Edgar Poe, as a personality, and his work have such an irresistible influence on me, that whenever I meet them I cannot stop thinking, 'linking fancy unto fancy', and 'dreaming dreams no mortal ever dared to dream before'*. It's all I have of him. I sit cross-legged on my bed with my eyes closed. My mother took me through the lives of the great composers. I've never heard of him.

'Everything I know about my father I found out on the Great Northern Highway,' says Finn.

We're sitting in the sunroom where he's set up his desk. He's rolling cigarettes for us both. I could do my own, but I'm so out of practice I know I'd be jamming the clear edge of the paper under the line of glue on the other side; making a crumpled, just smokable mess, whereas Finn does fat professional cylinders. I'm dizzy and relaxed. The branches outside Finn's window are crusted with cream and grey lichen. Beyond that the mist thickens and clears.

'He hated driving, so when he was in the car he'd say things he didn't mean to say because he was distracted by the road. I'd pitch him a question when his knuckles turned white on the wheel. You'd get anything out of him when he was passing a truck.'

He's found a photo of his parents somewhere in a cupboard. His mother is wearing a plain fine-waisted suit. She looks professional. She tips her face slightly, chin up, and gives a bright smile. This is her wedding day. It's the second marriage. Her first was to an airman, killed early in the war. She didn't marry my father. Easier to live with him, and say you've been married twice. In the picture Finn's father looks exactly like his son. The white hair. The noticeable eyes. When I cut Finn's hair I turned him into his father.

'He only had one war story, or one that he'd brushed up for me. I have to say he wasn't in the car when he told me this, he was in an armchair with a glass of Scotch. He poured me my first and only Highland Malt. I was around fifteen. I hated it.'

Finn's cigarette has a lick of brown at the tip. His fingers are brown and the middle one has grown a lump where he holds his pen. At night he'll pull on a jacket and call a cab to take him to the bottle shop; he comes back with a bottle of red or, once, some good champagne.

'What he wanted to tell me was that in Scotland a prisoner grabbed a revolver from a guard and pointed it straight at him. It wasn't a high-ranking prisoner. Afterwards the man's own officers were embarrassed about the whole thing. He didn't escape and my father wasn't shot. What he wanted me to understand was that he was afraid. He studied the art of war but it was clear that he felt the terror of war and he didn't want to tell me anything about it in a way that passed on a sense of adventure.'

Finn's manuscript about the General makes a tidy pile to one side of our feet. He's anchored it with a military history.

When a hat was passed around for Poe's family, just before Virginia died, an old general handed over five dollars. It was all he could afford. He said that true-hearted Americans ought to take care of poets as well as soldiers.

Finn's General hasn't given much thought to poetry, as far as I can see. Finn is having trouble with the material. There's a difference between plotting locations on a map, which I know he has done, and having something like a life on the page.

'My father never said very much at home but there was a sense of him being at all times connected with other men we'd never heard about. A name would come up with a certain emphasis, or he'd make a comment, in passing, over a story in the news. Intelligence always sticks together. So do sub-mariners. Something about being closed off and listening. Nobody else in the military links up in quite the same way.'

I'm watching the mist. A bird lands on a branch which is almost too fine to bear its weight. It sways and finally steadies.

'How are you going with the General?'

He doesn't speak for a while. I'm wondering whether I should tell him it doesn't matter, he doesn't need to reply, I'm just making conversation. Then he says, 'I'm starting to look at it like this. A captain gets shot at occasionally. My father was a captain. A major never gets shot. And a general? Well, it depends on the general.' He puts down his cigarette. 'Anyone would think I was enjoying this.'

The window in front of me is completely black. I can hear a chinking sound, the sound of a fingernail against glass. It's an insect, or something contracting in the cold. I've forgotten myself, and written into the early hours. I'm tired, I don't know what I'm writing any more. The words scroll up between me and the black windowpane.

I write, *I followed Edmund through the stink and mess at the rear of the battle-lines, where the shock of the clean slicing or shattering of flesh gives way to black swellings, to ache and old blood and stupe-faction. It rained and rained. There were whippings, and I saw the remnants of men who had been hanged for running away. The noise of gunfire came over the noise of wind and the water that seemed to leap back from the mud or whatever shuddering surface it cast itself against.* Then I stop, I can't go on. I don't know who Edmund is or what battle-lines I've written about. I wait, but there is nothing more.

Just these words, and the chink, chink of something in the room, or out in the dark.

I want to ask Finn how someone could go mad in a house in the mountains with a choice of lilac and rhododendron varieties and someone else could stay reasonably sane through battle and gunfire. I'm afraid he'd point out that his father was calm and sensible throughout the campaign in North Africa, but he lost his mind as a consequence of love.

My mother has a box in her wardrobe. It stays closed. It's a small leather suitcase belonging to our grandmother. It's full of letters, photographs and notebooks. Nothing valuable. There was a handful of sad jewellery to be given out after the funeral. Some of it had no history; it could have been straight from an antique shop display case, for all we knew about who had cherished it and passed it on.

Our grandmother's things were spread out on the bed beside us. Neither of us picked up the wedding ring. My mother asked if I was brave enough to wear it, but I said no. She gave me the watch. She told me she'd already opened the suitcase and looked at a notebook. Inside, our grandmother had written the date and left a space. There was over a year of this. Sometimes in the space she had carefully written *Help*. My mother closed the box for good and now it sits in her wardrobe. Next to the wardrobe is a table which is covered by a green damask cloth. If I push the cloth back I can look into the grain of the wood, which seems to be lit, far below the surface, with a deep red light.

My mother said, 'If you let yourself think about her life you would sink in shame.' Now I think about Poe, instead. Someone came to visit, after Virginia died. Poe wrote, in misery, to Louise, about how this visitor *stood smiling and bowing at the madman Poe.* At some point someone looked at my grandmother as if she were a madwoman and something inside her said *Yes, yes that is what I am*, and often, after that, she would need to be stitched up and put on a closed verandah in the annexe of a country hospital, or taken to somewhere more frightening, in the city.

There are no photographs, or at least none to put in a silver or bird's-eye maple frame on the piano for guests to pick up and comment on. I've seen a few pictures of her when she was young. I believe that one of the reasons my mother keeps the box of our grandmother's things so firmly closed is that in the photographs which I have seen, which are now back inside the box, the young madwoman looks just like me.

I'd like to have been able to take our grandmother from the hospital verandah and from the rooms she lived in at the end of her life, in the house which was turned into a museum. In fact it wouldn't have helped very much, to have taken her from these places. When Poe wrote about a lunatic asylum, in a story called 'The System of Doctor Tarr and Professor Fether', the lunatics have a grand dinner where they try to pass themselves off as sane, but their delusions break through into the conversation. They pretend to be animals or teapots; they take off their clothes and make so much noise that normal conversation is drowned out, Poe says, *like the voice of a fish from the bottom of Niagara Falls.* He makes a joke of it all.

I'll take our grandmother from her high metal bed, from her glass of water and her armchair. I'll give her a room next to the room where I have put the composer Karnovitch, so that in the night she too can hear a river pouring into a lake and the percussive sounds he makes with his breath or his pencil on the table edge when he is finding a rhythm. I'll give her cherries and rye bread and white butter and something fierce and evaporative to drink just before she goes to bed. Her suitcase will be open on the few plain things she has brought with her: glycerine soap and a hairbrush and, most importantly, skirts and shirts and a cardigan, not the kind of clothes which are packed to take to hospital.

She won't be disturbed by the mediaeval paintings in the town: the pursuits, the struggles with skeletons, the agony of those who are walled up alive and those who are strapped down. She's seen plenty of this kind of thing. I'd like to give her a morning on the lake and a discussion with another travelling woman which is so engrossing that neither notices they have sailed past a small jetty which is decorated for a wedding, with white flowers and wide white ribbon.

If I can't give her calm water and music in the evenings I'll try another thing. I'll make a new story out of Poe's asylum tale.

THE SYSTEM OF DOCTOR TARR AND PROFESSOR FETHER

A MAN TRAVELLING IN the south of France with a chance acquaintance decides to inspect an asylum which his medical friends have told him about. His travelling companion opposes the idea, and will not be part of it, himself. He knows the superintendent, however, and he introduces the narrator to the superintendent, before he rides away.

The superintendent is Monsieur Maillard. He takes our narrator to a parlour where a beautiful woman is singing and playing the piano. She is not, he insists, a lunatic. She is his niece.

He explains that his method of treatment has changed. Formerly, patients were entirely indulged, under a plan of treatment which he called the Soothing System. No patient was told that he was mad. All delusions were treated seriously, and catered for. The man who thought himself to be a chicken was given seed and gravel. All this has, apparently, been reversed, although we are not told the details of the new regime.

The traveller is asked to dinner. His fellow-guests are flamboyantly dressed and the food is over-plentiful. The orchestra is off-key.

As the meal progresses the discussion slips into anecdotes of lunacy. One guest describes a patient who thought he was a teapot. Another was convinced he was a donkey. The man who tells this story illustrates it by kicking a woman nearby. The asylum has held an impersonator of a champagne bottle, a frog, and a man who thinks he has two heads. All the delusions are demonstrated.

The traveller is told that the Soothing System has been abandoned because of the danger that the lunatics could take over the asylum.

As the conversation progresses, an angry crowd gathers outside the room, and finally what appear to be orang-utans burst in and attack the dinner guests.

The apes are the true keepers of the asylum. Everyone else is mad, including Monsieur Maillard. The keepers look like apes because they were tarred and feathered when the lunatics overpowered them.

The Soothing System

One morning a Russian landowner wakes in rare sunshine and remembers the great harm that he has done to a child. It gets in the way of his vision of the white shoulders of St Cecilia. It dissolves the satisfaction he takes in his travels and his land.

One morning a Russian woman wakes in a ruined chateau in the south of France. She's humming. It isn't a hum that can be heard. It's in her body, especially in the arms. Her heart beats hard and fast. It will be like this all day. The bumping heart and the hum in the arms. She closes her eyes and visits a particular room at a particular time, as M. Maillard has taught her. He wants her to remember a moment of stillness, directly after the events which have left her with this tremor, this palpitation.

M. Maillard advises her to begin to remember at the moment when the one by the door, the one who was last to rape her, finds a toothpick and a packet of cocaine in his pocket. The cocaine is a late kindness. She remembers how they hooked the arms of the landowner over their shoulders and lifted him clear of everything. Finally the door closes. She is suddenly alone and the cocaine they gave her is still having its effect.

After the cocaine all the colours in the room spring to

attention. Red, white walls, grey. Plaster looks suddenly hard, though it powders to the touch. Shadows drift into various blacknesses. This is important. This is what must be kept in the mind, after flesh and voices and the jingle of harnesses in the street drop away. The red blood on her legs will wipe clear. But the road outside the window is the most dense impressive grey and it continues to be so, as it lapses into tracks and climbs back into paved significance and crosses borders and mountains and follows the edge of a lake, all the way to other places. It is a part, right here, of the very far away.

A man who paints icons in the room above can't sleep. He lights a candle and turns to his square of wood. His brush thumps away like a ballerina on a practice floor. The mouth numbs. It is important not to look down at the red but to look out to the street, to the road, and to listen to what might be a pattern of footfalls on the floor of the room above.

Louise has fallen asleep in her own armchair beside a vase painted with delphiniums. She opens her eyes on a deep glittering blue. She has had the most terrible dream. Her chest constricts, fluid burns in the back of her throat. The letter in her hands is damp with sweat. She has never seen the frozen river or the building which appeared in the dream. The child with the wide face and straight black hair is strange, too. She knows children can be forced like this. She has helped a mother to clean and repair a child. She knows, but until now she has never seen.

The letter is from Muddy, letting her know that the wine she sent was welcome. There are some closely written pages in

Virginia's hand, as well. Muddy reminds her of how weak Virginia was when she first came to the house and what a difference all her gifts have made. Before Louise arrived, Muddy says, Virginia could not even speak. Louise doubts this. Then she thinks of Virginia, silent and staring, in the room near the kitchen, with her patient cat. She goes to pack. She folds the linen burial dress first, then goes looking for her bottle of good cologne. The dream is forgotten, but her ribs ache a little. It is all this sadness, she thinks, or else she has somehow exerted herself.

Louise makes herself breathe evenly. She makes herself relax into the chair by the delphinium vase. She falls into a light sleep and in this sleep Virginia's voice comes to her. Virginia's voice is very faint, above the cat and the eiderdown. Louise listens to the wind in the cherry tree and the purr of the cat, and to Virginia, who is talking about a Russian landowner waking, in horror, to the memory of what he has done. Virginia says, *It dissolves the satisfaction he takes in his travels and his land.*

Eugenie sits on the windowsill, looking down between her bare knees, onto the courtyard. The head and pelt of a grey cat sail through the kitchen window far below. There are older, hardened catskins on the cobbles. Eugenie decides not to eat the rabbit dish, tonight. Who knows what the cook believes about cats and rabbits? M. Maillard insists that everybody's confusions must be honoured, which allows the cook to serve whatever he traps, just as it allows Eugenie to sit naked in the sun. The old woman who mixed her own urine with her wine, to insult whatever it is inside her which insists that she drink and drink until she slides to the floor, was supplied with wine and fresh crystal and given her turn on the arm of M. Maillard when he takes his walk in the park, until she finally died.

Eugenie can see the path through the park from her windowsill. Two men have pulled their horses to a halt on the path. They talk for a long time. Neither looks up at the fans of iron spikes dividing one window from the next. Eugenie has found that hardly anybody looks up. She swings her feet in the void.

When she arrived M. Maillard helped her from the ropes and watched as she freed herself from the headscarf, the neckerchief, the blue dress, the cotton stockings and the clogs which the previous place had given her. She is a Russian woman. She doesn't feel the cold, especially now, in summer. And there can be no great offence in nakedness; after all, the prophet Ezekiel went naked. One of the women at the last place told her so. He was shaved and tied in ropes as well. The asylums are full of visionaries. Visions and blasphemies. It is entertaining. It is what the ordinary people come to see. M. Maillard countered by saying that he was closing the asylum to sightseers for this very reason. The ordinary people themselves, he said, often don't bear such close examination. The difference between the ordinary and the mad might be the difference between those who put their energies into concealment, as opposed to those who weep in full view. He offered his arm to Eugenie and together they passed through many open doors and wandered down the path by the tall summer grasses.

When Eugenie was quite small, on the day, in fact, that she

was visited by the landowner and his friends, she watched as her mother was prepared for burial.

Her mother earned her living as a seamstress. As the time for her death drew near she gathered candles, two coins and the strip of cloth for bandaging the jaw. Then she and Eugenie worked on the burial dress. When the sewing began her mother was pink and talkative. By the time the dress was complete she was a strange stinking yellow and in the night she opened her mouth on a single deep note, a cry which Eugenie was not to hear again until she paused outside the crates containing the truly mad in one of the great asylums. Eugenie blamed the dress. As it grew shapely and was embellished with the embroidery of her mother's region, her mother failed. She hated the dress, although it was full of her own stitches and speckles of blood from her fingertips. In her dreams she flung it into a furnace and her mother shook the coins from her eyes and drew her bare knees up under her chin and smiled.

Eugenie found herself telling M. Maillard about all of this as they sat on a garden seat in a circle of gravel to one side of the path. There were clouds in the sky and M. Maillard held a substantial umbrella which he thumped occasionally on the gravel as she spoke. He said nothing. Once he put an arm over the back of the chair behind her. Eugenie looked down at his polished tan shoes. Pigeons landed on the gravel, pacing, thickening their feathers at the throat, stepping in front of one another, baulking.

M. Maillard made no immediate comment about Eugenie and her mother. Instead he told her something of the history of the chateau, of his own methods and the characters of those she would join in the dormitory and at the table. She forgot them all, except the singer Augustine and English John the cook.

Eugenie sits across the warm stone sill and swings her legs. If it were not for the fan of iron spikes between each window she could edge down and along to the next window, which is fastened, but not tightly, on the family effects of the original owners of the chateau. The men far below say their farewells and one turns his horse back to the gates and the road. The other looks up. Eugenie is perfectly still. There are no visitors, no sightseers. He will not be allowed through the door.

An old woman passes through the courtyard, carrying a bag which sways with something soft and heavy. She opens a door and disappears. She is a bird gatherer. Today's dead bird will be stacked on a shelf in an old pantry, with all the others. Birds have living souls and the Lord says they must be fed, so their dead beaks have hardened around balls of dried bread which John leaves in a saucer for this purpose. The souls of the birds are, naturally, silent, but even if this were not so it would be hard for them to sing through each wad of bread. Eugenie suspects that John strips the flesh from the bigger birds, the pheasants and pigeons, even the tough African parrots which were once caged by the fishpond, and adds them to his stew. Some people add to their gold; John's currency is stew. It is part of M. Maillard's treatment to give him the cook's job.

In the dormitory a woman called Charlotte is praying noisily for the return of two thousand francs. The violinist who went mad for love begins to saw at his instrument. Someone is complaining that all the noise will wake her baby. Eugenie has never seen this baby. Augustine is the youngest in the dormitory, and she is no baby. It is true, though, that the front of the mother's dress is always wet, as if something has been drawing off the hopeful milk. It is true, too, that the francs are lost and may with God's grace one day be discovered.

Finally the prayer is over, the violin too is laid to one side and in the surprising silence Eugenie hears the snick of the outside door. The horse is wandering, free of his saddle, in the park. There is no sign of the traveller.

M. Maillard has been an important physician, but after a well-publicised lawsuit he left Paris in disgrace. He had confirmed the death of a woman who was, it was later discovered, merely in the deepest trance. An action was brought against the doctor by her lover, who was joined by her husband. M. Maillard was ruined. The position of governing the Maison de Santé was not his choice or vocation. It was all that he could do.

Some say that what he calls his Soothing System of allowing for the whims and imaginings of those who are in his care is not a restorative program at all, but an indication of his own helplessness.

Some say that he listens kindly to the patients' stories, but does not give them great weight, not, as he would claim, because he believes that simple events alone cannot cause such eccentricities and distress, but because he would prefer not to think about the stories, which exhaust him. His critics, and there are some even within the asylum, say that he is exhausted and dismayed.

Perhaps the traveller is a remnant of his happy life in Paris, and not connected with this place.

Eugenie angles herself so that she has an oblique view of the window behind the iron spikes. These rooms are locked, and the corridors which lead to them are locked. She sees a blur, the movement of drapes, or, and this is what has her tilting danger-ously forward, the face of Augustine.

She edges out onto the fan of iron. She is like the women strapped to the bars of bedsteads in the very bad asylums, except that she can move. The further she goes the more open are the bars. When she has almost reached the spikes they are wide enough to climb through. Then the palpitations start. She is trembling dangerously above the courtyard. This is because she has allowed herself to think of the bars as the bars of a bed. She is back in Russia, in the room by the frozen river. She closes her eyes as M. Maillard has taught her and willingly goes back to that room. She remembers stillness, colours, a throat numbed with cocaine, but she also remembers the flare of confidence which came with the drug. Her shaking eases. She is able to climb to the other side of the bars and force the loose catch of the window.

Down in the courtyard the violinist watches Eugenie climb across the bars. His eyesight is bad. Each day, it seems to him, he loses more of his vision, his hair, his skill with the strings. It seems to him that when he came here he had some of the radiance that followed his rejection of the great conductor and his own passion for the bassoon. He was hurt, yes, he needed rest and care, but surely he was still cruel and beautiful, when he came. He needs to be sure. He finds M. Maillard's notes in the caramel leather book which amounts to the administration of the place. The notes are brief: names, dates and a single word.

Catatonic. Anxious. Dangerous. Eccentric. Dead. There are no Recoveries. So often M. Maillard has simply written Grief. The word appears next to the violinist's own name. Grief.

He can hear M. Maillard explaining his methods in the next room. The doctor has made this speech so often that he doesn't need to think about the words. He thinks about something else, then loses his place, goes silent or repeats himself. The violinist wonders if M. Maillard is talking to someone, or simply rehearsing. Who could he be talking to? The asylum is closed to visitors. The violinist puts the caramel book back on M. Maillard's secretaire and leaves by a courtyard door. He looks up and watches a woman no longer than a finger perform over huge strings. Of course the bars are strings. Where might a bow be found to draw over these strings?

M. Maillard is not talking to himself.

The visitor is a narrow-shouldered American who is familiar with M. Maillard's publications; those writings which date from the first years he spent here, when something of his lost status and ambitions gave him the energy to apply his old habits of observation and imaginative treatment. The visitor has read papers which M. Maillard has forgotten that he wrote. It seems that his methods are the subject of dispute, even now, in the capital. His reputation surprises him. If the American is to be believed no one remembers his disgrace. The praise and denunciation which the American describes concerns only his position as a doctor to the mad.

In recent years he has thought of himself as one of the mad; eating the gristle that English John slops on his plate. He is the

Father at the head of their table and it is known that all madness is inherited. He feels different, with this American.

Then there is a knock on the door and Eugenie sweeps in, fully clothed. She is more than clothed; she is magnificent, in plain black from the previous century. M. Maillard is briefly speechless. He has never had the chance to write Recovery in his caramel-bound book. He forgets the long years she has lived under the practice of his methods. He makes a quick superstitious connection between the way she looks and the arrival of the American. Eugenie, who has an idea of what John has been chopping on his bench, is surprised to hear M. Maillard invite the stranger to join them all for dinner.

The closed family apartments that Eugenie climbed into were mostly bare and dazzling with light. The roofing had collapsed long ago. Walls were streaked with bird lime and the whiteness of the lime made whatever had been painted into the plaster beneath even more soft and indistinct. The floors in protected areas were thick with dust. If Augustine had been in these rooms she must have floated above the boards.

Eugenie quickly lost herself in rooms which opened into one another and guided her up stairs and through narrow empty galleries which had no equivalent in the familiar part of the house. She seemed to be retracing her steps, but the only footprints were those behind her. The light hurt her eyes; she had to narrow her eyes to see her own feet. Finally she lay down tiredly under a great wash of light and slept. As she slept the sun passed overhead and the room with its shadows and ordinary joinery took shape. Eugenie woke for the first time in ten years outside of her dread. Her heart was calm. There was no shaking in her limbs.

If she had to describe what happened, in a conversation with M. Maillard, she would perhaps have said that in these pathless brilliant rooms she realised that it was not one particular thing which stood for death: her mother's dress, the beard or the grip of the landowner. These distinctive things were signs of life. Death was a silent spaciousness, indistinct and very still. Her nakedness, her refusal to wear a dress which might be the burial dress, would not deflect death; and though it would protect her from seducers, who prefer a more gradual nakedness, it would not protect her from assault. She could have made a story of all of this. But it would be false to her experience of waking in rested awareness, so she never did.

Further down the next gallery she came upon the first of the family relics, a low wooden box. Inside was a mourning dress. Once she worked out how to arrange the laces which organised the structure of the thing she admitted to herself that it was pleasant to wear. She felt as if she were lightly held about the chest.

English John has forced the door of the chapel and taken the altar cloths to spread over their table. The linen can barely be seen for tureens and candelabra. Slices of bleeding roast fold over themselves. Wax drips, hissing, into the meat. The slices are immense. Eugenie hopes the traveller won't be needing his horse. Augustine lights a final candle and squints down at the silver, which she's cleaned and cleaned. She's black to the elbows. She stares for a minute at her hand, spreads her fingers and deliberately prints herself across the top of a milky jelly. Nothing a splash of anisette won't fix. John pushes past her with the bottle. Augustine is sent for the violinist and his music stand. For a brief moment John considers Eugenie, and the neck of the bottle. He holds it at his crotch to make his meaning clear. No. She says it in her own language, with an edge of irritation, as if he were suggesting a walk in the park during a storm, but with the authority of the Frenchwoman who first wore her mourning costume. John shuffles back to his kitchen.

Someone has dressed the grey hair of the birdwoman into a pyramid and cut away at her bodice to show off her unexpectedly pretty breasts. Women arrive arm in arm from the dormitory, talking about something other than money or children. The violinist turns his back to the room and touches his bow softly to his own eyelid and lip. The instrument lifts itself to his chin. Then, as M. Maillard opens the door for the American, he turns and skids his way up through an ordinary scale to a final easy note. He bows. His hands lift, he drops his head. Eugenie leads the applause.

The American says, *Never in all my life.* It's all he can say, for the moment. He is shown to his chair. Eugenie's keen ears hear his *Absolutely* drop softly to the word *barbaric*.

In the locked apartments where ribboned children float or dive across the walls one boy suddenly breaks free of the wall and stumbles away from his painted wings. The crouched outline he had fitted himself into is left behind. There is just enough moonlight to show that the trunk at the end of the gallery has been disturbed. The lid, which was too heavy for him to lift, is now propped open. He pulls out a piece of batiste. He sniffs it, shapes it to a point and begins to suck. It keeps him going until he finds his way back to the level of the courtyard and a hole where there was once a grille. A cat gives ground and he reaches for its kill. As he separates feathers from solid delicious blood he wonders at so much light and laughter in the dining room. He listens for the women, feeling the pull of a particular voice.

M. Maillard begins his familiar speech about the chateau, the fever which finished off the family who occupied it for centuries; the tragedy which destroyed the final heirs, twin boys, one well, one stricken with illness; the nurse who put the sleeping healthy child in the coffin with his mother and after the burial tried to wake the corpse of his brother; the spectacular madness of this nurse. M. Maillard never loses his way in this story. The American watches him closely.

The trouble begins with the talk about the Soothing System, the method for treating lunatics which was announced in the papers the American has read. English John refills M. Maillard's glass. He drinks from the bottle himself, and frowns at the birdwoman's breasts. Eugenie wonders where she found pink paste for the tips. Her earlobes are pink as well.

M. Maillard closes his eyes and stands. He says firmly of the lunatics at the table, 'I mean them to do harm or to do good as they please. They can hardly do more harm than those who are trying to do good.'

There is a silence.

The American pulls a scrap of paper from his pocket and begins to read M. Maillard's cautious official words back to him.

He nods, waving his glass, reciting, where he can, in chorus with the American.

M. Maillard says, deliberately, 'The sentence which I left off the end of the paper is, "They can hardly do more harm than those who are trying to do good."'

It is difficult to know what can be said, after this. M. Maillard will not continue. The American taps a fork handle against the paper he has been reading.

Eugenie decides to speak.

She is sorry, she tells the guest, but here in the country, in this particular house, some social nimbleness has been forgotten. We do not dance. We would not be here if we were able to perform. Our music, she says kindly, is unfashionable. All we have for entertainment is ourselves. So I propose that we tell our guest stories, in the course of the meal, each taking a turn, and each remembering, she looked sternly at English John, that what is of most interest to the self may not be interesting to the guest. M. Maillard has given us the history of the house. Who can match his story of the dead children and their nurse?

The Violinist's Story

The violinist stands and smooths his gloves, which he has forgotten to remove.

'M. Maillard's story of the nurse's error puts me in mind,' he says, 'of something which happened in another country, not so many years ago.

'The story takes place as a hard winter is beginning. The

days end early and squirrels with thin tails rush along branches and between tree trunks in the parks, scouring flattened grass for whatever might keep them alive in the months to come. We came through these parks in a carriage which slipped on ice at each turn in the road. There were just a few of us and our instruments. We were all dreaming of the big cream enamel stoves in the staterooms of the Schloss where we were to play; we knew the rooms well, we played there every year. The man I was crammed against was the oldest among us and the thinnest. His hands shook with fear or illness, as well as the cold. Finally the horses stopped and I saw the outline of the building through the white haze of the windowpane. A very young footman came to the door. His hand was soft in mine as he helped me to the cobbles. I stretched and found my feet. My friend was not so lucky. He could not move from his seat. The footman leaned into the carriage and half-lifted him. He lost his balance and they both fell to the ground. I waited for the apologies, the red-faced goodwill. Neither spoke. Later, in the porcelain room, under the gold monsters and garlands strung below the painted ceiling, the old man was unable to draw his bow across his instrument.

'The footman with the small cushioned hands came to me after the performance and proposed a walk through the long corridors, following a circuit about the courtyard which in time returned us to the cream stove of the porcelain room. I walked stiffly, holding myself at a distance in the most narrow spaces, because I wanted to brush against him so much. It became a habit with us, to walk a little, after the performances and the conversations expected by those who hired us all. One night we left the building altogether and made our way to the edge of a wood. Deer had scraped aside what they could of the snow. I could not warm myself. My cloak pulled the cold tightly in against my flesh.

'On my final night in this place I was invited to the footman's room. I took him the gift of a pin which had been given to me many years before, and which I kept, always, with the resin I used to smooth my bow. I had the idea that the old Roman spirit whose grave the pin had been taken from would watch over my bow, in the darkness of the compartment where I kept my piece of gum. I hesitated. It was, after all, a simple thing, pitted and unrefined, and looking so, to eyes which were used to the magnificence of the Schloss, where whole walls were panelled with green and gold fish scales and draped bodies tumbling through folds of pink or shadowy white. Nevertheless, the old pin was all I had.

'I did not have to part with it.

'The footman was taller than he should have been and he did not turn when I spoke to him. By the time I reached him, I understood.

'He turned so lightly under my hand, at the end of his rope. He had hanged himself. He left something for me, under his feet.

'I opened his letter in a carriage which was bearing me over the Alps.

'I too had been invited to the hunting lodge when I played at the Schloss the previous year. I did not go. None of us went, except the old cellist who slipped when he was lifted from the carriage. I remember that he told me the lodge was uncomfortable. The footman's letter told me just how uncomfortable it was.

'The cellist had offended a group of footmen. This was easy, for a man from Denmark who had come to their language late in his life, and who had spent his whole life so engrossed in the tones of his particular instrument that he did not measure his words, even the words he spoke in his mother tongue. His instrument was beautiful. There were the smallest serrations, like the drag of light teethmarks, in the grain. I often heard him give himself over completely to his music; the bow striking the instrument at the end of its long swoop, his breathing audible through an entire gallery. I watched him clasp the neck of the cello as if it were a lover's wrist, or the wrist of some inhuman creature that he loved.

'The footmen watched all this as well.

'A large angry boar was wounded in the hunt. It was bound and carried to the steps of the lodge where it struggled in the filth of its terror, throwing its head back again and again, as if the musculature of its neck alone could loosen the ropes, as if muscle and need were enough. Blood was drying and cracking open across its black hide and harsh black hair. It cried with pain and thirst, into the night.

'The young footman whose letter I held in my hands wished to recommend himself to an older man whom the cellist had offended. He made a suggestion.

'The cellist was taken from his bed and stripped. His knees were bound tightly about the frantic animal. Then the footmen cut the boar free. It was amusing to watch the pair stumble and jerk across the paving, to see the white skin and the dark hide, and the harsh black hairs of them both, and to see the cellist try to pull back from the animal, to save his hands from the sweep of the tusks. The rope loosened, the boar's hooves got a purchase on the thighs of the man and with a great thrust it pushed him aside. The cellist, bruised and stinking, limped back to his bed.

'The footman began to have the most sickening dreams. It was he who rode the boar through the low spaces of the forest, until he was, himself, the boar. His neck thickened, his back crested to a bristling ridge. He watched himself dragged down by dogs. He saw his own thigh torn from his side. He saw the white round bone which would never rest in the cup of its socket again. He cried and woke. But the fear returned in the course of the day. He was immobilised by certain smells and sounds.

'This lasted an entire year. But his worst moment came when he lifted the cellist from the carriage and the old man made a soft angry noise in his throat and suddenly the young footman with the angry bristling weight in his arms felt himself lashed to the boar, his body sinking to the centre of the boar and that animal body pulled down to its slow death.

'The idea of resting against another being, of holding another body in his arms, became unbearable. He realised this, after he had asked me to his room.

'I left the letter on the seat of the carriage.

'There was another city to be seen. Florence. I stood for a long time before a statue of a boar. Its heavy stillness comforted me; I was able to walk on.'

There is no applause. The violinist finds his seat.

English John seems most affected by the violinist's tale. He presses his thick fingers to his eyes. He says, in his own language, 'Thou shalt not follow a multitude to do evil.' Eugenie waits to see if he will give them a story. But no, he is not prepared to speak.

Charlotte says, 'In the laundry of the other place they brought in stiff dark shirts for us to boil. I thought they were huntsmen's shirts but then a horse's ear fell out of one and I knew they came from the men at the abattoir. These shirts made the water black and thick. We had to wring them with our hands and the smell was everywhere. But if a woman had a spot of blood on her hem she was taken to the cells.'

Eugenie asks if Charlotte was locked in a cell, in this asylum.

'Yes,' says Charlotte, 'but not for the blood. For scalding a man when he came to collect the shirt he'd wrapped around a horse's ear, to frighten me. I leaned a stick on a pot and gave it a great push and the boiling cloth flew over the floor.'

'Lord,' says the American.

'Yes,' says Charlotte, 'I prayed a good deal myself, in the old straw of that cell.'

'When I was a child I was taken to a forge,' says the bird-woman. 'I saw metal poured into a mould. None spilled. It was the hottest thing I ever saw.'

Eugenie wants to keep the talk moving, until the next story arrives. She asks what the mould was for.

'A bell. When I married I walked under the rim of that bell and the hands that pulled the rope so cleanly, so it sounded only once with every swing, were the hands of the man who should have been at my side.'

Charlotte makes a shushing, sympathetic sound. M. Maillard

and the American fold their arms as if they had silently agreed on exactly the same moment to shift position.

The Birdwoman's Story

'When I roll bread up and put it in the throats of the birds, it is not to give the birds nourishment. It is to fill their hard beaks with a tongue like the tongue of a bell.

'The young priest who sometimes forgot that he was a priest and the old priest who forgot everything, down to his very name, sprinkled water about and said prayers as the bell was poured. Later, after it had cooled and been smoothed down to its proper shape, the bell was inscribed with a verse from Isaiah. The young priest read it aloud in his fine Latin. Everybody stared at me when I spoke up and asked him what it meant. He waved me aside. It was not for me to know.

'As I sorted lentils by a window or stirred whatever steamed over the fire, I thought of the priest's flapping hand and I became determined, with a child's determination, to know what was written on the bell.

'I am my mother's only child. My father had a grown son in a great monastery in the south. My father often grieved over the loss of this son, although to hear him talk in the street and in the square you would think he was simply proud to have a priest in the family. My mother told me bitterly that he did not grieve for his son alone, he was crying over the loss of his first wife, and imagining how it might have been for him if she had lived, if it had been she who carried the water and sorted the grain of the household, if my own mother had not been invited to the door. When my father wept in the night, she said, he was wishing her away, and wishing that I myself had never been born to draw breath and eat bread under his roof.

'I tried to imagine what it might be like not to have been born, not to be. I climbed the stairs of the belltower and lay in a sprinkle of birdlime, in a place where no one would think to look for me, but I still knew I was there. I closed my eyes and tried to breathe in long slow breaths, so my chest was as still as possible. But positioning myself like one of the dead was not enough, for the dead have been born, in order to die, and each now occupies his hollow place, even a fingerbone or a flake of ash or dust itself has a place. I heard the sound of wings, far above, and opened my eyes. Birds vomited into the mouths of their young.

'Many years later, as I carried my father between the window and his bed, or wiped him free of the sweat of his fever, I did not think of him as the man who cherished me and carried me to my christening, and whom I had the chance to cherish and carry in turn. Instead I thought of him as a table I must scour with sand, as a water bucket which unbalanced me in the ruts along the road, as a broom which needed thickening with straw until it could be gladly thrown away. It was no wonder that he died.

'My brother returned from the monastery to see him put in the ground. My brother was a man from a different country, now. He had difficulty with our dialect. His Latin sounded well, though, as he helped with the Mass, and he was kind to me. He brought me a medal with a saint's face, from Rome.

'On the last day he spent with us he asked if he could be of any continuing help. He offered to send money. I said no. I asked him if he would come to a secret place and perform a small favour for me. He was surprised, but he did climb the tower behind me, and look up to the inscription on the bell. I asked him to tell me what it meant. He was puzzled. The first words were clear, although their meaning, in this place, was not. He read, *For the sake of my own name I was patient, rather than destroy you I held myself in check.* Then, he said, there was something about the furnace of affliction, but he was sorry, the words had been lost. He looked uneasy. It was an odd verse to place around a bell.

'Bishop's soldiers came for the young priest, who was no longer very young. The old priest had died, by then, and he was alone. We all heard that he had confessed, long before he became our priest, to having joined a forbidden brotherhood. He had been forgiven and absolved. The man who fixed the writing on the bell had now also fallen under suspicion. This verse was not the verse which was recorded as the inscription on the bell. It confirmed a connection between our priest and the brotherhood which was thought to have been severed many years before.

'We were for some time without a priest of any kind. I thought a good deal about sin. It was not the sin of heresy which occupied my mind. It was the sin of charity, which was what I had offered my father in place of kindness, and of love. I thought, too, of the young priest and the thirteen candles which are flung to the ground in the rite of excommunication, and of the bell which is sounded at that rite.'

The story is over. M. Maillard unfolds his arms. Charlotte is still transfixed. 'But what of the man who rang the bell at your wedding?' she asks.

'In the end,' said the birdwoman, 'that story is not so unusual. I took a lover who was not able to be with me. We saw each other for a few watchful minutes, an hour, an afternoon. The afternoon was most wonderful. I always dreamed of dressing myself for him as you see me tonight. Now the memory of it all is like any other hidden thing, any flake of ash or bone splinter which has its place, and that place is best left undisturbed. The bell sounds the Angelus, no one in the town or in the fields is to know anything about the particular hands at the rope.'

Eugenie catches sight of something in the shaft of light which falls through the window closest to her, overlooking the courtyard. When she looks again the quick flank and hand are gone.

The boy in the courtyard lifts his head from what is left of the pigeon's wing. How hard it is to be hungry; to eat and eat and never grow. He brings his face close to the window. There. The pink woman has covered herself in a dress. Something has happened to the face of the cook. Most faces thicken as they relax. The cook is resting his forehead on his fingertips. How fine his face becomes, with the grosser folds held taut. And his wrist and fingers are so thin. Everyone is able to change, year by year, or even moment to moment, depending on light and mood and the angle of the face, except this boy who will always stay the same. He understands now that his family is entirely gone, his nurse is gone, and the people who now walk through their rooms will change and leave and be replaced. He knows that he will always be hungry, and that he will be forever dead. He knows he should be out of sight and still, like the rest of the dead. But he is so hungry.

The woman with the wet chest asks Eugenie if she could tell her story next, because she must leave the table and see to her baby very soon. Eugenie nods.

The Mother's Story

'My story is not a story, but a dream. In my dream my baby lies face down in a tub of wax and I am a cat with sharp claws who must scratch a way down to him. Then in my dream I am a woman standing by the tub of wax watching a starving cat claw its way down to the corpse of a child. I am unable to brush the cat aside. I worry about what it might do when it reaches the child.'

'Do you want us to find a meaning for your dream?' Eugenie asks.

The woman says, 'Yes.'

'It is one of the dreams all mothers have,' Eugenie says, 'like the dreams of a child walking through a wall which turns solid when you try to follow, or the dreams of a child stolen to be raised by whatever might live in the hollow hills. It means that you are a good mother who watches over all possible dangers to her child, and is even alert for dangers which are impossible.'

The woman smiles. 'Are you sure of this?'

Eugenie said she was quite sure.

After the young mother leaves the room somebody tells the American that her baby died a year ago. She was brought here, demented, because her baby died.

'Then how is it,' Eugenie asks, 'that she has so much milk?'

Charlotte says that one night she herself dreamed that a growing child, a child of four or even older, naked, dirty and very lean, came into the dormitory and lay beside the young mother, nursing at her breast.

M. Maillard points out that there are dreams, and then there are events, and it is better not to confuse the two. Full breasts, in the absence of a child, have been noticed occasionally by physicians.

Eugenie wants Augustine to speak. 'Augustine?' In M. Maillard's book she is listed as mute, but she has been known to speak.

'Augustine has nothing to say for herself,' says English John.

'What if we were to ask her to sing?' The violinist would like to hear her sing.

'Please sing for us, Augustine,' says M. Maillard.

Augustine stands, then climbs onto her stool. She was trained at the Paris conservatory. She is determined to display her training and to bring credit to M. Maillard, whose relative was once principal singer at the Opera. She opens her mouth. The sound is truly shocking. Eugenie tries not to put her hands over her ears. The American doesn't try. Augustine bends at the waist, straightens, throws her arms in the air and lets them fall; she shouts and shouts. Then she stops.

'Ah,' says M. Maillard, '*la mode de l'aboiement*, I believe. The barking style. Also known as *urlo francese,* for the howling effect. It is a style which cost my aunt her voice.'

The food is cold on the table.

'Our guest may be sufficiently entertained,' says Eugenie.

'He may be,' says English John, 'but I have a story that I wish to tell.'

English John's Story

'When I was a young fellow of fourteen or so I enlisted and I was shipped away to France. I thought I was a man. I thought I could witness any horror calmly, as though I had no body of my own. I thought I could show such courage on the field that I would attract the notice of Lord Wellington himself. As soon as the coastline had faded I realised my mistake. It was only seasickness, but I felt I might go mad with misery. Every time the boat tipped into a trough I felt my heart sink down and it stayed down as the boat climbed to a crest. Each wave brought a deeper sinking of the spirits. In my fear and shame I thought about my mother. I was sailing hourly further from the one person who was obliged and inclined to care for me. If only there had been another person, just one reliable soul, whom I could be sure would provide for me.

'There was a young ensign on the ship who was immune to seasickness and who spent his time writing in a little book and sketching the sailors. He asked me if I would sit for his pen. I kept as still as I could, perched on a high coil of rope, gripping the rope as if it were the curve of an arm, against the movement of the ship. His name was Edmund and the sketches and writing were for a woman he was forbidden to see. The prohibition came from the woman's family, who saw no good in the ensign's prospects or his temperament. After he caught my likeness I climbed down from the rope and we barely spoke again.

'I found myself imagining that he was the one who would look after me in the terrible battles ahead.

'We landed just below the French border. I followed Edmund through the stink and mess at the rear of the battle-lines, where the shock of the clean slicing or shattering of flesh gives way to black swellings, to ache and old blood and stupe-faction. It rained and rained. There were whippings, and I saw the remnants of men who had been hanged for running away. The noise of gunfire came over the noise of the wind and the water that seemed to leap back from the mud or whatever shud-dering surface it cast itself against. The only boys my own age whom Edmund concerned himself with were the nephews of the colonel. How I envied them. They were faultless soldiers, which made it worse. Faultless, but their uncle worried over them, as did many of the older men in the battalion.

'Edmund took notes about the peculiar bodices of local women, or drew pictures of their hats. At the close of each day, wherever he was, under straw or cracked tiles or by a fire in the open, he gathered our excitements and our sufferings together for the woman he was not permitted to see. He named his mule after her, so he could speak her name. The journal was the glass through which he saw each day and what was behind that glass was simply local custom and the incidents of warfare, which might be useful in his appeal to her. It did not protect him from gunshot, it could have broken open fatally at any instant, but the notebook was not for protection, as one might carry a Bible in a

pocket above the heart. It was for connection, and to make the
stink of powder and blood and the staggering steps of those who
were about to die, those who had been shot but had not yet
fallen to the earth, into a pattern, with its own daily order and
purpose, rather than the sum of his life itself.

'I was one of the three who survived at Bayonne, when
Edmund was ordered to take a defensive position in a house
opposite a great array of French muskets and cannon. The house
collapsed. I was there when what was left of us retreated and he
came face to face with his captain, who asked after his men.
Edmund said, *You will see them again and I hope shortly*. The
captain asked for their whereabouts and Edmund replied, *Gone
to hell*.

'It was the bad orders of the Prince of Orange which
finished off the colonel and would have taken the lives of his
nephews, but for the presence of mind of a man whose horse
tripped as it was shot and shielded him as it fell. This man pulled
the young boys into a hollow in the earth. The Prince had
mistaken French for Dutch cavalry. I myself was in this charge,
running and yelling until it seemed that I took fire into my lungs
instead of air. Then I was lifted high and flung into a ditch.
Edmund was next to me. Whoever found us here would be
French and he would set us on our feet or else he would finish
us off. Either way, our pockets would be emptied. I could not
rouse Edmund and he was too heavy to lift. I thought of his
journal, that pane through which he saw the disorder of the
world. I pulled it free of his body and stumbled back to what
was left of our men.

'I met him again five days later at the door of a hospital in

Mons. An ordinary soldier was leaning on his shoulder. He recognised me, and took his little book gladly from my hands. He would have given me a franc for my trouble, he said, but the poor fellow he was helping inside was in greater need of it.

'I did not wish to be paid for my trouble. I could have wished for a way of seeing the world as a matter of foreign customs, as a mass of confusion some distance from myself, but this was not in his power to give.'

The American is asleep with his head on his folded arms. M. Maillard has glanced at his watch. If there was ever a child in the courtyard he has crept back through the space left by his rusted grille.

Eugenie thanks Charlotte, Augustine, English John and the violinist.

She may be mistaken, but she feels that something has passed between herself and M. Maillard in the course of the night. Nothing as obvious as the pressure of a foot slid against her own. Still, she is not surprised when he stands and offers her his arm. She knows he is much older than she. She remembers the delight she felt when her mother once took her to visit her grandparents and an old kind friend of her grandfather took off his shirt to wash at a tub. He had given her spoonfuls of cherry jam and taught her his favourite songs and she was warmly interested in everything about him. She remembers in particular a sweet hollow in the crook of the old man's arm, a hollow just big enough for a finger, or a tongue.

The American half-opens his eyes. Through the blur of sleep he sees a fine couple in a doorway, outlined in respectable black. He drops his head and dreams of the daguerreotypes above his family mantlepiece in Philadelphia.

The wind has calmed. I can't hear anything beyond this room except Finn's footsteps up and down the gallery, pausing once at the far end as he examines a detail of the framed engraving and hopes that his next sentence will come to him.

I look back over what I have written. I find that I can't imagine M. Maillard without his clothes. There's some shyness in this character. I'm happy to think of Eugenie slipping layers of cloth from his shoulders and leave it at that.

A woman I know showed me a photograph of herself, entirely naked, on a bathroom floor. The bathroom was in the Savoy in London and the photograph was taken from high above, as if someone with a camera had been crouching in the ceiling or lying flat on a rooftop with the camera lens against a skylight, waiting for the moment when she would lie unclothed on the floor.

It was a view from high above: the view of an angel, a lover, or a predator.

In fact the bathroom ceiling was one large mirror. She took off her own clothes, set her small dark camera on automatic, placed it on a small dark area of herself and waited on the cool floor for the shutter to close. When I looked closely I could see the strap of the camera across her thigh.

I think of this photo as I lie in the deep narrow bath next to my room. I loved this bath, when I was a child. I could float in it. I could lean over the side and drip fistfuls of water over the tessellated floor. It's brown and cream with the occasional soft blue tile in the pattern. The tiles continue under the lion's-claw feet of the bath, but nobody ever bothered to lean down and mop to the inner wall, so when I was small I crawled under there and in the greasy dust I found a garnet ring which my mother had lost years before, when she shook her hands free of water, over at the washbasin.

Lying here, in the warmth held by the thick iron under the enamel of the bath, I can almost believe, as plenty of physicians once did, that stories and sweet milk and baths can cure the mad, can give them back the power to arrange themselves to look attractive and promising to other people, and give them the sense that this power is worth having.

IV

LETTERS WITHOUT WORDS

It's the winter solstice and for weeks a street festival has been advertised in newspapers and shop windows. The drumming I've heard in the garden at night is someone keeping his hands in shape for the festival, or so Finn says. If I go out at twilight for an armload of wood there's a busyness in the air, a sense of energy spent on preparing for parties and ceremonies which won't be held in daylight, in the street. Fireworks crackle in backyards.

We're standing outside Woolworths in a bitter wind. Magic happens, or so the bumper stickers say.

We balance at the lip of the gutter and watch the parade. There are caps and bells and crushed-velvet dresses. Pointy hats. Devil's horns. Venetian masks. Then a group walks smoothly by on stilts. They're wearing black cloaks and death's-head masks.

One of them plays bagpipes. The bag is made from the fur of a red animal. It works. The skirl. The thin snarl of sound. Invisible hair lifts and prickles on my skin.

Finn yawns and offers me coffee.

'Let me tell you a story that did the rounds in the trenches,' he says. I'm licking cappuccino froth and sprinkled chocolate from the back of a spoon.

'A few good stout Britishers are manning a trench. There's an enemy advance and they know they haven't got a hope. So they all shake hands and take aim at the other side. In the thick of the fighting, when the artillery is blasting them to bits and everyone is yelling whatever comes into his head, one of them calls out to St George. The air is thick with smoke and everyone has his eye at his sights. But the Englishmen suddenly realise they're not alone. And the enemy is driven off, killed one by one by the arrows of the bowmen who stand shoulder to shoulder with the men in the trench. The army of Agincourt has joined the British Tommies. The dead are completely unmarked. Their command have thousands of losses to account for. They're German. They're scientific and rational. They put it down to poison gas.'

St George and England. A soldier stumbles on the words; the company is saved. I wrap my hands around my cup and stare into the back of the crowd. Someone is drumming, out on the road.

Finn wants to see how believable he is. But I won't meet his eye. 'It was all a story,' he says. 'Or it started out as a story. Ghosts and propaganda. Magic words.'

A man once sent me a series of blank pages. This was the man who brought me narcissuses, the man who took me to Boston, the man I left at Niagara by the waterfall in winter.

The spray from the falls drifts some distance in the winter, becoming lighter, colder, harder as it comes to rest. It weighs down trees on the Canadian side of the border until whole branches become the rafters of rooms made of living tree and ice. I must have lost the photographs.

I still have the gloves I was wearing. They're grey and close-fitting, with grey embroidery above the wrists. Many small lengths of fine leather have been sewn down into the insides of the fingers to make them so supple. I remember standing at a railing, after we said goodbye. I ran the stitched tips of the gloves over my mouth again and again.

We agreed to keep in touch. It made it possible to part. I had mail from the Max Plank Institut; from Johns Hopkins. I'd tear open the envelope to find that he hadn't written a word. I saved the pile of letterheads. This went on for years. Letters without words.

'Finn, do you still write letters? Do you like to write?' One year we wrote to one another. It was the lead-up to the final year. Each Wednesday for a year I got the letter Finn wrote on Sunday night. He wrote to me as if he were talking to me. It was very nice.

'Sure. I like to write a letter if I know I'll get one back.'

Back at the house I climb up onto my bed and cross my legs. I'm well into my notebook. I open the last of our grandfather's books on Poe.

For Poe, words were like torn cloth, like broken skin, like the buttons and laces that the dead fasten casually, on the last morning of their lives, never imagining that these same buttons will be slipped from their holes by sickened and inquisitive strangers, who are paid to decide what has become of them.

Poe wrote his second detective story a few months after he was certain that Virginia had tuberculosis.

The first was 'The Murders in the Rue Morgue', where a mother and a daughter are killed inside a room which seems to be sealed and impregnable. There is no clear motive. Nowhere is safe.

Virginia was singing when Poe realised that she might die. It was not the subdued, barely conscious private singing that goes with sunshine and wet washing. She sang formally, to entertain guests in the evening. She reached for a note, the sound crackled and her throat was flooded with blood. She was lucky to survive the night and the weeks which lay ahead. The household was lucky to survive, because Poe left his editing work.

He wrote the word *hopeless*. He wrote *illness* and *distraction*. He thought he couldn't work. But between the haemorrhage and the letter where he declares that he must *abandon all mental exertion* he wrote a long story, 'The Mystery of Marie Rogêt'.

He took it straight out of the newspapers. The body of a strangled girl was found in the Hudson. She worked in a tobacconist's shop. One Sunday she told the man she was to marry that she was going to church with her aunt. She didn't meet him afterwards as he expected. She was dead in the river and some of her things were thrown down in a clearing on the shore. The newspapers printed the little they knew. She had disappeared once before, with a sailor.

Poe followed the reports. He changed the name of the girl and the name of the river. The tobacconist's became a perfumery. The crime is solved by Auguste Dupin, who argues his case entirely from the newspaper reports. He doesn't walk the paths by the river in search of clues. He doesn't so much as handle a button from the dead girl's dress. He doesn't find things, he looks at words, then he makes up a story of his own.

The real case froze and faded. Then quite quickly it seemed to solve itself.

It looks like Marie died of a clumsy abortion, in an inn near where she was found. Her skirt was tied up high, out of the way of whatever was done to her. Her wrists were bound to stop her from fighting off the surgeon when the pain became extreme. She must have bled to death. Questions were asked about a secret windowless room behind a fireplace which was rented out to whoever needed a place beyond light and sound. It's hard to imagine why lovers would need such a secret place, unless one of them was unwilling.

I don't think of it as a proper room. I think of it as a narrow hollow space, very dry, smelling of builder's sand and lime. There must have been a bed, a lantern, a parcel of iron instruments, a length of rope and a broad dish. If something went wrong the dish would fill with blood in the time it takes to turn and wipe an iron instrument.

The innkeeper's sons probably tied a gag over the dead mouth and a strip of lace around the throat, then pushed the body out into the water, where it would swell, and soften, and disguise its own injuries.

Finn is leaving in two days. It's hard to believe. He can't take more than a few weeks' leave from his newspaper.

I didn't come to our grandfather's house for so long. I barely thought about the place when I was living in America. Sometimes I made it into a story over a dinner table. Dragons coiling above the summer house where my father took Finn's mother. The pair of them creeping naked below the windowsills because my father forgot to have curtains made, from one year to the next. Copies of old exchequer reports tilting down from the bookshelves.

Now I feel that I've lived all my life in this house with Finn, carrying armloads of wood from the shed to the great fireplace, climbing the stairs to the gallery and finally the table under the windowsill with my fresh jar of narcissuses, turning to take a mug of tea when Finn has made tea for us both and turning back to my page.

Before too long I'll have to leave, myself.

'Well,' he says, down in front of the fire, 'have you made up your mind about going to America?'

'I don't want to be like the people who stood about hoping to look at the bones of Annabel Lee, after Gill grabbed what was left of Virginia and put her in a box.'

'There's a difference between voyeurism and research.'

'Think so?'

I want him to leave me alone. I'm not sure about going to America. It isn't because I don't want to be reminded of the summer in Boston and the weekend at Niagara Falls. It isn't because I don't want to face packing away my books and my gold-painted Buddha and carrying my suitcase down these stairs for the last time.

'Fordham. The place where Virginia died. It might spoil it to see the place.'

'It's not like comparing a book to a film.'

'What did you get from all the notes you made in military cemeteries?'

He stops to think. 'I got an incredible charge from the difference between the mess of the war and the orderliness of the crosses. It was the difference between what I read and what I saw that was so incredible.'

This is so obvious I hadn't considered it.

'I didn't head off to France like a reporter with a notebook open for facts. I wasn't playing detective. I went because of a feeling that turned out to be worth having.'

'It's a long shot.'

He shrugs. 'Isn't everything? Coming here. Talking. Shutting yourself away at the top of the stairs. You don't need to do any of this. You've got a home, haven't you? You've got a desk and a pen at home?'

Yes, I've got a home.

At home in my mother's house I write on a verandah which has been closed in with plasterboard and big cheap windows. The floor still tilts a little because it was built so that if rain blew onto the verandah it could not pool on the boards. Around seventy years ago someone planted a bay tree next to the verandah. It flourished. It grows in a semicircle out from the windows of my room, so that I write from within this tree. I see wasps combing the branches for spiders; steadily, mechanically, sectioning and searching. I see struggles in spiderwebs. My desk is a table which runs across the width of the room and it is wide enough for me to scatter my work and leave or return to its separate pages. I have a desk. I have a pen.

'I'm sorry,' says Finn. 'I'm being hard on you. I'm telling you to go to America because I really want to take you home. I want to take all of this home.' He's looking around at the wood which we've piled up for the fire, at the relaxed sofa, the piles of books and the soda siphon on the mantlepiece.

I think of him with his hands in his pockets, at the door of my own writing room, or with his back to the interior of the tree. He stands there like a cheap special effect: a figure cut out and pasted on the wrong background and rephotographed.

I think of everyone else whose photograph I could prop up in this room. The narcissus man as he was before Niagara, pulling off his bicycle clips and handing me the two or three yellow flowers which had been pressed between his palm and the handlebar, as he rode. Marie Louise come to life, standing at my elbow, waving her finger over paragraph after paragraph, complaining that I cannot not write as well as Dickens. She did this with Poe. How much more exasperated would she be with me? She told Poe his stories were *unsatisfactory and unpleasant*. She helped him with the poetry. When he came to her with his emptiness and his great need she made up an opening line, in mimicry of his own style, and stayed with him, imitating, prompting, until the poem was done. I myself could put up with the complaints for the sake of the help she gave. Finn, then, and my mother, and the man with yellow flowers and Louise. It sounds like a crowd.

Long after Poe's death and the collapse of her final marriage, Louise cut her ties with her past. Her daughter wrote that *she retired to a remote country village taking with her her library of old books and baby Dora and for ten years seeing no new publications excepting an occasional newspaper*. There it is. The essentials of her life: old books and a new baby. She lost or stored a good deal of what Poe had given her. She was trying to retrieve Poe's scattered words, his letters, notes and verse, in the years before she died. She especially wanted to find the notes she took when Poe, delirious, told her about the novel he wrote, which a French writer stole and published under his own name. After she burned her journal she recovered some pages which had been left, for a time, in a vase.

It must have been a tall vase, to completely hide the leaves of her journal. It must have been so nondescript that it was untouched behind cupboard doors for some time, or so beautiful that it was kept in her formal rooms, closed away from the more turbulent everyday parts of the house.

I want it to be a blue and white Chinese vase, with a blue as deep and vague as the iris of a newborn child and a blue–white like the white of a newborn child's eyes. I want the blue to have been brushed across the white by a painter who did not know what it is to feel fatigue or hesitation. I want the leaves of her life to rest for as long as possible in this calm interior of bluish white.

She just wanted to find the scraps of Poe, among her things.

Perhaps somewhere in the Nile valley an old Egyptian spirit

glances irritably at his tomb walls, frowning at hunting scenes and platters of fish and pomegranates. He upsets gilded head-rests and folded linen and even his own viscera in its painted jar, looking for something: a taste, a favourite pin, so familiar in his life, and lost, now, for so long that he barely remembers what it is. I wonder if all the scattered broken treasures in Egyptian tombs have been scattered by grave-robbers, or by the dead themselves, longing for the lost details of their lives.

Finn breaks open a blackened log with the point of the poker. Heat and small slow flames move up and across. The logs have been burning for hours, until they are black and grey and patterned in small segments, like the skin of a dark crocodile. An old soda siphon from Paris is on one corner of the mantle-piece, next to a yellow enamel teapot filled with dry rhodo-dendron leaves. I've stacked our dishes on the hearth. I'm still thinking about him wanting to take it all home.

'It could look a bit stagey. The siphon. The books. The big engraving from upstairs. All packed into a townhouse, or wher-ever you live.' It would look like an Ibsen set. A European interior where something is wrong, or about to go wrong.

'Worse. I live in a flat over a shop on a six-lane road. That's why I stay awake half the night. No sirens. No smell of rubber coming up through the windows. No, I wasn't planning to walk off with the siphon and the books. What I had in mind was one of those dreams where you open a door and find yourself some-where you remember from a long time ago. If only you could choose the place, and do it whenever you felt like it.'

'And this would be the place you'd choose?'

'Yes. At least, until I'd got through all the things I thought I'd do when I first arrived.'

'Like what?'

'Write the last word of the General's book.'

'I'm sorry,' I say. 'I've used up all your nights with my stories.'

'Somehow I don't feel used up. You can talk or read aloud all night. I don't mind.'

'I haven't finished the next bit of Poe.'

Finn leans back in his saggy chair. 'Then tell me something you've never told anyone else.'

'Ah. Something I've never told. That would have to be very important, or trivial.'

'Or both.'

This rules out the parting at Niagara; a room with a ribbed architrave around the door, where I lived before I went to Niagara; so many things I can barely speak about.

It rules out things he already knows: the way I watched the bigger boys work the penis extender, for example. The way I frightened my mother by telling her that I woke in the night with a man curled at my back, and when I stretched he ran for the door. I made a lot of being able to feel the scratch of his beard at the back of my neck. The way I never, never answered her, although she called out 'Thea! Thea!' from the roof of the house until her voice wouldn't work any more.

'I trapped and killed something on purpose,' I say flatly, 'and I sickened myself.'

'That isn't a story. That's a confession.'

'I know, I know. I'll try.

'When I was small I was taken to visit an old woman in a big calm house. She had cake and blue china. She was childless, and in the district this was said to be a great tragedy. I think that waiting for a child had taught her patience and by the time it was clear that there wouldn't be a child she was eternally calm and smiling, as women are supposed to be in the earliest stages of pregnancy, before any symptoms appear, even to themselves. She had wrapped herself in the happiness of mistaken secret pregnancies for so long that she was simply happy out of habit, even when she grew old. I asked and asked to be allowed to stay with her.

'I got my wish, in the end. Remember my girl cousin, the one from my mother's side? I showed you a picture, once. She stayed with us while her own mother, my aunt, was in hospital. It was a bush hospital, and the surgeon was out of practice. He slipped. My aunt began to lose blood, then her blood stopped clotting properly and someone, it wouldn't have been my mother, told me that it was just like turning on a tap. That the body emptied itself fast, like a water-pipe under pressure. The only thing to do was to give a fast transfusion of whole live blood. My mother was in the waiting room. They checked to make sure that she matched, then they put her on a stretcher next to her sister under the operating theatre lights and hooked her up, and my mother, weakening rapidly, prayed that the shared blood would slow and clot before they both lost their lives. She prayed to the glowing disc of light, she told me later, because it was just as she had always imagined God, and the disc, or something, answered her prayers.

'My cousin and I were taken to the big calm house to be cared for while our mothers recovered.

'When I imagined visiting the old woman I always imagined that I would be alone. My cousin and I normally played in the garden or on the verandahs, well away from our mothers, who wanted to be sisters again, not mothers. Our favourite place in the garden was a may bush which had a big crucifix orchid growing up through the centre of it. The may bush flowered in great arcs, in wands, and the arch of the wands made a roof for us, as we crouched inside. The orchids grew on thin high branches and at the end of each there was a cluster of flowers exactly the same colour as our mothers' nail polish. I remember the sound of bees and pigeons.

'We didn't go outdoors because the old woman wanted us with her in the kitchen. We were children; she was hungry for children. We were hungry for her baking. She made pikelets and chocolate cake and orange cake and while we waited by the oven she opened a tin of sweet condensed milk and handed us two spoons. I was sick first, over a tablecloth embroidered with a willow pattern teapot. My cousin was sick later, in the bathroom and she cleaned up after herself so carefully that nobody except me ever knew. At the end of our visits we were both given presents. My cousin was given a pair of amber earrings. I was pleased to see that they were full of flaws. But when she stood in the light by the car door I looked more closely and realised that the marks in the amber were not tiny fractures. They were discs of gold: small leaves in the shape of lilypads; scoops of gold. I'd been given a willow pattern cup.

'We were told that our mothers had been close to death.

'The man who drove us home was a favourite neighbour, a man who often helped my mother with the heavy work. He

spent a good deal of time with my aunt. I remember sitting on
the bench seat next to him, lighting his Viscount cigarettes and
passing them across to his hand where it rested on the steering
wheel. My mother wouldn't have been happy about this, but
we'd done it often, before. My cousin was in the back seat.
I wondered if the neighbour was worried by the news about
our mothers. I wondered if he missed my aunt. I wondered
if he was afraid of death. I tried to console him. I told him
that by the time he was old and sick enough to die they would
probably have found a cure for death. He said when you're a
grown-up person sometimes you look forward to a time when
you might die.

'We lived with pigeons and bees and crucifix orchids, but
the warmth and water which made these things flourish also
made it a great place for snakes, and for termites which could
eat their way through the beams and have a house down in no
time at all. My mother's furniture was all plain bush furniture,
but it was made of cedar, which polished to a strong red colour,
more gold than mahogany. It was beautiful. It was also incor-
ruptible. Termites and borers have no taste for this kind of
wood. When I arrived home I put the cup upside down on my
mother's chiffonier. An oily grey lizard slipped from the back-
board and ran across the surface. I trapped it quickly under the
cup. I didn't forget about it. I left it there. Much later I came
back to the cup and lifted it, and when the grey head appeared I
brought the rim down hard across the place above the eyes and
leaned down until I felt the bones give way.

'I never know whether it was the brief loss of my mother,
or the sight of milk and bile splashing on the tablecloth, or the

small crunch of lizard bone under the rim of the cup which makes me avoid my cousin, now. She still sends me birthday cards. There was a time when I would have liked us to grow up like our mothers, whispering over cooling tea, but I've stopped opening her cards.'

Finn makes no comment about my story. He says, 'When I was at school one of my mates had a baby brother. Seventeen years younger. My mate said he was responsible. He was home for the holidays and one night his father called all the kids in the family into the kitchen. He told them their mother was pregnant and wanted to get rid of it. The youngest kid was ten. The father said they'd take a family vote on it. My mate knew it was a set-up. His father asked him first and he voted for the baby and the others fell into line. There was something wrong with his mother and the pregnancy made it worse. After the baby was born his father had to take her to the hospital for dialysis every few days, because of her kidneys. He was back at school by then.'

A crocodile log holds its shape in the hearth. Finn presses it here and there, with the poker.

I think of Mary Rogers; the lonely effort she made to get to the room behind the fireplace; the effort it must have cost her, to hold her wrists out so they could be tied.

When I flew back from Niagara, alone, I stayed with a friend who lived near a beach with Victorian railings and a promenade. There was an arched Chinese bridge over to an island and I climbed to the far side of the island and watched a cormorant dive and rise in the kelp. This was so flexible, so warm and strange, after Niagara.

At night I lay on a mattress and listened to an argument; first one voice, then the other. I waited for the moment when it would break. Suddenly there was a third voice. I waited for violence or for calm. Then I woke my friend. It wasn't an argument at all. It was only Shakespeare. *Measure for Measure* was performed each night in the rotunda by the arched bridge. I pulled on a pair of jeans and let myself out.

A man in ordinary clothes stared over the waves. I hadn't adjusted properly to the local accent. I made out a few lines, as he spoke about death and cold obstruction; about thick-ribbed ice; about a blind spirit thrown around in the wind. I reached the edge of the crowd. Someone in front of me corked a bottle of wine and wrapped a chicken leg in foil. A couple pressed themselves together; a single hand moved again and again across a forehead and down a length of hair.

At the end of the play the man who had turned to the waves was held by a woman who drew him into the padding over her stomach and as they embraced it gave way softly as a real pregnancy would not. He seemed to have put the idea of death and cold obstruction right out of his mind. When I think of this I'm suddenly fond of Poe, who knew that fear is unforgettable.

Finn hasn't really offered me a story about something trivial and important that happened to him, in his turn. I remind him.

'I don't tell stories,' he says. 'Apart from the odd anecdote I'm strictly facts and events. What I'm writing just makes sense of the facts and events.'

I have to smile. 'You've got the maps, you've got tapes and documents. Why haven't you finished then?'

He smiles back. 'There are plenty of facts and events. Sense is in short supply. There isn't a whole lot of sense in the world.'

We finish the wine. The last log dissolves into whiteness. Neither of us wants to say goodnight and climb the stair. I doze uncomfortably. I think I can hear footfalls in the room above.

Finn pushes something cold into my hand. When I open my eyes I'm alone. He's given me a button in return for my story. It's a button from a uniform. He must have picked it out of a furrow in the farmland above some French battlefield. I rub my thumb over it. If you were close to a shellburst, a button might be all that was left. Someone fastened it on his final morning, when a single button was the last thing on his mind.

When I come downstairs in the morning Finn is waiting for his taxi by the white ash of last night's fire. He has a suitcase and a leather briefcase with his manuscript inside. I can hear wheels on the gravel drive. He stands and puts his arms around me. It is the closest I've been to anybody for a long time. There's warmth and cloth under my hands. His sweater already smells of trains.

I carry the briefcase out to the taxi and pass it in to Finn.

'Write,' he says. Then he says, 'I'll write to you.'

I fill in the day and walk along the cliff paths, later. The valleys are solid with mist. I walk and walk. I have to remind myself that the paths are dangerous in the dark.

I have to remind myself to lay the wood for the fire, to pick wands of cotoneaster and put them in an enamel teapot on the mantlepiece, to pour myself a glass of wine and take a book from one of the piles which are still lying in front of the full shelves.

My chest feels tight.

When I run out of wood I go to the cupboard behind the front door and push aside the bright nylon umbrellas which I know won't survive the high wind on a night like this. Right at the back there's a tough black umbrella which looks as if it might rain moths when I open it. It doesn't. I'm spattered with black rain on my way to and from the shed where dry wood is stacked. It fights the wind for me. Poor old umbrella, I say to myself. All struggle, all ribs, and no head or heart.

Sometimes when I'm wandering about the corridors or leaning over the sink to push an extra stem into the bunch of leaves which I've left in a glass on the windowsill, I can hear Joan Baez singing about Annabel Lee. My cousin, not Finn, the girl on my mother's side, gave me a Joan Baez record for my fifteenth birthday. It was my first record, and I played it until the sound crumpled with scratches. By then I knew it perfectly. It was the sweet and forceful sound of California. It comes back to me more sharply than real memories of the place: the winter oaks, the milky Pacific. The track that most often turns up in my mind is 'Annabel Lee'. I didn't know then that the words were written by Poe, in the bleak East. It was one sweet woman's voice and all one America, to me.

In the early evening I walk up the bitumen road on the far side of the grounds. The great pines and the terrace which was once a tennis court are between me and my window. I have left the light on. Soon I'll be able to see, high in the distance, the gold of the little Buddha and a waterglass of fresh narcissuses. Soon. Everything is grey, or black, on this side of the pines. Someone is playing a swarm of guitar notes in a house by the road. The black birds, the currawongs, are too heavy for their branches. The branches plunge and steady. The currawongs sound like crows. Perhaps they are crows. Someone turns a knob on an amplifier. I say to myself, it's just a cold energetic guitar, it isn't a soundtrack, as I walk up this road, walking under black pines and crows. Then a heartbeat bass cuts in and I have to smile. You only let yourself be spooked by shadows and black birds when you feel deeply safe. That's the principle of scary movies. I'm smiling at the obviousness of it all when my window comes into view.

On my first night alone in the house I dream about the room with the ribbed architrave. It isn't mysterious, just a hotel room in California.

There are two doors. One leads to the corridor outside, where slow fans turn on the ceiling, day and night, although it is winter. The other door looks important enough to open onto a landing and a flight of stairs, or at least another room. It is heavy, panelled, fitted with brass. All that is behind it is a row of shelves. Next to it is an arched recess a little wider than a body. I have had enough time alone in here to imagine it as the niche for a statue; something from antiquity with the arms struck off. The niche contains a sink and a glass shelf on chrome supports and a shallow cupboard. The sink has lost both plug and enamel. It is a puddle of old rust. The window faces a set of black windows in the opposite wall. They all have lace curtains with uneven hems. Nothing except an agile cat could fall from these windows and survive. Lead piping and the glass and iron roof of the pyramid which covers the foyer would break a fall.

When I wake up the sky is blue with dawn. The wisteria under my window is bare like the winter branches of a Californian oak; branches which twist as if they tensed as they grew, as if growth was forced through some tense resistance.

I light a candle and watch the glow fade as the sun comes up. The house is bright and silent.

I miss the slight spookiness.

A parrot lands on a plum tree outside the courtyard. Under the plum there is a bed of strawberries which have been left unfertilised for so long that they've reverted to a berry flavour and shape: tiny, delicious, intense.

It seems like a good time to start on a big spooky story: 'The Murders in the Rue Morgue'. Finn isn't here to listen for too much morbidity but I'll write out a summary, anyway. It will be like writing for an unseen presence, though I'm sure he doesn't want me to think of him as a ghost.

THE MURDERS IN THE RUE MORGUE

THE STORY BEGINS WITH a long preamble about the pleasures of reason; of calculation and analysis. A certain kind of man is described with passionate admiration. The supremely observant and imaginatively calculating man is to be most admired.

Monsieur C. Auguste Dupin is such a man.

The narrator met him in a Parisian library and they have since become inseparable. They live for each other's company.

They have no wider circle. They share a mansion on the Faubourg St Germain.

There, they read a newspaper account of a terrifying murder. Madame L'Espanaye and her daughter, Mademoiselle Camille L'Espanaye, are the victims. Their house and belongings have been smashed, the hair has been torn from their heads, the older woman's throat has been cut and the younger woman has been strangled. No valuables are missing. There is no sign of a forced entry. Witnesses, or rather listeners, for the murders were noisy rather than visible, are not much help, although they did hear men's voices inside the house.

A clerk who delivered coins to Madame L'Espanaye earlier on the day of the murder is arrested. This clerk was once helpful to Dupin. Dupin suggests that he and the narrator investigate the murders, partly to entertain themselves and partly to vindicate the clerk.

Dupin has connections which make it possible for him to inspect the bodies and the house where the murders took place. The injuries are shockingly brutal. There is no obvious way for the murderer to have escaped from the closed room where the crime took place.

It is a complete mystery.

Dupin scrutinises the room and concludes, in the course of a long explanation, that the murderer must have scaled a lightning rod, swung over to the trellis on a shutter and climbed through a window into the room. He, or they, left the same way.

Dupin goes over the evidence. The violence was pointlessly brutal. There is no obvious motive. It is hard to imagine who could have the sheer strength needed to commit the crime.

The narrator suspects that a madman, escaped from an asylum, might have been responsible.

Dupin disagrees. He has found strands of hair in Madame L'Espanaye's hand. He has traced the span of the hand which strangled Camille.

He thinks the women were murdered by an ape. He thinks the voices which so many people heard were the voices of an animal in a state of rage and distress, and a sailor. He picked up a ribbon from near the lightning rod which was tied in the distinctive way that Maltese sailors used to bind the end of their plaits.

Dupin decides to entrap the sailor by fabricating an account of capturing an escaped orang-utan and putting an advertisement for the animal in a newspaper which sailors often read.

It works. The sailor arrives and offers a reward. Dupin names his reward. He wants to know the details of the murders. The sailor is deeply shocked. Then he confesses that he acquired the ape on a voyage from Borneo and brought it back to Paris in the hope of selling it. It was not a tractable animal. The sailor constantly whipped it into submission. It escaped with his cutthroat razor and he followed it to the house where the women were killed.

After all this has been explained to the slightly jealous Prefect of Police, the clerk who has been wrongfully accused of the murders is released.

The story finishes with Dupin's assessment of the limitations of the Prefect. The policeman's reasoning is too direct.

'In his wisdom is no *stamen*. He is all head and no body . . . The truly calculating man must have both.'

The Chimney

As Marie Louise pulls her front door closed and her coat tightly about herself she slips Muddy's letter into a pocket. The pages from Virginia, which were so finely printed that Louise decided to postpone reading them, are still in the envelope.

It is so cold, on the street. Before long her flesh numbs in the cold. If Louise were to pull her hand free of her glove and touch her face it would feel like the face of a stranger. Her breath is white. Her ears ache, in the cold. The linen dress which she is bringing for Virginia's burial is too thin for this weather, or so she thinks, knowing that it makes no difference. Still, how good it would be to take Virginia a shawl as white and warm as her own breath. Louise takes one glove off to wipe her eyes. Her face is like stone.

As Louise walks over the cobbles the weight of the letter makes the lining of her coat scrape slightly at the hip. The cold has made its way through the coat, through the lining and the wool skirt and the lawn underclothing, so that Louise's skin is numb and the scrape of the pocket does not register. There may as well be no envelope full of Muddy's thanks and good wishes, or Virginia's tiny words. But they are there, like the surface of the skin, which only needs a little shelter and warmth to soften and feel again.

Virginia has been drinking the wine which Louise sent. It

made her strong enough to tell another story. But the cat was outside and there is no point in telling a story to a bedpost or a wall. Virginia asked for her mother's pen and paper, and wrote 'The Chimney' in the smallest print at the head of the first page.

The old woman who tells fortunes behind the Rue St Roch is called Madame L'Espanaye. She tells Marianne she sees Red Indians making signs to each other with their hands. These Indians are here on the street, she says, standing about Marianne, their backs to Madame L'Espanaye with her clumpy uncombed hair and Marianne's topaz earring in her hand. Madame sees this, when she holds the topaz. If Marianne had given her a scarf or shoe to hold she would still see the Indians. All she needs is some object belonging to Marianne; something which lies against the skin. The Indians are moving their hands, hoping Marianne will understand.

They are invisible.

Then Madame blinks. She sees a man, she thinks it is a man, weeping in a locked cupboard. Outside a whip leans against the door. He can see the shadow of the handle through the crack under the door. It breaks up the strip of light at his bare feet. His toes are strangely long, according to Madame. He lifts them, kneads warmth into them with his hands, then lifts his hands to his face.

Marianne did not pay to hear about Indians and prisoners. She wants to know whether she is carrying a child. She gets to her feet. The old woman has shining white whiskers. Whiskers like sharp glass. She tells Marianne there is no baby, the baby she came to ask about is just a bag of water inside Marianne, which will break soon and leak away.

There is something else. A staircase, in darkness. No windows. Ledges, going down. And the top step does not lead to a landing, it abuts a wall. Someone has closed off the staircase.

The man in the cupboard is searching for something. He slips his long fingernails under the edges of splinters in the floor. He flattens his hands on the walls, smoothing over them with the whole surface of splayed fingers and palm. He finds books on the floor. He riffles, sniffs. Then he tears each page free. When the books are a mound of torn leaves on the cupboard floor he turns and lies in his narrow chair with his legs tucked up beside him. One arm reaches down repeatedly. He doesn't stop until he is covered with the leaves. Madame tries to read the writing, but the cupboard is too poorly lit. Madame L'Espanaye cannot break free. She longs for the catch to slip, for the smallest strip of light from the length of the door.

Marianne tries to prise open the old hand. She wants her topaz back. It sickens her to touch Madame. The skin lies thin and dry across the bones, or it rises over huge jellied veins, or pleats emptily under the limbs. There is no muscle for the skin to cover, no reason for it to be in any particular place. It is too soft. The eyes are open, but they don't see Marianne. She leaves the topaz where it is. She'll call for it tonight. Madame's daughter will keep it safe.

Marianne walks down the street alone and alight with happiness, forgetting the Indians. She is carrying a little liquid, that is all. A little liquid, which will pass through her and away.

The man she works for puts his shoulder to her door each

night until she thinks the panels will burst, until the bed which she pushes against the door skitters across the room. At least when he finishes, he goes. At least then, she is free of him. Or so she tells herself. Until her belly is high and tight, under her apron. Only a little liquid, according to Madame.

She stops at the edge of a crowd. The entire wall of a building has collapsed and the street is blocked with crumbled mortar and damp stone. One side of a chimney is exposed. Marianne sees the ledges of brickwork which make up the hip of the fireplace. She sees how it abuts the smooth wall of the flue. Madame's vision of a closed staircase comes to her, and she realises that the staircase is likely to be the hidden side of a fireplace. This is a comfort; Madame says there is no child, she also says there is a hidden stairway and within a street or two the stairway appears before Marianne. If Indians turn up Marianne will not be surprised.

It is twilight. The streets are narrow and uneven. Marianne is going back to her room, alert with happiness. She stops suddenly when she is startled by the sound of a shutter crash against a wall. She waits on the other side of the street for her heart to calm.

The window exposed by the shutter opens onto a room where two men sit, their eyes fixed on a game of draughts. The room is full of books bound in warm red leather, or in green cloth. The books are shelved behind glass, but they are also piled into steep hills through the interior of the room. Marianne notices an unbrushed hat, a tea cup, an ink stand with the ink gone hard and cracked in the glass. A violin balances across a high stable column of books. The men have full soft mouths and full soft beards. She moves under the shutter and listens to a conversation which barely makes sense; most of it must take place in the men's shared thoughts. As she listens she finds that she can follow this train of thought. They are talking about a woman who was pulled out of a river in New York. One of them knows exactly how long it takes for the drowned to rise from a riverbed.

She steps back into the street. It is now quite dark. As she watches one man leans across the draughtboard and places his finger on the other's lips. They smile.

Marianne stands for a long time in the dark. She is so calm that it is as if she has never had a troubled heart. She doesn't take the black street back to the room with the scraped floor. Instead she climbs the stairs by the open shutter and rings the bell.

Madame L'Espanaye cannot seem to free herself of the vision which shows her the interior of the cupboard. It interrupts every fortune that she tells. She can be seeing full canvas sails, or a fruiting tree, or a corpse with a rare faint smile; she can see a grey road leading from below a Russian window, over mountains and beside lakes, until it arrives at a particular door in France. Suddenly the vision fades to black airlessness; a crack of light broken by the handle of a whip.

The man in the cupboard has his memories.

He is running, running on a track in a forest like no forest Madame L'Espanaye has ever seen. The track is a tunnel in solid green. There is no clear air; the air is thick with warmth and damp must. Tree-roots stretch from unimaginable hidden branches. Madame would like to examine the flowers which brush past the crouching, running man, but he cannot stop and she is with him, as if she were lodged in him or as if she rode lightly on his back. There is no order here; earth is dispersed through the air, roots are not anchored in the ground. Madame is breathless. She catches sight of the thing the man is running from. It is the strangest carving she has ever seen. Horns curving out from the eyebrows, teeth bare. Her ears fill with a sound like a machine which might be the sound of blood in the ears, or an insect swarm.

The tunnel stops by a river. At the end of the path is another carving. This one has scales and a crown.

There is no warning sound. It must be something else, something invisible and protective surrounding the self like another layer of skin, which prickles and sweats and causes the crouching man to lift his eyes.

The net drifts slowly down from somewhere in the canopy. The view is divided into perfect lozenges. Madame L'Espanaye, dazed, can only admire the orderliness of the thing.

After the net falls Madame is free to return to the fortune at hand, free to return to her tree or her corpse.

The man in the cupboard has a bad effect on business. Nobody wishes to see her locked panting and wordless in her trance. Until she realised that the severed heads belonged to the vision of the forest she had a number of customers worried about the guillotine. Her predictions are usually good. She sees through her vision to whatever events are to come and she has plenty of kind advice for each customer. She is accurate and sensible. The gift of vision is only partly responsible for this. Her own shrewdness has a part to play. This is the first inexplicable vision she has had, and a vision without explanation is a frightening thing. There is something even more disturbing than being torn, inexplicably, from her work and dragged gasping through a strange forest. Something worse than the shadow of the whip. When the book is broken apart and the man sleeps under its sprinkled leaves the pages remind her of the pages of her husband's journal.

Madame opens her old hand on Marianne's earring, remembering. The hook has bitten into her palm. Marianne is nowhere to be seen. No matter. Tonight she will ask her daughter to help her wheel the iron chest out into the light. She will check that her husband's writing is still in its place. She will sit with the pages on her knees and ask for guidance into a future of her own.

When the door opens the man with grey in his beard barely seems to look at Marianne before telling her that her room is ready, her wage will be passed on by the cook, and while she is free to mop and shine, to lay fires and sprinkle the ash in the water closet, she is not to disturb the contents of the rooms, including the gentlemen themselves.

'He is M. Dupin,' says the cook, before sending Marianne down for a little coal. The cook explains that Dupin, who opened the door to Marianne, seems to be able to read minds, but there is nothing to be afraid of; it is skill, not magic, that makes him so knowledgeable. Marianne's clothes, the position of her eyes, her shoulders, tell him that she is a servant who needs work. Dupin is the clever one, and the cook has never been told much about the American, who pays for everything. She shakes coal into the fire and heats enough milk for two bowls of chocolate. Marianne lifts a cat to her knee.

The cook sits, too, and pulls a tatting shuttle and a ball of fine lace-like edging from a basket by her chair. Her fingers twist and flick. The shuttle jerks about and all this awkwardness produces an edging as perfect and repeatable as anything discovered in a laboratory. The cook holds the strip up for Marianne to admire the design. The fire is black and red behind the strip of open cotton threads and the strip buckles and drifts in the warm rising air. Like a mesh, thinks Marianne, like a net too narrow for any fish.

The cook stitches the edgings to the bonnet and hems of a baby costume. It is almost complete. It goes straight to the undertaker in the morning. The cook used to make these costumes for christenings but there was more demand from the undertaker and she prefers it this way. She can stiffen the cloth with a sugar solution and iron it to a perfect sheen which would quickly become dull and sticky on a live child. She knows her work will never be disturbed, her seams will never be pulled about or scorched. She always puts the costume on the child. There is an art to tying the ribbons under the chin, so the jaw is held closed but the ribbon still seems loose and decorative. If there are teeth the mothers like them to show. She adds a few touches of her own. A little soot and grease darken the eyelashes. Geranium petals give a natural blush.

The cat on Marianne's knee rolls and thrusts its head up under her palm. She strokes and the fur crackles and rises in small lines of electricity along the back. She feels a light shock.

As soon as it leaps down she misses the weight.

Later, as she stretches across her bed to push the far edge of a quilt into place, her skirt is suddenly drenched and the cloth chills against her legs. The candle which the cook is holding casts more shadow than light. Marianne hopes that the shadows hide the dark wetness of her skirt.

The cook passes her a grey porcelain footwarmer filled with boiling water from the stove. Marianne sleeps with it gripped in her arms. In the night it softens and twists against her heart, giving off the familiar smell of babies, of sweet grass. A hollow develops which is filled by the crook of her arm. Small fingernails find the inner curve of her breast and the breast aches until she feels the whole substance of herself pulled through her breast in gulped spray, in white threads which can never harden into something knotted or designed.

When the cook returns from the undertaker she tells Marianne that the corpse was a perfectly formed child who fell dead as it took its first few steps. There was some problem with the heart, apparently. The old man who laid the child in the coffin said you can never know what is going on inside, until it is too late. The cook thought she had a good idea of what was going on inside this old man, as she watched him work slowly with the shears which he used on the coffin linings, or straining to lift. But he was alive, whatever was slowing him down couldn't finish him off, and this child was suddenly dead. Marianne thought of the game where you are shown two fists and asked to guess which one held a coin. It was only possible to win if you were lucky, or if you knew which hand was favoured by the person who was trying to trick you.

In the morning while the gentlemen slept Marianne cleaned their drawing room. They read the same books, their plates held the same crumbs. They shared each bottle of wine. The Frenchman was clever, the cook explained over bowls of chocolate in the kitchen, and the American was rich.

That night Marianne dreamed again of the baby she had imagined with such sick fear, before she visited Madame L'Espanaye and discovered that she was not carrying anything more complicated than water. In her dream the swelling was definitely a baby. It had not turned, for birth. The head pressed hard under her ribs and one arm slid from side to side, then rested, still. She lay her hand above the place she thought its hand might be.

Her mother used to sing about sleigh-rides through a forest. It was a Russian song which failed to rhyme in the translation. Marianne hums the melody, in her dream.

There is no fire or chocolate in the house Madame L'Espanaye shares with her daughter Camille. The hearth has been cold for years. The women live on the fourth floor, sleeping, or resting beneath the eiderdown, talking softly between twilight and dawn. In the darkness they could be two old women. In the darkness Camille has caught up with her mother at last. She doesn't see visions like Madame does. She has plenty of her father's blood and her father navigated using stars and instruments. He loved the wind at his back. Camille reminds herself that sailors don't spend their whole lives in the rigging, or on deck. When she was small her father's boat docked and she was carried to his cabin and felt the tremor in the boards under her feet and breathed the scent of the tobacco that had once filled his own chest, out on the wide sea.

Madame does not often buy candles. With the shutters closed it is hard to find the old dish under the bed and the planks about the bed are soaked or sticky with urine, through the winter months. Camille only climbs down the stairs to empty the dish. She has no wish to go into the street, to leave her cabin. She remembers being led to a quay to meet her father when he returned from a voyage. She wore her communion dress, which is still in the bureau. She knows it is there because last time her mother was out she took it from the drawer and let her night-dress fall to the floor. She remembers her father lifting her high in the air like some white seabird, his hands on this very cloth, gripping so tightly that the starch scraped under her arms.

The communion dress slides over her shoulders. The sleeves are soft now. Her nipples rub against the rough interior of the embroidery. It distracts her; she cannot imagine swinging, laughing through the air in her father's arms when her adult breasts are so sensitive. Better to dream under the eider-down. Better to listen to the wind in the chimney and pretend it is filling great canvas sails on masts above the house.

Marianne is shaking coal into the grate while the gentlemen talk. She is hoping they'll wave her away so she can slip into the dark street and find her way to Madame. She misses her earring. The pair were barely worn, since she could hardly have them glittering at the edge of her cap as she did her work, but they are all that she has to remind her of her mother. They were given to her mother by a grateful Russian who said she had shoulders like a statue he once saw of St Cecilia. The Russian was Marianne's father. He was two weeks in Paris.

Marianne is on her knees, sweeping the hearth with a fine brush. She hopes to irritate the men, but they haven't noticed her.

The American is telling M. Dupin about the costumes worn by Indians: the hawk feathers and porcupine quills in buffalo cloaks; the tufts of human hair torn from their enemies which are fastened to the clothing of the men. He knows how they trap antelope, how they circle around a fire in the night. Marianne wants to interrupt, to ask if there are pictures of these Indians in any of the books, wanting to ask if they have a secret way of talking, using signs they make with their hands. The American is describing a friend of his, whose mouth was smashed with a rifle butt in the Indian Wars. He describes the broken teeth and the tongue which was torn almost beyond repair. It doesn't seem like the moment to ask whether Indians talk with their hands.

Madame L'Espanaye is unpacking an iron seachest which she has dragged to the centre of the room. Camille picks up a frond of white seaweed. Each stem is made of small firm pieces like pieces of an insect skeleton. They join loosely; the whole frond can be drawn over the back of a hand and it will follow the shape of the skin. It smells like old piss and salt. This was his treasure. Not narwhal horn or spice. He saved her shark eggs, grooved to spin in the current, a bottle of black sand, a few beads the colour of the sky.

Madame has the journal in her hands. It is intact; no one has torn it apart in a dark cupboard.

'Let me tell you,' says Madame, 'about your father in

the whirlpool. Let me tell you how he was saved from the great whale.'

'I can read for myself,' says Camille. She pulls the journal from her mother's hands. The mother grips more tightly. Suddenly the binding splits and as the stitching in the leather dissolves a pocket appears. It's packed with old letters. Madame glances at the first. A woman in an American seaport wrote these letters to her husband. Or so it appears, when they are unfolded and smoothed flat. The woman writes that the sound of the sea outside her window is like the sound of a man's breath next to her ear.

Madame L'Espanaye puts the journal and the letters carefully to one side. She thinks bitterly of the time when she and Camille learned to read English. She was shy with her well-travelled husband, and she had time on her hands during his long voyages. The English was a way of travelling with him. If she had never learned it the letters would be as safe and ordinary as the stove in the chimney. She finds that she has time to pull the dish out from under the bed before the hot uprush of vomit breaks from her throat.

Camille takes the loose pages and climbs into the bed.

The woman writes that she is sitting in the sun stitching a long linen seam, and every stitch is like a wave, every stitch is one wave less of the thousands of waves which lie between them and every stitch is over a second less of the days which remain to be filled, before they meet. The woman writes that today she misses him with her hands. Yesterday it was her ears and she closed her eyes and tipped her head about as she had done so often, under his mouth, and pretended that the sound of the sea outside her window was the sound of his breath close at her ear.

Camille reads this with great interest. She is so interested, and her mother is vomiting so noisily below, that she does not hear the window opening behind her and the movements of the strange beast which joins her on the bed. She puts the papers down and rubs her eyes.

An ape has the letters in his hands.

Marianne has at last slipped away, a few paces behind M. Dupin and the American, who often walk through the streets at night, their talk full of dreams and ideas, fitting stories to the faces they pass in the crowd; the gamblers, the pedlars, the women who stand close enough to the lamplight to be seen, but not close enough for the thinness and the pockmarks to show. It amuses the American to guess the profession of each passer-by. There is only one job for the women. Marianne wishes she had taken the street women fresh bread and roast chicken from the kitchen. It would not be stealing, not like giving her employer's gold away. Marianne does not like to remember her mother's final years in shadowed doorways. She caught the headlice so badly that her scalp wept and there were tight knots of infection in her neck. The old bonnet hid the worst of it when she visited Marianne. The nuns who plaited Marianne's own hair tight and marched her about with the other girls put a stop to the visits, although they were happy to keep the Russian gold, and there was enough gold for English lessons, for music.

The men pace as neatly as harnessed horses. If one waves his arm the other lifts his. They might be tied at the ankle and not notice. They turn, apparently without discussion, and

Marianne walks on alone. The street is empty outside Madame's open gate.

It is empty because everyone in the street has gathered before Madame's door.

A terrible screaming has been heard inside the house. Then silence.

Marianne is among the last to climb the stair.

The lower rooms are empty. She stands back from the upper locked door while a man puts his shoulder to the panels with as much energetic fury as her last employer used, to break into her room.

There is no proud frightened girl inside.

The room looks like a factory for making wigs. Or like a teepee strewn with the scalps of enemies. But who would want wigs of such pale, such dirty grey hair? Who would make an enemy of women so poorly provided for?

Boots track blood across the floor. As Marianne watches, a policeman picks up her earring and puts it in his pocket. She cries out, but everyone in the room is crying out.

One body is up in the chimney and another is down in the courtyard.

Marianne follows the policeman. He's walking at a great pace, striding importantly, but when he stops she can see, even in the poor light, that he is trembling. He pulls a flask from his pocket and drinks. Something flickers from the pocket to the ground. When he walks on Marianne creeps forward to the place where he stood. She picks a tight bundle of papers from the dirt. When she straightens and looks about the policeman is gone.

'I never was in love,' says the cook, 'and I never felt the lack of it.'

Marianne has the letters from the American woman unfolded on her knee. She reads them to the cook.

The American woman sleeps holding a pebble which Madame L'Espanaye's husband picked up on a beach and saved for her. The pebble is cream and a strange translucent green like a shallow sea where something is disturbing the sand. She looks deeply into the stone and pretends the disturbance is caused by one of the great rays he has told her about: a creature as oval as the moon one night before the full; a creature with a belly as pale as the moon.

'I never had more than one dress,' says the cook. 'More than one is vanity.'

Marianne has to be firm with the cat, which is bewildered by her refusal to take it up on her knee. She reaches down and moves her fingers and the cat pushes the velvet behind its ears into Marianne's fingertips, sliding from one side to another and pausing at the underside of the chin.

Marianne reads that the woman in the American port is stitching a dress in cloth as hard and glossy as wet sand. The dress is for a merchant's wife. She is rolling the hem and as she rolls it under her thumb and stitches it into place the fabric stretches and flutes like the edges of a creature which moves through water; like a great ray. She is to sew a length of fringing directly under the hem. It will touch the ground first and protect the hem from dust and floor-wax. She is the same size as the merchant's wife and before she finishes the fringing and the final beading at the chest of the dress she tries it on herself, and walks the length of her room with her eyes closed, and stops when she feels the sunlight from the window fall across her face, and pretends that the tightness of the cloth and bone under her breasts is the pressure of his chest as he tightens his arms about her.

Marianne stops reading aloud and the cook says that it is a bad case. A very tough case.

The woman in the American port writes about tucking the sailor's pebble in her cheek as she sits and sews. She is like a woman in a desert with a stone in her mouth.

'Enough,' says the cook. She tells Marianne that M. Dupin has a mourner's book. She overheard the American translating it aloud to him. It read well. She sends Marianne to the gentlemen's room to fetch it.

The mourner's book was written by A Lady and published in Philadelphia. It is full of verse and sermons.

'Give me an Infant poem,' says the cook. She leans back dreamily as Marianne turns the pages.

> *Sleep little baby! sleep!*
> *Not in thy cradle bed,*
> *Not on thy mother's breast,*
> *Henceforth shall be thy rest,*
> *But quiet with the dead!*

Marianne stops reading. She hopes the dead are quiet. The room was strewn with the torn hair of Madame L'Espanaye and her daughter. There were pools of dark liquid which the policeman splashed through on his way to the chimney. The fireplace was empty, except for a sweep of hair, and a face. The daughter had been wedged upside down in the chimney. The face was hard and very still. Madame's throat was cut and her body was thrown into the courtyard. At first the crowd thought it was a bundle of old rags. Marianne is sure that her own mother is dead, and she is never troubled by her presence. The baby she dreams about is different. In the morning there are fine scratches on her breasts.

'More,' says the cook, voluptuously.

> *Thine upturned eyes glazed over,*
> *Like harebells wet with dew,*
> *Already veil'd and hid*
> *By the convulsed lid*
> *Their pupils darkly blue.*

'Exactly so,' says the cook.

Marianne rushes on.

> *To meet again in slumber,*
> *His small mouth's rosy kiss;*
> *Then wakened with a start*
> *By thine own throbbing heart,*
> *His twining arms to miss.*

Marianne coughs unconvincingly. When the cook smiles across at her she shakes her head.

In the early hours Marianne dreams again of the baby at her breast. She draws her long nipple from the baby's mouth and props the baby against her updrawn knees, where it yawns in pink happiness. It doesn't look dead. She asks it if it is flesh or spirit and it yawns again. She asks the empty room if this baby is the spirit of one of the children the cook dresses for burial.

The baby doesn't look like the child of a stranger. It has a dimple in the same place as Marianne. It has her colouring. Then Marianne notices something odd about her hands. They are too small. She wears a ring which she can barely remember that her mother wore.

This is no haunting.

In her sleep she is her mother, nursing the baby daughter who is herself.

The men have finished a bottle of Bordeaux and a fine meal of kidneys and rice. Each wears a foolish smile of satisfaction. Marianne is clearing the plates when the American begins to speak.

'Imagine if we never saw evidence of the dead,' he says.

'You are asking me to imagine Paradise?' asks M. Dupin.

'No, not immortality,' counters the American. 'I am thinking of a world where graveyards stood empty, except for the few mourners attached to each particular funeral; where a funeral itself was an oddity. Imagine no plumes, no black, no enamel mourning rings, no wisps of saved hair. Imagine if you only removed your hat for a pretty girl.'

'Impossible. It would be easier to imagine a world where hats were not worn in the street.'

'I have read an argument that we need daily reminders of

death to avoid being paralysed by terror when a death occurs.'

'But in the country where death is hidden and occasional, would not the general indifference to the subject carry a man through the spectacle of death?'

'For the sake of argument, I report what I read. Here.' He waved Marianne to the mourning book which she had replaced on the shelf. 'Here it is: "Were death a rare and uncommon object, were it only once in the course of a man's life that he beheld one of his fellow-creatures carried to the grave, a solemn awe would fill him; he would stop short in the midst of his pleasures; he would even be chilled with a secret horror."'

'Chilled in secret, briefly, yes.'

'No,' said the American, following the words with his fingertips. 'Chilled so as to "render men unfit for the ordinary business of life".'

'Then there could be no reasonable enquiry into the circumstances of life, or more importantly, the circumstances of death. There could be no justice in your world. Murderers would roam free.'

'Or be so disabled by their crime that they could never commit another.'

The sailor's journal is open on a piece of guttering outside Madame L'Espanaye's highest window. Pages flick over as if the wind had fingertips.

'Today at last the fever took the Greek,' Madame's husband wrote. 'It was he who plunged into the opened gut of the whale where I lay senseless and bleached by the juices of the animal.

The Greek strapped me to his back and climbed out over the ribs. I never knew a man so strong.

'During the fever I never knew muscle to shrink so hard. There were hollow pockets under the collarbones. The jaw. As if skin could creep in toward the centre of a being. As if the bone could swell. The stout hair fell away. He shone like oiled wood. All this in a matter of hours. Me assuring him that the thing would break and he would soon be well.

'At the end the Greek pointed to his seachest and lifted his hand to make me understand that I was to open it.

'I found a wrapped cotton gown with a cross dripped in wax above the breast. He had shown me this before. It was his baptism robe from the river of Jordan. He made the pilgrimage as a young man. The robe was soaked as he sank beneath the water, and dried in the hot sun of Jericho, and he kept it with him ever since.

'The men on deck tried to distract me from the horror of the whale by laughing about making a shroud of the inner muscle of the fish. Then the Greek fetched his own shroud and explained how the Jordan water would keep him safe from the flames of Hell. As I wept and trembled he made me hold the cloth. He told me that holding it would keep me safe.

'He stared resolutely at the chest. I thought he had composed himself for death, but there was one thing more. I understood suddenly, and I withdrew a flat packet and held it above his hands. He blinked. I opened it. It was a daguerreotype of a woman. I put it under his hands.

'I know the woman, a seamstress, American, who always looked so fair on the arm of her Greek. We are on course for the port where she is waiting. It will fall to me to give her the terrible news.'

The wind moves over the sailor's words. The sky is bright with dependable stars.

Marianne is in bed at last, with a candle by her pillow. She cannot help opening the letters once again. She feels that the woman who wrote them is as dear to her as any of the girls who slipped into her bed on cold nights in the convent dormitory.

The dates on the letters are long past. The woman is likely to be dead; her fluted dress will be worn out and unfashionable, in the rag-basket of a merchant's wife. Marianne does not care.

'You were first alone with me in the great ugliness of grief,' wrote the woman. 'You wiped my face clean and held me as I crouched, rigid with misery, unable to stand, unable to loosen my elbows or my knees. You told me he was safe in the water of the Jordan, far, far under the sea. You poured a little wine into the side of my cheek and it seeped through my clenched teeth. You sat the whole awkward shape of me on your knee and patted me and sang in your own language, which I could not understand, and told me in mine that there was only one other person in the world you would do this for, and that was your daughter, far away in France.

'You sent me turquoise just when I was recovering, and a note letting me know the month when you would return.'

Marianne sees the woman like a great cat on the lap of the sailor.

Marianne sees her gradual relaxation; the stretching like the long stretch of a cat.

The wind has got to the end of the sailor's journal.

The final entries are brief.

Under each date, a few words: 'Calm and well provisioned.'

'Birdless skies. Calm. Too deep for a plumbline. Provisions, still.'

'One sighting of waterweed. No wind.'

'Calm. All stores gone.'

Then, 'Calm.'

And, 'Calm.'

'At least it was a sudden death,' said the American.

'All death is sudden,' said M. Dupin. 'Even when you've been waiting for a long time, death is sudden.'

They have the newspaper reports of the murders in front of them. Crumbs of pastry leave butter shadows on the newsprint.

'I do not see how a head can be all but severed in one blow. I cannot conceive of the strength required to thrust a body in a chimney.'

Marianne puts fresh coffee before the gentlemen. She closes her eyes on her tears. She is ashamed of herself. She works out the name for the way she feels. Shame. She could not bring herself to touch Madame, when the old woman lived and spoke, yet she rushed as fast as any of the others for a glimpse of her poor corpse. She is ashamed.

At night, by candlelight, Marianne re-reads the letters of a woman who lives for everything that has no place in her own life. Sea and sunshine, the shiver of a flank under a sailor's hand, the sound of the drunken accordion and voices singing by the quay.

'Thank you,' writes the woman, 'for the sketch of the wild

man your friend caught in the forest. The face was as frightening as death, to me. The black skin and sunken nose. The sister of the man who sells me thread died last month in Philadelphia, leaving three small children. Her husband had been living in New York but he rushed to her side and kissed her, I was told, for a good thirty hours. He wrote in a letter to his brother-in-law, and I have seen this letter, "I kiss her cold lips, but their fervour has gone." What can he have expected, I wonder? She was buried in Brooklyn and just last week he had the coffin opened so he could kiss her again. Her brother is scandalised. The woman was damp and black and her nose was gone. Her forehead was the only bit left to kiss. When I see the dull eyes and shrunken lips of your wild man I think of the woman from Philadelphia. Thank you too for the lock of the wild man's hair. It is as red and coarse as the wigs of the old women who work by the quay. I wonder if the wild man, or as you say, orang-utan, has a red woman weeping under some thick scentless flower in the forest you have left behind.'

In the creases of the letter Marianne finds a few odd rough hairs. One flies into the candle-flame and burns with sudden foulness. The smell fills the room; it draws the goodness from the air in the room. Marianne wipes her streaming eyes with the edge of a sheet.

'Since you are sending me the hair of an animal,' the woman writes, 'I will return the favour. I have snipped some white silky hair from the throat of the cat which belongs to my friend Stella. Stella and her cat came through a great shipwreck alive, so I believe this to be a lucky gift, as well as beautiful. You will wait many long years before my hair shines as whitely as the hair of Stella's cat. And I know that you will wait.'

It is an unfamiliar language, but one that Marianne is prepared to translate.

Marianne knows the letters must go back to the police. She plans to bargain with them, for her earring. They should have been returned the day before, but it is hard to part with all this information about ears and breasts, about ways of measuring the ordinary time it takes to load cargo and ballast and calculate the direction of a voyage, which the ears and breasts know nothing about.

Down in the kitchen the cook is cutting butter on marble while the cat floats on hind feet about the table, paws stretched up to the edge, and drops to the floor and reaches up again.

The gentlemen have gone out.

The cook talks about the murders and the strong agile murderer. M. Dupin thinks he can work out who it is. The corpses were shockingly cut about. A razor, according to the newspaper, and a strong pair of hands. The cook is frightened. She asks Marianne if she would share her bed.

In the darkness Marianne wakes and hears the cook cry out in her sleep.

The cry interrupts a most unusual dream. She is exhausted in the hands of a man she is sure she has seen before. He turns her, or she turns. His chest has a dip above the heart which is a perfect cup for her cheekbone. The hollow at the top of her thighs when he lays her on her front is a nest for some loose and heavy softness of his own, and she feels a long stripe of hardness as if it had grown from the crease of her own flesh. There are fingers well known to her tongue in her mouth. She turns and nestles and is turned again, and everywhere it is as if their bodies are socket and bone in the body of some animal which moves and feeds in sunshine, unaware.

She has seen this man before. If only she could remember where she has seen him before.

The cook cries out again.

Marianne breathes shallowly and keeps her own eyes closed. The cook is not a child to be woken and calmed, or a young girl at the convent who might make a prayer shape of her cold hands and slip them between another girl's thighs.

In the end Marianne cannot bear the sound. She pushes her arm beneath the shoulders of the cook, sliding and digging her way between the mattress and the heavy flesh. The cook rolls towards her. Dry grubby hair falls over her. Breasts move limply, like dirty hair. Marianne makes her mother's shushing noise.

When the cook has calmed a little she tells Marianne she hates to be alone in the night. She brings the cat up to the bed with her so she can hear the breath of another creature in the room.

Marianne asks if she was shut away when she was small.

'Not when I was small,' says the cook. 'When I was a grown woman I was shut away.'

It is Marianne's turn to feel cold and afraid. The woman may have been a prisoner or a lunatic.

'I had a house in the rue du Faubourg-Saint-Denis. I helped women rid themselves of their pregnancies. I was careful and clean and I took their bloodied linen afterwards and washed it out myself so they would not be discovered. I asked a hundred francs but I would do it for thirty. I delivered live births too. I had steady hands and a name for gripping the wombs that had begun to bleed. I could stop a woman bleeding with my hands.

'I made a mistake. I misjudged a girl.

'It was not a child she was carrying, but a great cyst. My needle caused her pain, but not the loss we were expecting, and in her confusion she told her master about me.

'I was sentenced to eight years, to be served in a single cell, alone.'

Marianne keeps holding and shushing until they are both asleep.

In the morning she tells the cook that she slept soundly through the night.

The gentlemen are eating white peaches and cheese. They send Marianne to open a particular wine which smells of sunshine on peaches. She breaks M. Dupin's rule of silent service, and says so. 'Sunshine on peaches.'

'Yes,' he says. 'Exactly so.'

The American says that it is not the evening to be drinking a heavy red wine. They have seen the aftermath of murders so strange and terrible that it is as if the air itself opened and allowed a demon from under the sea to commit this crime. He pauses; he has frightened her. He gives her his glass of wine.

Marianne remembers that the sailor trickled wine into the cheek of the woman who wrote the letters she has been reading in her room. Marianne has only tasted communion wine. She drinks it like medicine. Immediately she is aching and relaxed. She stretches distant fingers to the tabletop and sets the glass neatly down. There is something familiar on the tabletop. She stares.

'I found this in the hand of one of the victims,' says M. Dupin. 'It is a most unusual lock of hair.'

Marianne lifts it to one of the candles. She burns a strand. Her eyes begin to stream. 'It is the hair of an orang-utan,' she says.

M. Dupin and the American walk on either side of Marianne, their cloaks pulling from one side to another like the wings of a bat. The policeman she had followed from Madame's house opens his door to them. Marianne has lost hope of recovering her earring. But there is something else about him, something she can't quite place. His hand. The faint dip of his chest. Surely he is the man in her passionate dream. She smiles with such rapture at the policeman that he drops his hat.

Finn has written to me.

He wants me to visit him, on the way to America. He's sure that I'm going to America. He says he's a bit short on roaring fires and whisky-and-sodas and the sound of the wind through pines, but he can make up a bed on the floor and hang a beret from the doorknob.

He's been to the State Library and photocopied a pile of stuff on Poe for me.

The front of the postcard is a portrait of a young man looking at himself in a mirror above a fireplace. Or perhaps it is a wide lectern, with the edge of an arch under the shelf. The man doesn't look like Finn. There is a window behind him, and a moon showing in the window. His shadowed eyes are as round as the moon. When I look closely the eyes themselves are narrow. It's the arch of the brow, the bone, which gives them this appearance of astonished circularity.

V

VALENTINE'S DAY

F inn left the key with his neighbour.

I came down on the train from the mountains.

In the seat behind me a man was telling a girl about his time in jail. Another prisoner had the same name and this could have been a real problem, for each of them, if they hadn't known how to stay out of trouble. He told her about listening to rumours about himself, in the yard and the cells, nothing interesting, just rumours about where he'd been and what he'd done, and they were all so wide of the mark he started to worry. The girl interrupted to ask if anyone ever mentioned her. The prisoner said women all think the men inside have got nothing better to do than talk about them.

I shifted about on my orange plastic seat, trying not to listen. I thought about the men inside, getting on with their weight-lifting and university extension courses, while the women in the visitors' queue talked about the men inside.

'Where do you go,' Finn asked me, 'when you've finished with romance?' It was just before I cut his hair, before I turned him into his wartime father.

When I'm dreaming lightly on a train or aeroplane I often slide back to romance, back to Boston and the ice rooms under the conifers at Niagara.

We went to California, between Boston and Niagara.

The man I was in love with had to do some work on blood with people he knew in California. He was interested in platelets: the things which clump together and stop you from bleeding to death after you cut yourself. He planned to work hard, to cram six months' research into two. I was to go for walks and make necklaces from antique African beads and bake rye bread and take day trips to San Fran to look at frayed quilts and Chinese lamp-bases in second-hand shops.

There was no oven. He was working so hard that he barely had time to eat and sleep.

We stayed in a big single room with a sink and a grill. One wall was glass. There was a deep recess in the other which held the garbage chute for the whole building.

It was winter and when I went out walking the sky was like mother-of-pearl. Buckling. Luminous. Soon to be dark. There was no light, lamplight or candlelight, under the plastic sheeting which the homeless had tied to fences and tree trunks in the gully by the shopping centre. I walked and walked past the homeless and a car lot and a Safeway with a Payless Drugs sign and a frozen-yoghurt place and a hospice thrift shop and a psychic palm reader and a man with a sign which read Homeless, and it started all over again.

Every few days I took our laundry down to a windowless room with a washing machine and a dryer.

The corridor and the lift were almost always empty. Once I stuck my head around an open door and introduced myself to the neighbour, who was sitting with her back to her own wall of glass, so at first she was in shadow. I said my name but she didn't say hers. When my eyes adjusted to the light I saw that she had a ribbed silver pipe like a microphone coming out of her throat. She was wearing a man's satin smoking jacket, as shiny as the pipe. She must have had throat cancer. She couldn't say hello.

The women in the hospice thrift shop talked and talked about their nails and their hair. I bought two plates. I couldn't think of anything to say about my hair.

I stopped on the bridge over the gully. Below me a rope was stretched between two trees with a blanket drying, or airing, over it. Thick semitransparent plastic was carefully taped around a tree trunk to make a tent shape. There was a drift of knotted supermarket bags on one side of the tent.

The same people stood inside the bus shelter each day. A woman asked where I had bought my coat. The bus was never going near her street. After a while I worked out that she had no home, only the bus shelter.

I shouldn't have been noticing all of this. The sky was like mother-of-pearl over the palm trees in the evening. Glossy squirrels rushed up the trunks of the palms. There was a shopping centre with cyclamen in window boxes and a cinema with a wurlitzer which rose up on a platform through the stage.

Once I was sure that someone followed me through the shopping centre, his footsteps placed exactly in my own, his fingers lifting every object I examined, every weaving and carving, every plastic useful thing, each glass and tablecloth.

The man I was in love with knew that something was wrong.

I had a light vibration, a kind of humming, in my bones. I couldn't phone my grandmother and ask if this was the first stage of going mad.

Next time I was out on a walk I turned under a railway bridge and took a few short streets to a hotel with a glass and chicken-wire elevator and top-floor corridor where the fans never stopped circling and each door opened on a room a little wider than a double bed.

I checked in. The hem of an old lace curtain swayed across a windowsill. The window opened on a wall. The walls were painted a thick pale grey. I slept into the early hours and then lay awake until the first train shushed its way across the overpass.

Everything lapsed away so easily.

I had jeans and boots and a sweater and underwear which I rinsed each night in the basin, after I had screwed up newspaper and plugged the drain. I kept the door closed and watched the curtain sway. I drank from the basin tap and used the bathroom in the corridor. I didn't think to speak or eat. After a week I went to the foyer to pay for more time in the room and the coffee smelled so good that I poured myself some and read a magazine.

In the second week I went for a walk in an unfamiliar direction and found my way into a church. Voices came from the choir loft. Someone was giving an organ lesson. She said that this is as close as an instrument gets to the sound of a human voice. Even through the bass notes I could feel the humming in my bones.

In the second week the blood researcher was waiting in the foyer of the hotel. He said that we could work it out. Whatever it was. We could go away for the weekend. We could fly to Seattle, and then on to Niagara.

Sometimes I think of the yellow narcissuses which he carried between his palm and the handlebar of his bicycle. Sometimes I think of the place beside his mouth where a line was just beginning to form. It comes to me, when I'm on a train or an aeroplane.

The humming, the sense of an invisible trembling in my bones, gradually went away. I got on an aeroplane after Niagara, and flew back to Australia, to a friend who lived close to the beach.

I like everything about trains. I like the way that stations still smell of coal smoke. I like the slow weighty movement of old trains. Mostly I like to be inside that noise: the shushing, the ring of metal rails and wheels, the horn like a single note on a cornet. If I close my eyes I'm back on the bed in that hotel, dawn turning the old lace curtain grey.

The train slowed past the platform which was built in the last century specifically for funerals. Part of the mortuary station was dismantled and put together in another city. The arches were filled with glass and the coal smoke was cleaned from the old sandstone and then the whole structure was consecrated. I've been inside, with my father, who took a special interest. It was the right shape for a church but the carvings were disturbing. Opium pods and animals with open snarling mouths.

We swayed on until the bitumen of our own platform showed beneath the windows.

The prisoner helped me out with my suitcase and my box of books.

Finn sent me directions: two steps up from the street beside the video shop, double doors with bevelled glass, more wide stairs and a landing with letterboxes and names under scored plastic, then more stairs.

He left the keys with a neighbour.

It was exactly what you'd expect. Books. Velveteen chairs with a polished wooden platform on each arm, where you could rest your glass. A bakelite ashtray on a chessboard. More pictures of his mother, in tight pants and a scoop-neck top, in jeans. One with my father. They've grown alike as they've aged. She looks better older, lined and clear-eyed. The kitchen had a noisy round-shouldered refrigerator with a door full of beer. I knew all the clothes on the floor beside his mattress; I'd seen them on the line in the drying yard in the mountains. Perhaps he kept secrets in biscuit tins on top of his wardrobe. I had the feeling that all I needed to do was ask.

I tucked myself entirely into one of his armchairs and rolled up a little pinched tobacco and let myself fall back into dizziness and old velveteen.

It was then that I started to talk to Finn in my head, to address some of my thoughts to him.

I am thinking of all the small things Poe gathered and lost in the course of his life. An inkwell given and then retained by his foster-father, so that he had to insist on the right to take it away. A coat that stayed with him like the pelt of some animal with a big loose skin. A rug and silver tea service which visitors to the Fordham house noticed, then later visitors don't notice, because they disappeared or lost their shine. Pictures and books and letters to be shown to other people, or burned.

In late daguerreotypes he looks crumpled and oily. His eyes are dull. He is past the fresh shock of losing Virginia. It's no clean wound. He looks clotted and unhealed. A newspaper infuriated him by reporting that his pointy chin made his head look like a balloon. The newspaper was right. He looks like a balloon with seams which are not strong enough for any volatile gas. Thin-boned and pressured from within. A biographer says he looks *emotionally electrocuted*, and he does.

Finn, did you know that the first man in the electric chair would not die, after almost a minute of strong current? His limbs were in buckets of water. Smoke rose from his skin. He breathed.

Listen: this is what I most like about Poe. He took some terrible current. He lost almost every small forlorn thing. An inkwell. Virginia. He kept breathing, just, and he refused to pretend that he was healed.

Poe was dug up, a while after he died, and buried somewhere else. I've read about the details. The sexton who lifted

Poe's skull heard a thud when he shifted the thing from hand to hand. The brain had dried and it fell from side to side, he said, just like a lump of mud. Long after his death, his brain was still clattering away.

I must have gone to sleep in Finn's velveteen chair. When I opened my eyes the rooms were soft and dim and the noise was huge. I leaned on the windowsill and watched an ambulance run up over a curb and speed neatly along a footpath, cutting into the column of traffic ahead of the lights.

Finn would probably appreciate some fruit and fresh milk.

There was a woman on the stairs.

I glanced across at her, and while I was looking away from the door a hand closed over my shoulder. Finn.

'Photocopies,' he said, holding up the old briefcase which had been bumped about so much that the edges were rubbed down to suede. 'Photocopies from the State Library, and all for you.'

More welcoming than flowers and champagne.

I handed over his key so he could let himself in, and went out onto the street past the video posters and the laundromat, hoping not to get in the way of a footpath ambulance, and since there were sunflowers and delphiniums in black buckets around the door of the bottle shop, I picked up flowers to go with the wine and food.

In the early hours the highway was almost silent. Finn put on some Debussy and we both listened to the pretty, rippling sea. My mother played this, in the house in the mountains when the families were all together. My father asked her to.

Finn lifted his glass to America. America and Poe.

Poe again. Poe.

Finn was filling my glass, holding the bottle with both hands and great seriousness. It was the hour when kids tell each other ghost stories and watch for the dawn. We told each other stories ourselves, sitting on the windowsill above the wisteria courtyard, swinging bare legs and waiting for the dawn. Now if I asked him for a ghost story he'd tell me he only works with facts and with remains.

A skull with a dried fist of a brain rattling from side to side, that's Poe; and there's the white linen of Virginia's burial dress and her teeth and her dark hair with all the gloss long gone – telling us nothing, nothing about a man standing by his writing desk looking down on a girl in a box hardly wider than a manuscript.

It must have taken a lot of strength to lift Virginia from the top of the desk and carry her out over the snow to a borrowed space in the vault of the family who owned the Fordham house, who were called – most painfully, under these conditions – the Valentines.

Poe couldn't stay inside the house.

At night he walked over to the tomb. I think of snow and absolute stillness, except for the rhythm of the feet, the heart, the breath, turning like cogs, linking and forcing each other on like cogs in some simple machine whose work is grief.

Finn was lying flat on the floor with a wine glass upright on his chest, eyes closed, not held closed, just relaxed and shut. One

arm was crooked so he could hold the wine glass and the other
fell away a little from his side.

'You know,' he said, 'I like to hear you talk. When we were
in the mountains I liked the way you whispered on one night,
something about cake and lizards and a may bush. I don't know
how hard I was listening, I just liked the way you talk.'

'I was trying not to talk.' I could say this, because his eyes
were closed. 'I was trying not to tell you about miserable Poe.'

He smiled. He reached over and stroked the inside of my
ankle. His finger circled a small round bone. It's about the size
and shape of a button, but it can never come unfastened.

I was listening to the Debussy slipping faultlessly, deli-
ciously, over and around the scale, and wishing I could hear
recordings of Debussy himself, who was said to play so
awkwardly that he was almost an embarrassment.

Finn looked as if he had drifted off to sleep. But one hand
reached out and closed warmly over my ankle and he said, 'You
know sometimes I think that the chariot doesn't swing low over
the sunny plain where all the happy people are. It swings down
over the pit.'

When I woke up Finn really was asleep next to me on the floor
in front of the velveteen sofa, flat on his back, his palm across his
forehead as if he was trying to keep something in.

I poured myself a glass of cold milk in the kitchen and
drank it quickly, so it felt as if there was no pipe down from my
throat to my stomach; it felt as if the whole inside of my chest
was washed in coolness.

A cat crouched on the wall of the courtyard below. It

stretched and shrugged. Then it spotted me and settled down to stare. The fur and skin were loose, as if the real cat was well inside and the covering was there to be stretched out and licked and enjoyed, to protect the cat from boredom as well as from cold or accident.

It broke off the stare to rub its chin against the ledge of stone on top of the wall. It swept its whiskers again and again across the stone and at the end of one long sweep the whole body tucked under and rolled. It didn't fall.

I suddenly remembered the light scrape of stubble over my cheek or the side of my throat when a man is teasing, after or before a kiss, using the morning's beard like a wide tickling fingertip, and I remembered smiling and tipping my head from side to side.

The delphiniums were in a spaghetti jar on top of the fridge. They glittered deep blue in the streetlight. Egyptians garlanded their mummies with delphiniums. The blue must have looked so fine against gold necklaces. I read about this in my grandfather's books. Cats were mummified, too. Gutted, wrapped and closed up in gold replicas of the bodies of living cats, with precious masks to lay over the bandaged fur and whiskers. And why not? They were loved. Tomb painting after tomb painting shows a cat sitting confidently under the legs of a woman's chair, sometimes calm, sometimes excited by a flapping fish which has clearly been rushed, alive, to the cat.

Poe loved his cat and his cousin Virginia. He got up repeatedly in the night to let the cat in or out, and the cat wouldn't eat unless he was home.

He wrote about a man who kills his wife with an axe and

walls the corpse up with a live cat. The worst thing about this story is the tone of patient reasonableness. The murderer describes all this as if he were a modest inventor, detailing the steps which led to an advance in engineering or in medicine. *When I had finished*, he said, *I felt satisfied that all was right.*

X-rays of the cat mummies in Egyptian cemeteries show the Egyptian cats often died young. Their necks were snapped, or else they were strangled.

There wasn't much point in going back to the couch, curling up and waiting for the dawn. At that point sleep seemed to be Finn's greatest achievement, more impressive by far than the pages of the General's biography, which were stacked at the end of the kitchen table. He must work here, I thought, looking down on the courtyard where the same fern that arches over the mountain paths is growing out through a crack in the stone.

I made myself coffee and opened the briefcase full of bits of Poe.

It was more than bits of Poe. He'd copied anything he could find about New York, around the year that Virginia died.

English visitors complained about the noise of the traffic over the cobblestones on Fifth Avenue. Timber and bricks were dumped along Broadway and the city looked fresh and unfinished; as mobile as democracy itself.

Bonnets with long veils were in fashion, and so were big white shawls, which made everyone look like tablecloths and ghosts and desert Arabs.

I read about a girl who had the strangest dream. She was out on the harbour in a boat. It wasn't a floating palace, like the steamers on the Hudson. It was a boat for one, and the whole harbour was thick with flexible gold, moving on the surface of the waves, and as she reached out and cut pieces from the gold and stacked them on the floor of her little boat they disappeared.

The cat was still stretched out on the stone coping of the courtyard, out of reach of the window or the street below. Occasionally it sleeked itself against the light curve at the top of the wall, enjoying the cool impersonal pressure of the stone.

Stairs, a landing, more stairs ending just above street level, a list of names beside letterboxes and heavy glass doors: carrying a suitcase down to wait for a cab should be easier than dragging it up, especially since Finn is doing the carrying, but it isn't.

I'm not afraid to fly. I like that long droning stretch of time where a day folds into the day before and is lost completely, or pegs itself so wide across the hemispheres that it repeats itself. I'll have two February elevenths. If the body had more respect for the calendar you could put off death for ever, unless the plane went down. I like a long flight.

I don't like to leave.

Finn needs a shave. He smells like toast and warm cotton. I've told him not to wait with me, but he wants to.

He talks about how cold it's going to be when I arrive. He doesn't think much of the scarf I bought in the mountains. He's given me his own. He talks about the view from the rooftop room of his hotel, last time he was in New York. The pigeons. The tops of the yellow cabs. He makes me promise to have a hot dog.

I'm saying, 'Yes, yes,' until suddenly a cab stops dead in the traffic and pops open its door. It's for me.

The driver is saying my name, Finn is shoving my suitcase in the back, the car stuck behind the cab is blaring away on the horn, and suddenly I'm in tears, turning aside from the cab and the suitcase and Finn, saying, 'What if I can't do all this? What if I can't make anything of this?' It's going to be like cutting up light on water and trying to stack it in a little boat.

The driver watches calmly.

Finn says, 'You'll be fine, Thea. Just take your pen in your hand and let it all balloon out.'

I'm following the morning, all the way around the world.

Twice I've looked across to the black porthole window and seen a line of whiteness which could be the edge of a wing or a reflection from inside the aeroplane itself. Then the darkness pulls apart. The sky is suddenly all white and there is ice on the outside of the window and a film of sweat in the cavity between the panes. We fly against the turn of the earth. A white stripe widens in the blackness. We nose through the American dawn.

I think of my mother on a wooden step which has weathered to grey, or silver. She's thumbing peapods open and the peas scatter into her iron saucepan with a sound like rain. If I wait she'll pass me a handful. She's elsewhere; her hands work mechanically, her eyes are on some horizon. She's in her own trance of hope and memory. She passes me peas instead of words. Each one has a powdery cream bloom. Each one tastes as sweet as a soft nut.

Poe thought he could hear the sound of darkness coming down over the countryside. Perhaps what he heard was a soft drone, like the noise that surrounds me as I stretch out with my arms folded, under the airline rug.

I'm making my way to the Fordham house, like Marie Louise who travelled to Virginia's death with her big sensible heart and her bottle of cologne. Louise always said that she couldn't go mad because her brain was too small and her heart was too big. She met an old sweetheart of Eddie's on the way; there was a flurry after the death when it was realised that there was no picture of Virginia; then someone did the quick skilled sketch of her face, freshly relaxed in death. She looks enraptured, exhausted, like a woman in the deepest trance.

The Fordham house is a museum, now.

I'm not bringing a linen burial dress to comfort a stricken mother, or something to sweeten the air in a room.

Moisture was trapped inside the window panes when the aeroplane was fitted together. It gathers and then evaporates, and gathers and evaporates. I'm thinking of a line from somewhere, a line I read in one of Finn's books, standing in front of his brick and plank bookshelves. The book with a red cloth cover. Yes, I remember. A Russian in exile in Prague begins to weep *the way windows weep in a room heated for the first time in many weeks.* Warmth and tears; the combination works like the first benchtop experiments in high-school physics, which let you think the subject will be easy.

Louise thought that guava and open windows would help Poe. The guava was to soothe his throat. But if it worked and his misery evaporated, it was only for a little while.

I've had a quick sleep, and a dream, in between watching the dawn and thinking of my mother.

In my dream I'm standing in front of Finn's bookshelves with the red book in my hands.

Finn is standing between me and the window above the bitumen courtyard. He's brought me some tea and I take it from him and put it on the windowsill. He slides the edge of his hand lightly across the space between my breasts. It's a light slide, again and again. Less personal than fingers. I can hear the traffic in the street on the other side of the courtyard. If my shirt were open I feel I could look down on shiny young girl's breasts. Finn cups his hand and strokes my face and neck with the backs of his fingers. He barely touches the skin. He may be a little distance away from the skin, in that space above the surface where the warmth of another creature registers, before there is any actual touch. He opens his hand and drags the fingertips down lightly between my breasts. I'm watching, now. The tip of his middle finger moves over the buttons of my shirt.

If the cat in the courtyard looked up it would see the square of Finn's shoulder and my eyes.

Then the dream slips into a memory of my mother's wrists, of the iron saucepan on her knees, and the way she leaned forward to stare at the place where the land meets the sky.

New York is climbing into the crown of Liberty.

New York is watching the Yankees from the bleachers with Coke and fries.

New York is a carriage ride in Central Park.

Somehow I miss out on all these things.

New York in winter is white and silver and deep water-colour brown. Thin squirrels rush and pause, rush and pause, through crusts of snow. The ground lifts slowly and unevenly under my feet. It's jet lag. Cigar smoke seems to pool and remain in the air.

I spend hours in the Egyptian rooms at the Met.

The linen is folded like manchester in a department store. This Egyptian linen, according to the sign, is finer than anything which can be made today. The stonework, the painting, the calm symmetries of the jewellery, the coffins which have nothing to do with fear and misery: it all looks finer than anything we've made in the last few thousand years.

The floor wavers with jet lag, the glass wavers; the air is bitter outside.

I'm thinking about Isis gathering the pieces of Osiris from the sky and the earth and the waters of the Nile, collecting the wreckage of the body to make it loved and whole.

I'm thinking of all the poor dead who once lived in the Fordham house: Virginia, Poe, Muddy, then later, everyone who gathered a few facts and ideas and wrote about them, trying to use words to make them whole, until they themselves died, and I am standing for a moment at one end of all of this, a little Isis, until someone reads what I have done and takes up the position behind me.

I told Finn I wanted to put the love back into Poe. Now I can see that I didn't mean passion, as if love packaged as romance could be lifted from a shelf and added to a line of words. I meant something like this process of gathering torn scattered pieces and smoothing them into a shape.

A woman is selling pretzels outside the Met, big, warm and bready as New York pretzels are, and I buy one and hold it in my glove in the pocket of my overcoat as I wander along the edge of Central Park. My camera is in my other pocket and as I walk and walk I'm watching for that rectangle which will fit itself into the viewfinder and lock the whole place into an image for me. The stone lions outside the Public Library. The Flatiron building. Further down. Washington Square. No.

It is so cold on the street that my face numbs. Legs numb, as my coat blows open in the wind. If I pull my hand free of a glove and touch my face, it's as hard and cold as the face of a stranger.

It's seventeen days after the anniversary of Virginia's death.

I'm standing at the window of my hotel, my cheap camera held at my waist, against the glass. There is a quick answering flash from the building opposite. This is the photograph. This is my real souvenir. There is no view of the ground or the sky. The buildings of 42nd Street are flattened and overlapping. The colours are soft black, warm brown, grey. There's an off-centre splash of intense white and a few curves of white beyond this. The flash has shown up the dried half-circles of some window cleaner's work.

It might snow. Snow changes everything. The air warms before snowfall. Afterwards a great city can be silenced, except for the laughter that comes with skidding to avoid a snowball. I think of a snowball landing on stone like the flash in a window of the building across the street.

I'll send a copy of this photograph to Finn.

Tomorrow I'll go to the Bronx, to the Fordham house.

Early in the morning a newspaper shuffles under my door. This is one of the best things about travelling: newsprint so fresh it leaves shadows on your hands.

There's no snow outside.

There's no one on the streets except the people who have spent the night on the streets.

I remember the cold yesterday, how it feels like ice applied to the face in a mask, how even the space between the teeth and inside the lip numbs with the cold. The inside of the mouth is suddenly strange.

I don't have to worry about this, not now, not sitting up in bed with the paper on my lap.

It's Valentine's Day.

Love is just around the corner almost anywhere in New York, and not just on Valentine's Day. It beckons on Riverside Drive at 122nd Street, where it hovers on a high (it's one of the highest points in the city), and can go far higher, ascending the tower staircase of Riverside Church to the carillon for a kiss in the clouds.

There are Valentine walks down in the Village on the weekend and hotels serve tea and heart-shaped desserts.

I won't have time to get out to Riverside Church, to the place where you can kiss in the clouds.

The man who put up the Empire State Building had just one question in mind: *How high can you make it so that it won't fall down?*

Where I come from in Australia there's a long beach where people go in the heat of summer, after work, and sit on the lawns above the sand with wine and fish and chips, or wade out into calf-deep water in the shelter of a rock wall, waiting for twilight. An old biplane from the first war flies back and forth over the water, trailing a long sign. Lovers spell out messages for one another, behind a droning Tiger Moth.

In 1846 Fordham was set among dairies and fruit trees.

There aren't any cows or flowers, now. The streets are busy and littered.

There are cars, pavements, shabby buildings that were doorman apartment blocks a very long time ago, and lots of people in padded down-filled plastic jackets and runners. The yellow cab takes me under subway arches and pulls up behind an NYPD squad car with a siren on hard. We wait. I look out the window at a man jerking past, the victim of some spasticity. He stops outside a newsstand and drops something, yes, a pencil, and bends, jerking, trying to pick it up. He has a slit in the back of one trouser leg. There is a little snow on the ground. The trousers are made of worn dark-brown cloth. His bare skin is visible. Through the other window I can see a tall young man with headphones, rocking on the balls of his feet, belting out a song, under the noise of the siren. The police car moves on.

Suddenly it's there: a small timber farmhouse on a patch of ground with a fence of iron spears.

I walk up the path. There are clumps of snow on the ground and grey squirrels with white-tipped tails are moving between them. I can hear the single thin notes of starlings above the grind of trucks changing gear.

A man in a black turtleneck sweater walks around the side of the house and waves me up onto the verandah. He's unlocking the door. As I come closer he says, 'I tried to plant wildflowers but they didn't last. The place is cursed!' He laughs and laughs.

I find myself laughing, too, as I give him my name and tell him I've come all the way from Australia to see the museum.

It must be the smell of fresh paint that makes me so dizzy. Sixteen layers, he says, and the latest is pretty recent. Paint fumes or jet lag. The most comfortable-looking seat is Poe's rocking chair, in a roped-off part of the main room. I can't ask. I breathe more deeply and that makes it worse.

The rooms are painted white and a glossy turquoise blue. 'Not the original colour,' says the guide. 'That would have been white or bone, and the floors would be limed. We know they had a chequered rug on the parlour floor. The shutters are probably original, and some of the shingles outside. The stove is a true copy, the foundry kept the mould and we had a new one made from that. The house has been moved. This was an apple orchard, in Poe's day.'

There's another visitor behind me: a man in an anorak with two warmly dressed small boys. I move away to the stairs, climb up until I'm out of sight and sit with my face resting against a wall. The stairs are hollow with wear, cup-shaped and narrow. I can see why they put Virginia in the room at the bottom of the stairs when she was dying. You wouldn't want to have to get a body down.

After a while the dizziness lifts and I climb up into a space with ceilings so low that I can press my palm flat against them. The roofline comes down to hip-height at the side. There are three small rooms, one with a television and a fireplace. I settle to listen to the video about Poe. I can hear the anorak man and his children climbing the stairs. Somehow I don't want company. I pass them in the first of the three small attic rooms, while the voice on the video booms out.

Virginia's room still has Virginia's bed. It's very small. There would once have been high acorn-shaped knobs at each corner of the bed, marking the points where four angels are supposed to stand, arguing over the life or death of the sleeper. Or so ghost stories say. The acorns have been sawn off on one side, when the bed was cut down to fit under the slope of the ceiling upstairs. Her room is at the corner of the house, small and light, and a long way away from the iron stove. I've slept in rooms like this, in winter. The timber seals in damp, but the walls don't hold the warmth. You wake to a slick of cold dampness on the boards, from the moisture in your night-time breath.

There's a half-door blocking the way into Virginia's room, like the door of a horse stall. I can hear the guide talking to more visitors, over in the kitchen. The half-door has a bolt inside. I reach over and slide it across and suddenly I'm in the room, still dizzy, my palm fitting exactly over the dome of the acorn at the foot of her bed.

After a death from tuberculosis a room was supposed to be completely sealed, with brown paper glued over all the cracks and joins which might let in the air. Then sulphur was burned in a shovel, propped across a tub of water in case of fire. At least that was how it was done in my own country. Phenol, sulphur, plenty of thick paper and glue. Even the keyhole had to be papered over, after the nurse lit the sulphur and left the room. When the room was opened up again it had to be whitewashed.

Never mind the odd strand of hair. That was picked up in the first sweeping, and burned. Everything had to go: finger-prints, a dried slick of breath against a wall. All possible contagion.

I don't know if Muddy went to all this trouble after Virginia died.

I don't know if anyone else slept in the room.

I'm thinking about what has been written about Virginia. I *was a child and* she *was a child*, wrote Poe in 'Annabel Lee', and he might have been writing about Virginia, who really was a child when he married her. Someone wrote that his women *all had the inert bosoms of boys or angels.* Someone else wrote that Virginia *always unbound her hair when Eddie was with her. That was the way he liked it, the way he had liked it when she was a child, when he had first loved her.* Someone else wrote that *one can never visualise Virginia as a woman.*

I'm thinking about the paper that was used to seal a room like Virginia's, and the sulphur that burned away all traces of a breathing self.

I can't stand here forever like the last angel at the corner of her bed. I can remember an asthma attack but I can't imagine what it's like to fight for air through a chest full of blood, as Virginia did, and to know that you won't win.

I take my hand from the acorn that fitted it so well.

There's a postcard stand in the kitchen and a glass case with copies of Poe's manuscripts on stiff sepia paper. I'd like 'Annabel Lee' but he's out of them, except for the one in the display case, which is stuck down with double-sided tape. So I buy a copy of 'The Raven'. It comes in an orange envelope. There are raven's feathers scattered inside the case. I ask if I could take one. He says 'Sure,' and reaches into a cupboard on the other side of the fireplace. There's a plastic bag full of them. 'They're not really raven's feathers,' he says. 'Just dyed.'

I want to go out and find a dry place to sit in the park with iron spears on the fence. I want to close my eyes for a little while and dream.

The anorak man and his children are coming downstairs. The guide goes off to show them Virginia's room and Poe's rocking chair, which is made of a dark wood with red striations in the grain, like the red colour which is showing through on the quills of my raven's feathers.

The anorak man raises his voice.

'He watched over his wife, in that bed, as she died?'

There's a murmured 'Yes,' from the guide.

'It's kinda tough, you know, for a human being.'

THE VOICE OF A FISH FROM THE BOTTOM OF NIAGARA FALLS

MARIE LOUISE IS WALKING swiftly down Carmine Street with a parcel in the crook of her arm.

The parcel has a linen dress inside, and a bottle of cologne. The linen dress was stitched by a young girl who had just learned pintucking, so every line on the bodice is proudly perfect. As the girl stitched she sang a song that her cousin had learned in the south, a song about a chariot, swinging low to carry her home. The sewing girl thought that the dress she put so much care and so many little speckles of blood into would be worn by a girl exactly like herself in every way, except the girl she imagined would have the means to buy a fine linen dress and the leisure to sit about in it, waiting for a man to bow deeply over her hand. She would have been better off embroidering a bishop's glove.

Marie Louise examined the seams and the row of pearl-shell buttons and then she bought the dress.

Marie Louise is concentrating on holding the parcel and keeping her coat closed against the cold.

She doesn't feel the slight rasp of the edge of an envelope against the skin of her hip. She will forget about the pages Virginia tucked into Muddy's letter until long after the death and the bitter funeral. Then one day at the beginning of summer when the window is open on the sound of the bells of St John's and she can look out at her guava tree she will be mending a tear in the lining of her coat before she packs it away in cloves and lavender, and the envelope will show through the lining, and she will take it out and read about Marianne and the woman who longed with her eyes and hands and heart for the becalmed French sailor.

She will sit with the thickness of grief in her throat, and she will long just to hear Virginia's voice, the voice so soft, Virginia once said, that it may as well have been the voice of a fish at the bottom of Niagara Falls.

Or so I imagine, sitting on the big unfolded manuscript of Poe's 'Raven', with squirrels pausing and darting about on the bark of the trees above my head. 'The Raven' makes an excellent groundsheet. No earth or dampness can get through.

The traffic is as bad as the traffic under Finn's window.

This is the second house I've come to in a spirit of familiarity.

I went to the house in the mountains and I found the umbrellas and croquet hoops and the clay dragons of my childhood. If I'd looked hard enough I would have found some of our baby teeth. I found Finn again. I climbed a ladder and stood up on the widow's walk.

The Fordham house has been moved.

In Poe's day this ground was an apple orchard. The guide thinks the apple orchard was the place he came to when he wanted to avoid his visitors. The visitors are all he's left with, now.

Virginia's coffin was carried down those verandah steps, but she didn't travel out to that particular road and on to the Valentine's vault. After the last step she slips into pathlessness, into a place where there are no acorn-headed beds, no languorous sketches, no scraps of manuscript or rocking chairs.

Louise is on the train to Fordham. Her eyes are closed. She's warmer now, and given over to the sound of shushing, the ring of metal rails and wheels, the single note of the horn. Her hands relax over the parcel. The cologne was given to her by a reverend gentleman who is hoping to make her his wife. He didn't give it to her thinking she would sprinkle it about on Virginia's floor. Louise just might marry this man. She likes him enough to marry him. Later she'll regret the whole thing, but for the moment she likes the way the cologne makes an envelope of hope and goodwill, even love, about her when she is wearing it. She wants Virginia to lie within this envelope. She wants Virginia in pintucked cotton in a brief atmosphere of love. Her hands rock lightly on the parcel. She sleeps.

In her dream Louise is still leaning into the bitter wind on Carmine Street. She walks and walks. Her eyes are wet at the corners and she struggles to keep the ends of her scarf tucked in.

There's a crowd at Washington Square, looking up into the grey sky and shouting excitedly, making as much noise as a great waterfall. The wind has suddenly dropped. People have unwound their scarves and some coats are even unbuttoned.

Louise has no time for a public spectacle. She tries to make her way through the crowd. But she seems to be baulked at every turn. A space opens and she steps forward and someone moves in close behind and the next step isn't in the direction she wants to go, but she takes that step anyhow, hoping to circle up and across through the crowd, but it doesn't work. Soon she's in the front row, just behind the rope which tethers a huge balloon.

The rope is as grey and silky as a grandmother's plait.

The envelope of the balloon is white and hard.

Louise can see Virginia in the basket, with bare arms relaxing on the lip of the wickerwork. The flame below the envelope has created so much warmth that the air ripples all around. Louise hands the cologne and the burial dress to one of

the women in the crowd. She levers herself over the edge of the
basket and lands neatly inside.

Virginia is sitting up high on woolwork cushions with piles
of books around her feet.

Louise glimpses a few names and titles on the spines.
Swedenborg's *Heaven and Hell*. Tieck's *Journey into the Blue
Distance*. There are many, many more, some with pictures
under shiny covers that look as if they've been shellacked; most
without the stitched bindings and hard covers of every other
book she's ever seen. Many of them have the name *Poe* somewhere in the title. There are hundreds of books. Louise picks
one up from the top of a pile. It has a picture of Eddie, looking
worried, on the cover. He looks so worried that Louise almost
cries out. There are other pictures all around him. An ape with
sharp teeth. A church spire. An exhausted girl with a lot of
yellow hair. A bound-up corpse with its arms crossed over its
chest and a raven's head.

'Ballast,' says Virginia.

The crowd is still making the loud sighing noise of a waterfall, but nobody moves in close to the balloon. Louise picks up
the newest book. She opens it and reads: *The bones under the bed
are long and hard with slightly porous ends. They're wrapped in dark
hair which is dull, now, dull with dead sweat and traces of old soap.
The teeth are dry and glossy but all are still in place. Scattered
through bones, teeth, hair and the white linen threads of the burial
dress are polished guard hairs from the coat of a well-groomed winter
cat.* Virginia smiles and reaches her hand out for the book. She
adds a few more and throws them all over the side. Then she
gives the rope a sharp tug and it immediately pulls clear. As she

winds the rope into a coil the upturned faces of the crowd shrink and slip away, and the only noise that can be heard is the roar of the great flame.

The balloon sways up over Manhattan, over the cobble-stones and lumber. If it had been eighty-four years later they could have tethered the balloon to the Zeppelin mast on the Empire State Building, and watched the opening ceremony. The city is soft deep brown and silver, below. There are steamers out on the Hudson. Louise thinks she sees a woman, alone, in a little boat.

'This is the sweetest travel I've ever known,' says Louise. She pulls off her scarf and coat. Virginia's feet are bare.

The balloon moves about just as it pleases, but even when it's moving fast it feels like a boat at anchor in a safe harbour: lifting and sinking in a light rhythm which the body comes to expect, and to enjoy.

'When I was small I used to watch for cracks,' says Virginia. 'Cracks in plaster or china. Any edges. A seam. The crease between the pages of a book. I put myself to sleep by pretending I could slip through into another place, like the space inside a wall, or through wet tea-leaves, into China.'

'You've seen buildings being pulled down,' says Louise. 'There's nothing so very fine about the space inside a wall. It's just empty and dry. It smells of builder's sand and lime.'

'No, no,' says Virginia. 'It's like this. Remember how it is to be kissed? When you're half-awake with half-closed eyes, and it's dark, and the only edges are those you sense or touch. And then there is the pressure and the light slide of the kiss. It's soft and cushiony, and your mouth opens into warmth that feels so vast, so endless, an endless expansion. But a mouth is such a small space, really. Kisses end. It's just a trick of happiness and the night.'

'I remember,' says Louise. 'I know.'

'When I slipped through a crack in a wall I came to a whole new country where there were easy paths by the water and Chinese bridges across to an island. I could sit and watch birds spear down after fish and come up to dry themselves on the branches above my head. It felt as calm and wonderful as this. The birds held their wings wide open. Nothing came to any harm.'

'Except the fish.'

'And they were only the fish of my imagination.'

They drift above Knightsbridge Road and out to Fordham.

'I've seen your sewing,' says Louise. 'Twenty stitches to every inch. I thought you liked to close up the edges of things.'

'It was my mother who taught me to sew.'

The balloon has plenty of seams. When Louise looks up she can see the outside of the canopy and the inside as well, through the hoop above the flame. There's nothing hidden or mysterious about the balloon. It's all visible. Yet the balloon only exists because of all the curved edges of silk, carefully stitched into the shape of a globe, that hold in the warmth. Any small errors in the stitching would be safely held closed by the pressure of the warmth inside.

The balloon sails on through the limitless atmosphere. There are pastures under snow, and barns for dairy cows, and sharp bare orchards. Smoke rises from the chimney of the little house. The balloon begins a slow descent.

People in black are standing on the verandah. The cat

moves between them, sliding against the trousers of the man, dipping its nose to the wrist of the woman who is suddenly bent over, gripping a verandah post. Nobody looks up. The cherry tree catches at the basket, then the basket frees itself and they travel on at shoulder-height above the earth. The shutters are open on the far side of the house. Louise can see in through a parlour window.

There's an open box on Eddie's writing desk. The lid is propped against the wall. Virginia leans across Louise to get a better look at the white face in the box. 'Sad, isn't it,' she says. 'I should have brought the cat. She'll only die, down there.'

Sources

In the course of researching this book I have consulted various texts and numerous accounts of the work and lives of Edgar Allan Poe and Virginia Poe. In the making of the novel, I have drawn on and imaginatively recreated historical and literary material for my own purposes. However, for the benefit of interested readers, the following list acknowledges certain original citations or inspirations.

I THE WINTER HOUSE

Osip Mandelstam's *Stone* provides the lines on page 11 of *Poe's Cat*. 'The fire tongues my dry life away' (Osip Mandelstam, *Stone*, translated and introduced by Robert Tacy, Princeton, New Jersey, 1981). Mandelstam mentions Poe and 'The House of Usher' in another poem in this volume.

The boats in Thea's grandfather's garden are partly inspired by Mandelstam's comments about the inclusiveness of the work of art: 'The century falls silent, culture goes to sleep, the nation is born again . . . and this whole moving current carries the fragile boat of the human world out into the open sea of the future, where there is no sympathetic understanding, where dismal commentary takes the place of the bracing wind of our contemporaries' hostility and sympathy. How is it possible to fit this boat out for its long voyage if we do not supply it with everything necessary for a reader who is at once alien to us and so precious? Again, I compare a poem to an Egyptian ship of the dead. Everything needed for life is stored in this ship, and nothing is forgotten.' (Mandelstam, in Tacy, *Stone*.)

Poe's biographical note on page 13 of *Poe's Cat* draws on a number of sources, but in terms of biography I found Kenneth

Silverman's *Edgar A. Poe: Mournful and Never-ending Remembrance* (HarperCollins, New York, 1992) crucial to my work. Wolf Mankowitz's *The Extraordinary Mr Poe* (Summit Books, New York, 1978) was also helpful because it combines biography with the repro-duction of significant documents and visually arresting material on Poe's life and work. Gustave Dore's engraving, which is mentioned on page 72 of *Poe's Cat*, is reproduced here. I first came across the suggestion that Poe died of rabies in Matt Crenson's 'Poe "Died of Rabies, not Drink"', which is based on inquiries and statements by Dr Michael Benitez of The University of Maryland Medical Centre. (Matt Crenson, 'Poe "Died of Rabies, not Drink"', *The West Australian*, September 13, 1996).

Poe wrote directly about the effect of Virginia's illness and temporary recoveries in a letter to George W. Eveleth: 'it was the horrible never-ending oscillation between hope and despair which I could *not* longer endure without total loss of reason,' in Raymond Foye, *The Unknown Poe: An Anthology of Fugitive Writings by E. A. Poe, with Appreciations by Charles Baudelaire, Stéphane Mallarmé, Paul Valéry, J. K. Huysmans and André Breton* (City Lights, San Francisco, 1980).

On pages 16 and 17 of *Poe's Cat* I've used Marcus Clarke's comments about the desolate, Poe-like Australian bush in his preface to Adam Lindsay Gordon's *Sea Spray and Smoke Drift* in John Barnes, ed., *The Writer in Australia* (Oxford University Press, Melbourne, 1969).

The line which Thea remembers writing into her notebook on page 20 of *Poe's Cat*, 'The life still there, upon her hair – the death upon her eyes', is from Poe's 'Lenore' in *The Complete Tales and Poems of Edgar Allan Poe* (Penguin Books, London, 1982). My paraphrasings of Poe stories rely on this collection.

I first read an account of the history of Virginia Poe's bones in Wolf Mankowitz's *The Extraordinary Mr Poe*. John Carl Miller, in

Building Poe Biography (Louisiana State University Press, Baton Rouge and London, 1977) writes that, 'It was not until 1885 that Virginia Poe's bones were brought from Fordham – after having remained for some time in a small box in William F. Gill's possession. Gill said he had rescued the bones in the nick of time to save them from being destroyed when the Fordham cemetery was razed in 1883, and he brought them to Baltimore where they were reburied on Poe's left.'

Philip Lindsay in *The Haunted Man* (Hutchinson, London, 1953) argues that, 'One can never visualise Virginia as a woman. She remains a pale shadow, an Annabel Lee to be mourned as a spirit rather than as a once living human animal, and when she is spoken of, it is usually as though she were a child.'

Mary Gove Nichols' account of Virginia Poe's deathbed, including her comment that, 'The wonderful cat is trying to keep Virginia warm,' is quoted in *The Extraordinary Mr Poe*.

Marie Louise Shew Houghton's account of 'Mr Poe's cat [which] always left her cushion to rub my hands and I had always to speak to the cat before it would retire to its place of rest again . . . She seemed possessed and I was nervous and almost afraid of her, this wonderful cat', appears in John Carl Miller's *Building Poe Biography*. General comments in *Poe's Cat* about Poe and Marie Louise Shew draw on Marie Louise Shew's letters in *Building Poe Biography*.

The idea of the 'cluster' marriage on pages 26 and 27 of *Poe's Cat* is mentioned in Edward Wogenkecht's *Edgar Allan Poe: The Man Behind the Legend* (New York, Oxford University Press, 1963): 'It has often been said that Poe married two women – Virginia and her mother: the workaday functions which are ordinarily performed by the wife were taken over by Mrs Clemm, and Virginia was there to be loved.'

Virginia Poe's 'very youthful appearance' as a bride and her 'abandon' with Poe before their marriage, used on page 29 of *Poe's*

Cat, derive from contemporary comments made by Jane Foster, a wedding guest, and Mrs Mackenzie, Rosalie Poe's foster mother, respectively, quoted in Wolf Mankowitz, *The Extraordinary Mr Poe*.

Henry Lawson's 'Poets of the Tomb', which Finn recites to Thea on page 34 of *Poe's Cat*, may be found in Henry Lawson, *The Poetical Works of Henry Lawson* (Angus and Robertson, Sydney 1925).

Details of Weber's music which Virginia considers on page 44 of *Poe's Cat* are to be found in John Warrack's *Carl Maria Von Weber* (Hamish Hamilton, London, 1968).

II A WOMAN HAD FIRST TO DIE

Information on fairy tales, including the rape of Sleeping Beauty, which appears on pages 54 and 56 of *Poe's Cat*, is taken from Iona and Peter Opie, *The Classic Fairy Tales* (Oxford University Press, London, 1974).

The judgment that, 'In order that Poe might become the kind of artist he was, a woman had first to die' used on page 61 of *Poe's Cat*, is made by Marie Bonaparte, in *The Life and Works of Edgar Allan Poe: A Psychoanalytic Interpretation* (The Hogarth Press, London, 1971).

The sentence from 'Ligeia' which Thea quotes to Finn on page 62 of *Poe's Cat* may be found in *The Complete Tales and Poems of Edgar Allan Poe*.

Marie Louise Shew's criticism of Maria Clemm: '[She] was like a cat, often, treacherous and cruel' and 'She had a hard side to her nature like many Southern persons who are, or have been brought up with slaves as servants and associates in childhood', appears in John Carl Miller's *Building Poe Biography*. Maria Clemm's distress, 'I feel every hour more *desolate*' is from the same source, as is the remark that the dead have 'gone to dwell with the angels'. Marie Louise Shew's declaration about her 'elastic soul' and her marital 'emancipation' is to be found in *Building Poe Biography* and Poe's disparagement of Stella and 'literary bores' is also from *Building Poe Biography*. The original published account of Poe in church is in *Building Poe Biography* and Marie Louise Shew's criticism of Maria Clemm as a woman who could 'never respect the intellect or judgment' of other women is from *Building Poe Biography*.

The legend that the markings on cat's fur were left by the fingertips of Mahommed, used on page 85 of *Poe's Cat*, is taken from Jaromir Malek, *The Cat in Ancient Egypt*. Malek's book also supplies information on the strangling of Egyptian cats.

The drowning child 'deep beneath the murky water' which Marie Louise remembers on page 93 of *Poe's Cat* is from Poe's 'The Assignation', in *The Complete Edgar Allan Poe Tales*.

The absolution on page 98 of *Poe's Cat* is from 'Eleanora', *The Complete Edgar Allan Poe Tales*.

III SMILING AND BOWING AT THE MADMAN POE

The Captain who is quoted on page 108 of *Poe's Cat* tells the extravagantly faithful husband that he is 'mad' in Poe's story, 'The Oblong Box', *The Complete Tales and Poems of Edgar Allan Poe*.

Rudolf Hess' advice to climbers, which Finn reads to Thea on page 111 of *Poe's Cat* is taken from Wulf Schwarzäller's *Rudolf Hess: The Deputy* (Quartet Books, London, 1988).

The comments of the Lithuanian composer with such creative affection for Poe, quoted on page 114 of *Poe's Cat*, may be found in May Garretson Evans' *Music and Edgar Allan Poe: A Bibliographical Study* (Greenwood Press, New York, 1968).

Poe's description of a visitor 'smiling and bowing at the madman Poe', page 119 of *Poe's Cat*, appears in Kenneth Silverman's *Edgar A. Poe: Mournful and Never-Ending Remembrance*.

The Russian landowner on page 122 of *Poe's Cat* is based on the reminiscences of Mme Kovalevsky, in J.A.T. Lloyd's *Fyodor*

Dostoyevsky (Eyre and Spottiswoode, London, 1946).

The woman who contaminates her wine on page 124 of *Poe's Cat* is originally to be found in Yannick Ripa's *Women and Madness: The Incarceration of Women in Nineteenth Century France* (Polity Press, Cambridge, 1990) as is the bird-woman in *Poe's Cat*.

The American asylum visitor on page 133 of *Poe's Cat* is echoing the thoughts of the narrator of Poe's 'Doctor Tarr and Professor Fether' when he murmurs 'Absolutely barbaric'. From *The Complete Tales and Poems of Edgar Allan Poe*.

A line from Isaiah 48: 9–11 appears on the bell in the bird-woman's story in *Poe's Cat*, page 143.

Augustine's singing style on pages 146 and 147 of *Poe's Cat* is based on a description of 'la mode de l' aboiement' in Patrick Barbier's *Opera in Paris 1800–1850* (Amadeus Press, Portland, 1995).

Edmund Wheatley's *The Wheatley Diary*, in Christopher Hibbert (ed.), *The Wheatley Diary* (Longmans, London, 1964) provides the information for English John's story in *Poe's Cat*, pages 147 to 150, including the exchange between Edmund and the captain, page 43.

IV LETTERS WITHOUT WORDS

The story about the ghost army which Finn tells Thea on page 154 of *Poe's Cat* appears in Arthur Machen's 'The Bowman', in Trudi Tate (ed.), *Women, Men and the Great War* (Manchester University Press, Manchester and New York, 1995).

Poe's conviction that he must 'abandon all mental exertion. The renewed and hopeless illness of my wife, ill health on my own part, and pecuniary embarrassments have nearly driven me to distraction' which I partially use on page 156 of *Poe's Cat*, is quoted more fully in John Walsh, *Poe the Detective: The Curious Circumstances Behind 'The Mystery of Marie Rogêt'* (Rutgers University Press, New Brunswick, 1968). This section of *Poe's Cat* uses general information from *Poe the Detective*. Raymond Paul's *Who Murdered Mary Rogers?* (Prentice-Hall, New Jersey, 1971) has also provided useful speculation and information.

Marie Louise Shew's assessment of Poe's stories as 'unsatisfactory and unpleasant' and her daughter's description of her withdrawal 'to a remote country village taking with her her library of old books and baby Dora and for ten years seeing no new publications excepting an occasional newspaper', quoted in *Poe's Cat*, pages 160 to 161, appears in *Building Poe Biography*.

On page 175 of *Poe's Cat* Thea quotes Dupin's complaint about the Prefect who fails to solve the murders in the Rue Morgue: 'In his wisdom is no *stamen*. It is all head and no body . . .' from *The Complete Tales and Poems of Edgar Allan Poe*.

The dead baby verse on pages 191 and 192 of *Poe's Cat*, as well as the discussion of a society where death is rare or hidden, are taken from *The Mourners Book*, compiled by A Lady (W. Marshall and Co, Philadelphia, 1836).

The Greek sailor's baptism robe on page 195 of *Poe's Cat* was inspired by a description in G. Belzoni, *Narrative of the Operations and Recent Discoveries within the Pyramids, Temples, Tombs and Excavations in Egypt and Nubia* (London, John Murry, 1821).

The sailor's lover on page 198 of *Poe's Cat* describes the excessive grief of a husband hwo is based on Rufus Griswold, as he is described by Kenneth Silverman in *Edgar A. Poe: Mournful and Never-ending Remembrance*.

The abortionist who is comforted by Marianne on pages 200 and 201 of *Poe's Cat* is based on an account of Mme Foriat in *Victorian Women: A Documentary Account of Women's Lives in Nineteenth Century England, France and the United States* (Stanford University Press, Stanford, 1981).

V VALENTINE'S DAY

Kenneth Silverman is the biographer quoted on page 210 of *Poe's Cat*. His description of Poe as 'emotionally electrocuted' seems valid, and is from *Edgar A. Poe: Mournful and Never-ending Remembrance*.

The graphic description of Poe's exhumed skull, quoted on page 211 of *Poe's Cat*, appears in John Henry Ingram, *John Henry Ingram's Poe Collection at the University of Virginia* (University of Virginia Library, Charlottesville, 1994).

The line from Poe's story 'The Black Cat' which is quoted on page 215 of *Poe's Cat*, may be found in *The Complete Tales and Poems of Edgar Allan Poe*.

The description of the weeping Russian exile on page 218 of *Poe's Cat* is taken from Viktor Schlovsky, *Zoo, or Letters Not About Love* (Cornell University Press, Cornell 1971).

'Love is just around the corner . . .' on page 222 of *Poe's Cat*, is from *The New York Times,* February 14, 1998.

The aspiration behind the Empire State Building: 'How high can you make it so that it won't fall down?' quoted on page 222 of *Poe's Cat*, appears in Reinhart Wolf, *New York* (Benedikt Taschen Verlag, Köln, 1980).

The quotations about childish women in general and Virginia Poe in particular on page 226 of *Poe's Cat* are from the following sources: '*I* was a child and *she* was a child' is from Poe's 'Annabel Lee', *The Complete Tales and Poems of Edgar Allan Poe*; 'all had the inert bosoms of boys or angels' is by J. K. Huysmans in *A Rebours: The Unknown Poe*; 'She always unbound her hair when Eddie was with her. That was the way he liked it, the way he had liked it when she was a child, when he had first loved her' is by Cothburn O'Neal, *The Very Young Mrs Poe* (Crown Publishers Inc, New York, 1956); 'one can never visualise Virginia as a woman' is from Philip Lindsay, *The Haunted Man*.

'The voice of a fish from the bottom of Niagara Falls', on page 227 of *Poe's Cat*, appears in Poe's story 'The System of Doctor Tarr and Professor Fether', in *The Complete Tales and Poems of Edgar Allan Poe*.

Abbott, Ethel B., *A Diary of a Tour through Canada and the United States*, London, 1882.

Allen, Hervey, *Israfel: The Life and Times of Edgar Allan Poe*, Rinehart and Co Inc, New York and Toronto, 1934.

Barbier, Patrick, *Opera in Paris 1800–1850*, Amadeus Press, Portland, Oregon, 1995.

Bonaparte, Marie, *The Life and Works of Edgar Allan Poe: A Psychoanalytic Interpretation*, The Hogarth Press, London, 1971.

Bryson, Bill, *Made in America*, Secker and Warburg, London, 1994.

Burns, William, *Female Life in New York City*, T. B. Peterson, Philadelphia, 1850.

Carlson, Eric W., *A Companion to Poe Studies*, Greenwood Press, Westport, Connecticut and London, 1996.

Clarke, Marcus, 'Preface' to Adam Lindsay Gordon's *Sea Spray and Smoke Drift*, in John Barnes (ed.) *The Writer in Australia*, Oxford University Press, Melbourne, 1969.

Darling, H. C. Rutherford, *Surgical Nursing and After-Treatment*, J&A Churchill Ltd, London, 1941.

Evans, May Garretson, *Music and Edgar Allan Poe: A Bibliographical Study*, Greenwood Press, New York, 1968.

Foye, Raymond (ed.), *The Unknown Poe: An Anthology of Fugitive Writings by E. A. Poe, with Appreciations by Charles Baudelaire, Stéphane Mallarmé, Paul Valéry, J. K. Huysmans and André Breton*, City Lights, San Francisco, 1980.

Grossman, Joan Delaney, *Edgar Allan Poe in Russia*, Jal-Verlag, Würzburg, 1973.

Halliburton, David, *Edgar Allan Poe: A Phenomenological View*,

Princeton University Press, Princeton, New Jersey, 1973.

Hoffman, Daniel, *Poe Poe Poe Poe Poe Poe Poe*, Paragon House, New York, 1990.

Ingram, John Henry, *Edgar Allan Poe*, AMS, New York, 1965.

Ingram, John Henry, *John Henry Ingram's Poe Collection at the University of Virginia*, University of Virginia Library, Charlottesville, 1994.

Lady, A, *The Mourner's Book,* W. Marshall and Co, Philadelphia, 1836.

Lindsay, Philip, *The Haunted Man*, Hutchinson, London, 1953.

Machen, Arthur, 'The Bowmen', in Trudi Tate (ed), *Women, Men and the Great War*, Manchester University Press, Manchester and New York, 1995, pp. 252–4.

Malek, Jaromir, *The Cat in Ancient Egypt*, British Museum Press, London, 1993.

Mandelstam, Osip, *Osip Mandelstam's Stone*, translated and introduced by Robert Tracy, Princeton University Press, Princeton, New Jersey, 1981.

Mankowitz, Wolf, *The Extraordinary Mr Poe*, Summit Books, New York, 1978.

Mendell & Hosmer, Misses, *Notes of Travel and Life*, self-published, New York, 1840.

Miller, John Carl, *Building Poe Biography*, Louisiana State University Press, Baton Rouge and London, 1977.

Muller, John P. and Richardson, William J. (eds), *The Purloined Poe: Lacan, Derrida and Psychoanalytic Reading*, Johns Hopkins University Press, Baltimore and London, 1988.

Nichols, Roger, *Debussy Remembered*, Faber, London and Boston, 1992.

O'Neal, Cothburn, *The Very Young Mrs Poe*, Crown Publishers, New York, 1956.

Opie, Iona and Opie, Peter, *The Classic Fairy Tales*, Oxford University Press, Oxford, 1974.

Paul, Raymond, *Who Murdered Mary Rogers?*, Prentice-Hall, New Jersey, 1971.

Poe, Edgar Allan, *The Complete Edgar Allan Poe Tales*, Guild Publishing, London, 1986.

Ripa, Yannick, *Women and Madness: The Incarceration of Women in Nineteenth Century France*, Polity Press, Cambridge, 1990.

Rosenheim, Shawn and Rachman, Stephen (eds), *The American Face of Edgar Allan Poe*, Johns Hopkins University Press, Baltimore and London, 1995.

Schlovsky, Viktor, *Zoo, or Letters Not About Love*, Cornell University Press, Cornell, 1971.

Schwarzwäller, Wulf, *Rudolf Hess: The Deputy*, Quartet Books, London, 1988.

Silverman, Kenneth, *Edgar A. Poe: Mournful and Never-ending Remembrance*, HarperCollins, New York, 1991.

Smith, G. Elliot, *Catalogue général des antiquités egyptiennes du Musée du Caire: The Royal Mummies, Nos 61051–6110*, La Caire Imprimerie de L'Institut Français d'Archéologie Orientale, 1912.

Stuart-Wortley, Lady Emmeline, *Travels in the United States etc During 1849 and 1850*, Richard Bentley, London, 1851.

Symons, Julian, *The Tell-Tale Heart*, Faber, London, 1978.

Toksvig, Signe, *Emanuel Swedenborg: Scientist and Mystic*, Faber, London, 1948.

Victorian Women: A Documentary Account of Women's Lives in Nineteenth Century England, France and the United States, Stanford University Press, Stanford, 1981.

Walsh, John, *Poe the Detective: The Curious Circumstances Behind the Mystery of Marie Rogêt*, Rutgers University Press, New Brunswick, 1968.

Wheatley, Edmund, *The Wheatley Diary*, edited by Christopher Hibbert, Longmans, London, 1964.

Wolf, Reinhart, *New York*, Benedikt Taschen Verlag, Köln, 1980.

READ MORE IN PENGUIN

In every corner of the world, on every subject under the sun, Penguin represents quality and variety – the very best in publishing today.

For complete information about books available from Penguin – including Puffins, Penguin Classics and Arkana – and how to order them, write to us at the appropriate address below. Please note that for copyright reasons the selection of books varies from country to country.

In the United Kingdom: Please write to *Dept. EP, Penguin Books Ltd, Bath Road, Harmondsworth, West Drayton, Middlesex UB7 0DA*

In the United States: Please write to *Consumer Sales, Penguin Putnam Inc., P.O. Box 12289 Dept. B, Newark, New Jersey 07101-5289.* VISA and MasterCard holders call 1-800-788-6262 to order Penguin titles

In Canada: Please write to *Penguin Books Canada Ltd, 10 Alcorn Avenue, Suite 300, Toronto, Ontario M4V 3B2*

In Australia: Please write to *Penguin Books Australia Ltd, P.O. Box 257, Ringwood, Victoria 3134*

In New Zealand: Please write to *Penguin Books (NZ) Ltd, Private Bag 102902, North Shore Mail Centre, Auckland 10*

In India: Please write to *Penguin Books India Pvt Ltd, 11 Community Centre, Panchsheel Park, New Delhi 110017*

In the Netherlands: Please write to *Penguin Books Netherlands bv, Postbus 3507, NL-1001 AH Amsterdam*

In Germany: Please write to *Penguin Books Deutschland GmbH, Metzlerstrasse 26, 60594 Frankfurt am Main*

In Spain: Please write to *Penguin Books S. A., Bravo Murillo 19, 1° B, 28015 Madrid*

In Italy: Please write to *Penguin Italia s.r.l., Via Benedetto Croce 2, 20094 Corsico, Milano*

In France: Please write to *Penguin France, Le Carré Wilson, 62 rue Benjamin Baillaud, 31500 Toulouse*

In Japan: Please write to *Penguin Books Japan Ltd, Kaneko Building, 2-3-25 Koraku, Bunkyo-Ku, Tokyo 112*

In South Africa: Please write to *Penguin Books South Africa (Pty) Ltd, Private Bag X14, Parkview, 2122 Johannesburg*

PENGUIN AUDIO BOOKS

A Quality of Writing That Speaks for Itself

Penguin Books has always led the field in quality publishing. Now you can listen at leisure to your favourite books, read to you by familiar voices from radio, stage and screen. Penguin Audiobooks are produced to an excellent standard, and abridgements are always faithful to the original texts. From thrillers to classic literature, biography to humour, with a wealth of titles in between, Penguin Audiobooks offer you quality, entertainment and the chance to rediscover the pleasure of listening.

You can order Penguin Audiobooks through Penguin Direct by telephoning (0181) 899 4036. The lines are open 24 hours every day. Ask for Penguin Direct, quoting your credit card details.

A selection of Penguin Audiobooks, published or forthcoming:

Tales from Watership Down by Richard Adams, read by Nigel Havers

The Brontës: A Life in Letters by Juliet Barker, read by Sian Thomas, Sean Barrett, Susan Jameson and Patience Tomlinson

Cleared for Take-Off by Dirk Bogarde, read by the author

An Ice-Cream War by William Boyd, read by James Wilby

Junky by William Burroughs, read by the author

Oscar and Lucinda by Peter Carey, read by John Turnbull

The Log by Craig Charles, read by the author

Excalibur by Bernard Cornwell, read by Tim Pigott-Smith

The Waste Land by T. S. Eliot, read by Ted Hughes

Ben Elton Live, performed by Ben Elton

10-lb Penalty by Dick Francis, read by Martin Jarvis

The Diary of a Young Girl by Anne Frank, read by Sophie Thompson

Jesus the Son of Man by Kahlil Gibran, read by Eve Matheson and Michael Pennington

My Name Escapes Me by Alec Guinness, read by the author

v. and Other Poems by Tony Harrison, read by the author

PENGUIN AUDIO BOOKS

Thunderpoint by Jack Higgins, read by Roger Moore

Tales from Ovid translated by Ted Hughes, read by Ted Hughes

A Mind to Murder by P. D. James, read by Roy Marsden

Wobegon Boy by Garrison Keillor, read by the author

One Flew over the Cuckoo's Nest by Ken Kesey, read by the author

Rachel's Holiday by Marian Keyes, read by Niamh Cusack

One Past Midnight by Stephen King, read by Willem Dafoe

The Black Album by Hanif Kureishi, read by Zubin Varla

Therapy by David Lodge, read by Warren Clarke

Rebecca by Daphne du Maurier, read by Joanna David

Amongst Women by John McGahern, read by Stephen Rea

How Stella Got Her Groove Back by Terry McMillan, read by the author

And when did you last see your father? by Blake Morrison, read by the author

Felix in the Underworld by John Mortimer, read by Michael Pennington

Into the Heart of Borneo by Redmond O'Hanlon, read by the author

Walking Lines by Tom Paulin, read by the author

The Queen's Man by Sharon Penman, read by Samuel West

The Bell Jar by Sylvia Plath, read by Fiona Shaw

Culloden by John Prebble, read by David Rintoul

A Peaceful Retirement by Miss Read, read by June Whitfield

The Marketmaker by Michael Ridpath, read by Samuel West

Perfume by Patrick Süskind, read by Sean Barratt

Kowloon Tong by Paul Theroux, read by Martin Jarvis

Jane Austen: A Life by Claire Tomalin, read by Joanna David

The Chimney Sweeper's Boy by Barbara Vine, read by Michael Williams

Victoria Wood Live, performed by Victoria Wood

READ MORE IN PENGUIN

A CHOICE OF FICTION

The Beach Alex Garland

'*The Beach* is fresh, fast-paced, compulsive and clever – a *Lord of the Flies* for the Generation X. It has all the makings of a cult classic' Nick Hornby. 'A highly confident début ... this incisive novel may well come to be regarded as a defining text in the history of imaginative travel writing' *Daily Telegraph*

Love of Fat Men Helen Dunmore

'Helen Dunmore is one of the brightest talents around and these stories show the full scope of her talent ... Exquisite writing adorns every page, marvellous flashes of poetic insight' *Sunday Telegraph*. 'Dunmore's new collection of short stories have the crisp delicacy of a snowflake and a snowflake's piercing sting' *Sunday Times*

Felix in the Underworld John Mortimer

Writer Felix Morsom's existence is comfortable if uneventful, until he meets Miriam, who proclaims him the father of her son Ian, and he becomes the prime suspect in a murder case, encountering more drama than he could ever imagine ...

Chasing Cézanne Peter Mayle

Camilla Jameson Porter's magazine *DQ* drips with flattering portrayals of the rich enjoying their riches. André Kelly, her favourite photographer, is away in the South of France when he discovers a highly lucrative art swindle that involves a shady art dealer who just happens to be Camilla's lover ...

After Rain William Trevor

'Each of the twelve stories in William Trevor's glittering collection, *After Rain*, surveys a quietly devastating little earthquake. Tremors that ensue when pressure is put on a fault-line running through a marriage, family or friendship are traced with fine precision' *Sunday Times*

READ MORE IN PENGUIN

A CHOICE OF FICTION

The Memory Game Nicci French

When a skeleton is unearthed in the Martellos' garden, others rattle ominously in their cupboards. For the bones belong to their teenage daughter Natalie, who went missing twenty-five years ago, and the murderer must be very close to home. 'A beautifully crafted psychological thriller ... electrifying' *Harpers & Queen*

Gaglow Esther Freud

'[Freud] sweeps us back to Gaglow, to its tensions and mysteries, to three sisters who love their brother and detest their mother, whose adored governess vanishes into an uncertain world ... her fine prose holds the reader to the end' *The Times*

The Brimstone Wedding Barbara Vine

Unlike the other elderly residents of Middleton Hall, Stella is smart, elegant and in control. Only Jenny, her young care assistant, guesses at the mystery in Stella's past. 'Out of the mundane accessories of past existence, Vine fashions a tender, horrifying mystery ... The story, beautifully written, emerges delicately, yet with shocking, ironic force and breathtaking imagination' *The Times*

Grianan Alexandra Raife

Abandoning her life in England after a broken engagement, Sally flees to Grianan, the beloved Scottish home of her childhood. There she begins to heal, putting behind her a whole lifetime of hurt and rejection. 'A real find, a new author who has the genuine story-teller's flair' Mary Stewart

Shadow Baby Margaret Forster

'An unfailingly intelligent novel, full of lucid observation of a phenomenon, mother-love, too often seen through a gilded haze of false feeling and wishful thinking ... Forster is a fine storyteller' *Sunday Times*

READ MORE IN PENGUIN

A CHOICE OF FICTION

Quarantine Jim Crace

'A story-teller of unique gifts ... One of the finest novels I've read in years' *The Times*. 'Splendid ... a novel so original that its prose will ring in your ears, and its theme – man's potential for faith and brutality – will haunt you long after you have read the last page' *Daily Telegraph*, Books of the Year

Kowloon Tong Paul Theroux

'Hong Kong in 1996. Here, as the days tick away towards "the Handover" to China, two last-ditch Brits become belatedly aware that their time is running out ... Theroux's taut tale quivers with resonance, menace and suspense ... The work of one of our most compulsive story-tellers on peak form' *Sunday Times*

Distance Colin Thubron

Edward Sanders, a young astronomer, has lost two years of his life, his memory obliterated by a trauma. In the days following his awakening, one memory fades in and out of focus: his love for a woman he cannot name. But as the elusive image becomes clearer, so too does the terrible event that plunged Edward into his private abyss.

Libra Don DeLillo

'DeLillo's monumental novel *Libra* concentrates on the inner life of the people who shaped the Kennedy assassination ... It's DeLillo at his chilling best: he constructs the very human faces behind a monstrous event, creating fiction which trespassed on reality' *Time Out*. 'As testimony to our crimes and times, this is an original, unignorable book' *Observer*

The Destiny of Nathalie 'X' William Boyd

'The intense visual quality draws the reader into a world where betrayal and fear are the dominant themes. This pithy and evocative style is reminiscent of the young Hemingway ... a master of fantasy, farce and irony' *Sunday Express*

READ MORE IN PENGUIN

A CHOICE OF FICTION

The House of Sleep   Jonathan Coe

A group of students share a house in the '80s, fall in and out of love, and drift apart. A decade later they are drawn back together by a series of coincidences involving their obsession with sleep. 'A remarkable book ... Perhaps most strange of all, for a novel about insomniacs, *The House of Sleep* is a wonderful bedtime read' *Sunday Times*

Original Sin   P. D. James

The literary world is shaken when a murder takes place at the Peverell Press, an old-established publishing house located in a mock-Venetian palace on the Thames. 'Superbly plotted ... James is interested in the soul, not just in the mind, of a killer' *Daily Telegraph*

The Actual   Saul Bellow

'A brilliant new novella ... Bellow conducts his narrative through fond territories – big businesses, small crooks, murder contracts, exhumations, marriages "in the final stages of black underwear" ... exceptionally smart' *Independent on Sunday.* 'Bellow's prose remains a source of constant pleasure' Martin Amis

All God's Children   Thomas Eidson

Pearl Eddy's belief shines out like a beacon. She is a widow, struggling to raise four young sons. Hiding a black man from a lynch mob is her first crime. Protecting an immigrant family her second. But when the town turns against her she faces their cruelty with a heroism as boundless, beautiful and dangerous as the Old West itself.

Idoru   William Gibson

'A five-minutes-into-the-future novel which parallel-plots its way through the twin efforts of a psychic "netrunner" and a naïve fangirl to solve the mystery of a rock 'n' roll hero's "alchemical marriage" to a Japanese "idoru" or virtual media star. This is sharp, fast and bright ... a must' *Arena*

READ MORE IN PENGUIN

A CHOICE OF FICTION

The Regeneration Trilogy Pat Barker

'Quite simply a masterpiece – a devastating, deeply moving account of the suffering of soldiers in the First World War and the effect of the war on those left behind at home ... Fiction of the highest order' *Express on Sunday*. 'Harrowing, original, delicate and unforgettable' *Independent*

In the Beauty of the Lilies John Updike

'Lovingly registered, epical narrative of a twentieth-century America caught between God and celluloid dreams, Victorian certainty and modern doubt, the new humanism and a grim millennial age. It takes its place among his finest books' Malcolm Bradbury, *The Times*

Reality and Dreams Muriel Spark

Tom Richards wants to make a simple film about an ordinary woman. As his ambition becomes an obsession, he draws his wife, daughters, lovers and friends into a maelstrom of destruction. 'In this her twentieth novel, she remains inimitable – surely the most engaging, tantalizing writer we have' *London Review of Books*

Of Love and Other Demons Gabriel García Márquez

'García Márquez tells a story of forbidden love, but he demonstrates once again the vigor of his own passion: the daring and irresistible coupling of history and imagination' *Time*. 'A further marvellous manifestation of the enchantment and the disenchantment that his native Colombia always stirs in García Márquez' *Sunday Times*

Heat Wave Penelope Lively

'An extraordinarily good novel, intelligent and perceptive, cool yet very moving, concerning the universal matters of love, death and the affairs of the human heart ... Buy it' Susan Hill, *Daily Telegraph*